THE ROAD HOME

NIGEL STEWART

Published in 2023 by Provoco Publishing who own the publishing rights.

ISBN: 978-1-7395012-1-1

DEDICATION

To Andy, Dave & Steve - The best friends anyone could want.

FRIDAY

7.10pm

I don't want weeks like that. Gazing, forlorn, over the dying embers of a customer's enthusiasm, rekindling it with goodies that made them clap and cheer. We won a deal, but I lost something.

'Usual, Joe?'

'Hello, James. I feel like I want something different.'

I generally don't like beer. Not the ale kind, which this cosy bar excels at. I don't actively dislike it but prefer the fizzy zing of lager. And they have very good lager here.

He's smiling at my own dying embers, knowing I'll stick with the tried and tested. I smile back. 'Nah. Okay. The usual.'

It would be quiet but a bloke sitting in the next booth, his legs along the whole bench seat, is more or less shouting to a couple he may or may not know across the way. It's a one-sided conversation because they don't want to shout back, especially not about football. But he keeps going, incensed by the notion that Player X is being picked for Team Q ahead of Player Y. They smile back, mute, and disinterested, grateful for the well-lit empty tables in the space between them and him, desperate to get back to their own, more confidential dramas.

I sip through the chilly foam and touch an envelope shape on a screen. My boss's email still makes my chest heave.

Hi Joe

I wanted to back up the conversation we had earlier

with something more formal. I really want you to think hard about what I told you, because I meant what I said. The work you put in during the last month has been astonishing, and the result is amazing. But you're not functioning right. There is so much anger in you. No one can handle it, least of all you. The deal and the bonus and all the backslapping won't mean a thing if all they do is gloss over your broken spirit. So please think about what I suggested. This isn't an instruction. I just want you to consider it. Call me any time to discuss.

He'd phoned me this morning, immediately after the formal announcement about the new contract with Caddy-Hill. It's worth a couple of million over three years, and it's all down to me. My selling, negotiating and personal touches. No one else got close. I literally did it all. Late nights. Early mornings. Face to face. On the phone. Emails. Contracts. Letters. I was in their faces, and mine never faltered. I even paid for the bubbly and flowers sent to the owner's wife.

Once he'd acknowledged all that, Neal slid his real agenda down the line. If there'd been a table between us, he'd have pushed a piece of paper towards me, smugly. That's how it felt. He told me there'd been a complaint. A customer pissed off that I was ignoring them. I wasn't, but Neal took their side. You're due some time off, Neal said. You should take it. Not just a long weekend. Not just a week.

'We need you out of the business for a fortnight, Joe. You're hard work right now. I need you to re-set. Go and lie in the sun, or play golf, or read books. Then come back, ready for the next challenge.'

He's mostly all right, is Neal. A decent manager. He's looked after me since he joined the company, learned quickly that I don't need direction or handholding. A father figure is the last thing I want. He knows what makes me tick and makes every second count. He just doesn't know, because we've never discussed it, that I hate golf and haven't ever read a book.

Maybe I should tell him? He should know that kind of shit. And, while I'm doing it, I can mention that I don't want to lie anywhere all on my own.

But today was the day that he stopped being mostly good. He mumbled his way through that stuff about the customer. He sidestepped anything I said in my defence. He made out this was concern, feelings shared by the whole management team. It was pathetic.

There it is though. He wants me out, perhaps permanently.

Someone is talking.

'Do you ever find what you're looking for on that phone of yours?'

Gordon is often here when I'm here. On those days, between seven and half past, he shuffles up the hill from Market Square. Always immaculate in brogues, suit and tie, plus a jaunty hat. He's a lady's man, and neither his walking stick nor being in his late eighties are a barrier to that.

I stand, and we shake hands then he orders his half of stout. James raises an eyebrow at me but I'm not ready for a second.

I hit the side button and slide the phone into my inside pocket. All the knowledge and networking and opportunities I might find in that tiny conduit are unimportant alongside Gordon's amazing tales. It won't be long before his fan club is here, so I sit back and listen.

The angry football fanboy has decided to go and stand next to his audience, but he hasn't turned down the volume. To be fair, I think he did this because two couples arrived and sat at one of the tables between the booths. So, he had to take action.

Gordon tells me he wishes the AFF would shut up and learn some manners. We agree he never will, and G leans in closer to resume his anecdote about a lover in

Augsburg. This was during that time he spent working in aerospace, sorting out the Germans and Italians. He always makes out I'm a trusted partner, so I don't mind that, really, I'm not. Gordon doesn't care who he talks to. It could be anyone. I like the distraction his monologues create. They give me the excuse to be inert, with nothing to do other than nod and grin, or throw in occasional gasps of delight, disbelief, or dismay.

Over his shoulder, through the window, I see the smokers and vapers huddled under the awning. They need safety in numbers to counter the elements. Like penguins. It's dry and not that cold, but a gusty wind is funnelling between the buildings out there.

Then two-fifths of Gordon's fan club pull up in their battered old SUV. Before they've crossed the pavement their drinks have arrived on the table. That's quite classy, isn't it? Phoning in your order. A pint of ale and half a cider, plus packets of crisps with fancy flavours.

Now I'm ready for my second pint.

Liz and Gary join us, her next to Gordon, him on my right. They live on St George's, are nice people, and always say *hi,* or wave if our paths cross. Gordon doesn't break stride. He's not one for interruptions. Gary necks half his pint in one go and Liz greets me with theatrical pouts and winks. And a smile.

The AFF bids his audience goodbye. It's very welcome to all concerned, and the silence created by his departure is like a blessing and relief. There's music playing that no one could hear because of him. It's a selection of things that, mainly, I don't recognise.

My phone vibrates. After two more buzzes, I decide I'd better look.

It's Carly.

Hope ur ok hun.

Everyone's a bit worried x

A song comes on that I actually know. 'Brand New Day', by Kodaline. It was Nat's favourite album for a while. When we were getting to know each other, she used to play me songs, usually at home, sometimes in her car. That was one of them.

Gary gets a word in while Gordon takes a sup. 'We finally got the doors done on the conservatory today. Weeks, it's taken them. Months.' Liz rolls her eyes and mutters something under her breath.

Gordon turns to her and asks what she said so she repeats it at normal volume. 'I said *the useless fuckers*, Gord. Been living with boarded up windows all that time.' They embark on a review of the useless fucking company and how much fucking money Liz got back from them for their poor fucking service.

I'm back to my phone.

Hi Carly. All good. I just needed to bail. What you up to this weekend?

She tells me her hubby is treating her to a couple of nights away but it's a secret destination.

We're in the car now hun. Somewhere out in the sticks. Could be anywhere. LOLZ. Glad ur ok. xxx

I look at Neal's email again. At face value it's well-meaning. So was what he said to me on the phone. He is consistent. But this has never happened before. In all my time at the company I've worked my cock off and had plenty of flare ups. It's part of the deal. No one has ever cared. Why now? I don't see what's changed or why I am suddenly some sort of liability.

'How was your week, Joe?'

I tell them about the contract I won with our new client and how many hours I worked. Gordon's eyes glaze over, and he drains his glass. Gary gestures to the bar that service is needed. I finish my reply with a hint that

I'll get a pretty massive bonus and when James arrives, he's told it's my round.

I walked into that one.

It's past eight now and the tables are full. The atmosphere is good, full of chat and laughter. It's why I like being here, rather than in a pub or posh wine bar. This always feels like the kind of place I was born to be part of. It's comforting, with none of the entitlement and gloss that I've never craved. Here, I don't need to dress up or smell nice. I just need enough money for beer, and enough smiles and chat for whatever confronts me.

'What happened to that gorgeous girlfriend of yours?'

He means Nat. Gordon never remembers names. I don't recall them meeting but they must have. She and I came here sometimes, from different directions. A date night to mark the end of a working day or week. It was one of the things we both liked. Quite a long list of things, I thought.

He is immune to the *not now, Gordon* nudge from Liz.

I stick with the facts. 'She didn't like my other love.'

'Playing away, were you? Good lad.' No one joins in with his suggestive laughter.

'I think he means his job, Gordon.' I give a nod of resignation. Liz is primed with a change of subject, but Gordon has a bone to pick.

'I'd never have let her go, not with legs like that.' He's caused tension but we relax when Gordon moves on to another anecdote about one of his women. He's distracted his own train of thought in just one sentence.

My nods and grins are in play again, but my mind is stripping the words out of Neal's email until I have just two to analyse:

suggested...

instruction...

He is *suggesting* I should take a break. He will not *instruct* me to do so. That's quite pointless, but it's a good indication of how bad he is at decision-making. If I ignore his *suggestion*, he will say he tried. If I insist on a mandate to take leave, he will back down. He won't issue *instructions*. Neal isn't a bad human being; he's just a bad leader. Today's exchanges prove that he thinks he cares, but he doesn't care if I care.

Is that what's going on?

Gordon has decided to go home, and Liz gets up to let him out. He pays for his own drinks with cash. He doesn't do rounds. Gary walks him to the door and then stays outside to make a phone call. When he comes back, he tells Liz the curry is on its way, delivery in forty-five minutes. They have time for a third drink. He heads to the bar, then onwards to the toilets.

Liz shakes her head. 'Time for *him* to have another drink. I'll make do with a softie.' She's holding my gaze with those searching blue eyes. She knows what happened. A few nights after Natasha left me, I was here in the bar and spilled all the details. It was like the conversation I might have had with my mum or with Leigh if either of them had been there. Liz is too young to be my mum or my sister, but she listened and learned. She's checked in on me whenever we get time together without Gary, or anyone else, in earshot.

'Gordon's a lovely old chap, but sometimes...'

I wave away her regret that he mentioned Nat. 'I'm over it.'

'Are you over Natasha?'

'I'd like to think so.'

'It's not like you to be evasive. But what you just said sounds like you are being.'

'I really wasn't. Let me say it another way. I have no doubts I'm over Natasha.'

Time has passed, even though time was sometimes on hold, sometimes lost in lockdowns. Maybe all those weeks in pandemic custody were the right time for me and Nat to try again. But we'll never know.

'Have you been looking for someone?'

I maintain eye contact, wondering if I should say more. The dating sites were a decent idea but too remote, too virtual, too abrasive. Nights out an option, but I never had a wingman. I don't doubt that I want someone in my life. Eventually. And I don't doubt that there is someone who wants me in theirs. Eventually. But I sometimes really do doubt that I can go through it all again, just to end up back behind the starting line.

'No, not really. Maybe I need to get myself sorted.'

'No, I don't think you do. Don't push too hard, Joe, on anything. What you've had to cope with is mind-blowing and still raw. It really shows in your face. You look a bit desperate. Don't risk making wrong choices or decisions.'

I can no longer hold her gaze. She's right.

'Someone will drop into your life in a way you might never expect. And she will be perfect for you, and you for her.' Liz places her hand over mine. 'You're lovely, you're kind, and you're great company. Don't ever forget that, Joe.'

Gary returns during those last statements and adds, 'And fitter than a butcher's dog.' Liz slaps him half-heartedly but gives me another wink.

We talk about today's headlines and disagree about everything, but we don't fight. None of us is perfect. None of us is evil. We can be civilised without agreeing and argue without pettiness. This fixes nothing, but it means our friendship doesn't bend and break. When they get the call that their curry is five minutes from home, we kiss and hug and shake hands.

I'm left with the background conversations of others and whatever thinking time I can fit in while I finish a fourth pint.

When I finally get up to pay it's a few pence short of a tenner. That's another thing I love about this place.

<>

In the toilet mirror, my reflection weighs me up while I wash my hands, accompanied by the sounds of a flush. I look stark and haggard, like someone has used a piece of charcoal to draw highlights on a monochrome photo of my face. I can't tell if that's anything new. The pressure has always been there. Partly that's why I do the job. I like the buzz of engagement, of playing to win, of making customers think they've screwed me with some petty, predictable finesse. I want to be good at my job and it means I work hard. It's important to me. I can cope. I can take it.

Another gaze into my own eyes. For the first time ever, I wonder if that's true. That I can cope. Being good at my job means I am often running on empty, means I'm... something. Full of anger? Really?

It's time to get out of here, out into the semi-darkness.

<>

My walk should last ten minutes, max, if I turn right to go through the memorial gardens. But that also means I pass the house with all the smackheads. So, I stay on the main street.

Across the way, every other retail unit has whitewashed windows. One of them was a bank until they all decided to close and leave us in the lurch, we happy debtors. Those TV adverts. Nasty lies. They really aren't by anyone's side.

An old VW accelerates up the hill. The noise of its engine is appalling, a long, drawn-out blast of sound, almost physical in its intensity. Then another nothing car, tuned to the edge of reason, rushes past in the opposite direction. The lights must have changed further down because a stream of vehicles heads past towards Preston. Almost all of them have music rupturing the airwaves.

I've reached the pedestrian crossing and two kids are on the other side, pretending to step off the pavement to wind up drivers. One car pulls over and a guy jumps out to chase them, swearing and threatening. His mates stay in the car, laughing. When I join their laughter, one of them mouths *fuck off* through his window.

Further on, a young man is pestering two young women outside the burger place. He's standing. They're sitting on a step. I can't work out what's going on. Some of what he says and does sounds and looks aggressive. Some of what they say back sounds accepting. Which of them is winning? His mate stumbles out of the burger place and hands over a package. The two blokes make an incongruous pair: one in shorts, trainers and outsized hoodie, the other in a tightly fashionable three-piece suit.

The scene is obliterated by another cavalcade of cars, a mobile nightclub. There's a tailwind, heavy with the smell of weed.

On my side of the street, I pass the other takeaway place with its piled-high boxes for pizzas and those giant insulated bags for deliveries. There are no customers inside the shop. That sweating, thigh-shaped lump of doner meat is there, spinning its glistening magic, dripping whatever it can't contain.

Down the hill, to where the smell of Indian food always fills the air and my nostrils. The aroma seems to be working. The takeaway has people sitting, waiting. The adjacent Chinese is empty.

Should I eat? There are bits and pieces back at the house, but a curry might be good. No. There are things back at the house.

I keep walking. A gang of people, hooded and noisy, makes me decide to avoid my next available shortcut through the supermarket car park. While I'm thinking about that change of plan, I'm nearly hit by a car racing in from the street. More soundless abuse on a face behind a screen.

Opposite, the Compass has a bouncer on the steps, and he's looking down on people. It seems good-natured, but he's guarding the entrance, barring their way. Discarded glasses and bottles stand on most of the tables. A bloke sits on one of the benches, slumped forward as if he might throw up. Smokers stand, knotted together for their fix.

The massed traffic signals go to green, and it changes the way everything looks. Bathed in the red miasma of a stop sign, those littered pizza boxes, polystyrene cartons and half-chewed morsels of chicken skeleton were unseen. Green makes them visible, like shitty kryptonite.

A sound from my right makes me tense up. I take a wide berth around the alley's entrance, but it doesn't conceal potential muggers. The man is gasping. The woman is kind of whining. He is swearing the encouraging abuse she seems to need to make her come. Her legs are up around his waist. His rhythm is fast and occasionally makes her head hit the wall. They're oblivious that someone is watching. They're oblivious to everything except their own needs: pleasure, pain, fucking.

Up the hill towards the station, and it's less frenzied here. For a few moments I can hear my footsteps, then a small group of lads' lurch towards me, hoods up, mumbling so quietly it might as well be silence. There it is again, the smell of weed. It's overwhelming and seems to cling to me. I wish I understood the appeal.

Across the road, a couple holds hands. They're happy in those alternating pools of streetlight and shade. I want them to stop and kiss. They keep strolling.

On past the plastic display case, a memorial to the town's last ever loom. Past the place, whatever it is, with its tall white pole and drooping flag. Past the funeral directors with its proud stone about being a business since 1946. Past the terrace of houses opposite and the care home on my side.

I need to cross. I'm on the wrong side of the road for my turning. The traffic's light, so I stride off the pavement and head diagonally to the far side. Not long to go now.

There's a mound of dog shit on the path. Not just a couple of tapered turds. A mound. A curling, glistening pyramid, street-lit and proud. I swerve around it and turn into my road.

The house is there. The car is there. The overgrown bushes are there. The three windows and a door are there. In the border, there'll be the usual dribs and drabs of litter that people provide for me, free of charge. I stop and look across the threshold of two houses. Next door is still empty, waiting for a sale. The driveway I share with it is eerily darkened. I should get a safety light for back there. Maybe the new neighbours will get one if anyone ever buys it. The get-rich-quick prick that did it up is asking a fucking fortune. The glossy new paintwork and sexy kitchen units a mask on the corner-cutting by his unpaid contractors. It will end in court, and I'll happily be a witness because of all the misery that cunt caused me.

Flashing neon makes me turn to watch an ambulance head towards the far end of the road. No siren, but it's accelerating. That's what all the traffic does down here, down this rat run. A road linking other roads. Surges from nought to sixty in a twenty mph limit. Someone will get killed out here one day. It won't be one of the lads in their hot Fiestas or the lofty set in their mobile armchairs. There'll be more ambulances that day.

I'm still lurking by the pillars that once held gates. Their art deco crowns are jarring, somehow. Was this place ever that grand or arty? This question leaves me stuck, here between street and house.

Someone walks towards me, her face lit by the garish glow from a phone as it broadcasts the other half of a conversation.

It's time to get inside.

After I close and lock the door, I stand with my back against it and inhale.

More breathing. Rehabilitation with this haven.

Inhale.

Exhale.

Calm.

9:47pm

Shouting starts outside, then more. Running feet. Many of them. I look through the small window in my front door to see who's out there. The view is distorted by the decorative glass. It's a bloke, shaven head, bulky but toned. He's fast but being chased by three uniforms, then, soon, more neon fills the night. A van and a car screech up. Back-up uniforms. He's caught but puts up a massive fight. I have to see this and, when I get back outside, the whole street's watching. Maybe not the whole street.

He's struggled clear and got into a garden - number 13, I reckon - and one of the bizzies uses a baton. It doesn't stop him swearing and resisting. It takes five of them to restrain him, then move him to the street and into the cage inside the van. Even once he's in there, it needs two bizzies to put their weight against the door so another one can lock it. The lad is still going mental inside, the van rocking, and his shouting barely muffled. The bizzies don't make any effort to reassure us or tell us *nothing to see here*. Instead, they just stand there chatting, laughing, their body language suggesting they're competing for who got the most shots in.

It's over. I step back inside and shut the door. Locked up tight.

I make a cup of tea and debate what to have on my toast. I change my mind and stick some fish fingers under the grill then some frozen bread in the microwave. It's pleasant enough to sit in the yard, so I head out there and look at the sky. It's peaceful and the tea is good. When everything's ready, I make my sandwich in the full knowledge that my choice of sauces would cause outrage in one of those pathetic debates on social media. It tastes good the way I make it, so fuck 'em.

That's it, then. That's the end of a week in which one segment of life was a triumph. And what is my reward? This sandwich. This mug of tea in dusk's calming comfort. That social scene. Those slivers of boozy charm, chats with the people I met. This place where I live, a mass of drab, ordinary, broken redundancy, and its ever-present menace.

The world in my eyes.

I go inside and grab my phone. Several app icons have numbers to tell me how much I'm needed. But I go to email and open Neal's. Back outside, in the deepening dark, I type:

> *Hi Neal. I will take my two weeks holiday with immediate effect.*

SATURDAY

4:07am

It's morning and I can't tell if I slept. It feels like I didn't, so I lie there trying again but the need for a plan ends up being too distracting. I get up and shower, wondering why I never wake up with a hard-on anymore. Showers used to be a kind of fun. These days, all the hot water does is stimulate my mind.

I keep trying to make a plan.

Downstairs. More tea. Laptop. Map.

It's too late in the year and too early in this process to go somewhere hot and sunny. Probably too expensive as well. I hit *Current Location* on Maps and I'm swept back from the Adriatic in an instant. There is my house in my road in my town. A blue circle with a cartoon symbol in it equals the heart of my home. But it isn't one.

There are all those interconnected main roads and, away to the left, another symbol that represents where I work. Just above my home circle is the railway station.

I open a railway ticketing app and tell it I'm going from my local station. Then I tell it I want to go to Edinburgh. I've no idea why. This is a random, perhaps dangerous, decision. Anyway, there's a train in ninety minutes. One change, and I will get there in about three hours. The price isn't a problem. I could even afford to go first class. Wouldn't that be a treat?

I'm on a roll now, not sure why. From Edinburgh I could go on, deeper into Scotland. I've never been, but I'm sure it's great. Dave, one of my customer contacts, is from Stirling. Now I'm looking for trains from Edinburgh to Stirling. It's really quick, and cheap.

The roll hits the buffers. What am I doing? I'm thirty-five, yet it's like I'm much older. Looking at maps and train times and nice places to go. I need to act my age and do things with spontaneity and a carefree spirit. Instead, I'm seeking validation, like someone lost in a needy vortex. My brain is fried from over-planning. That's the problem. Everything lately has been about delivering the needs of others.

I'm going to drive.

No trains. No tickets. No being herded. No destinations governed by wherever the lines are drawn. My car is enough. I've got nowhere to go, so I'll leave with nowhere in mind. Take a small bag of essentials and, if I need more stuff, buy it wherever I land.

Good plan.

I need more tea and, while the kettle boils, I sense that the house wants me to stay. I don't know how I feel about that. All the disintegration outside these walls, the endless happiness with nothing, the unyielding monotony of routines, are countered by the comfort and simple pleasures in here. Do I run or hide? Fight or fly?

Nat always said she found this place appealing because I kept it simple. Don't know what she'd make of it now. Since we split, I've become bored by material things and how they make people compete. I've decluttered to an insane degree. The charity shops and their customers won big time.

I still want this house to be the one place I've ever called home, even on the days when I can't say *home*. Maybe I should stay another day?

What was it Derek used to say as we worked the punters? *More haste, less speed*? I laugh. Isn't it the stupidest possible statement? I mean, what does it actually mean?

In fact, Derek was far from stupid, or so it seemed, and perhaps the things he often called *wisdom* were worth understanding, even by me in my teens. While a voice in my head whispers *stay*, I hear his saying *get on the road and do one*.

I go to fetch something from my car and find a half-dried lake of vomit by my gatepost. That settles it. Time to get away. I can't be in this place. I need change. I'm not going to change. I just need to be somewhere I can call *away*. Somewhere without symbols on a map on a screen, like anchors that let me drift without leaving. Somewhere I'm not head of sales for a company. Somewhere I'm not me.

6:30am

I've enough fuel for 178 miles, it says. Are cars reliable? Are computers? I've a pretty basic concept of distance, but I imagine those 178 miles would take me to any number of places I've never been.

Work occasionally takes me to big cities, mainly here up north. We feed businesses who like to boast about all their green credentials. They are mainly local, but the word is spreading.

I slap the steering wheel and tell myself to stop thinking about work.

Cruising quietly along, I think ahead to the end of the motorway and what I should do there. Left? Or right? North? Or South? This feels happy. It grounds me. I see that my choices are much simpler for now. It doesn't matter which way I go. Instead, I start thinking about what I might see that I haven't before. A real marketplace? City walls? A coal mine? Cobbled streets? A cathedral?

That's it. I decide I'd like to see a cathedral. Or several cathedrals. I don't know why, but now the thought has happened, I need to learn. Ten minutes later, I pull into a hotel car park to search for the nearest cathedrals. Some are nearer than others.

I've got a revised plan but, once I'm back on the road, I feel troubled about how little I've travelled. I mean, yes, I've been on holiday. Natasha made all that happen. We toured, sometimes grandly. What about this country though? Why don't I know about the places with cathedrals?

Neal's words seem to be written on the windscreen.

...suggest...

...instruct...

The steering wheel gets another slap.

Instead, I focus on the scenery. It's early morning but things look nice. The weather is fine but, so far, not sunny. Places come and go. I know some of the names. A farm shop, where Nat and I went to get stuff for special occasions. The aerospace site with its old warplane on a stick, like a massive model. It reminds me of its sister site back near my place. Then of someone I sometimes forget I used to know. She was connected to these sites and buildings and runways.

A sign to Balderstone makes me smile, then the one to Osbaldeston makes me laugh. I'm childish like that. Easily made silly. When no one's looking.

The road's straight and there's no traffic. The surface rolls at me as I aim my car between the lines of kerbstones, and I wonder if I'm driving or being moved by the buttons and joystick of a gamer's controller. I slow for the roundabout and drive around it twice, just to confirm it's me making the decisions. Then I race away up the hill.

It's mainly fields for a while. Nothing special, but green and pleasant. Old pubs, re-branded as places to eat. A reminder of some very posh places around here, and one is coming up soon.

How do I know they are posh? What has ever brought me here? When did I ever break out of the simple cell where I've existed these few years and travel along this road to eat fine food? How many people might have accompanied that? I remove my left hand from the wheel and count them. A thumb and three fingers. Then I curl two of the fingers back into my palm so just my thumb and forefinger are raised, in the shape of a letter L. It makes me purse my lips. In the rear view mirror, my eyes are stony grey. When I look at the empty passenger seat, it also looks like a letter L.

The sun, watery and weak, has made an appearance ahead of me and my reflected gaze is back to the pale blue version. I cover it with the shades I often use to hide my eyes. I don't like them to be looked into in case someone gets to see what I've known and seen. All that.

I want to fold my arms and bury my chin on my chest. To drive all that away, the seen and the known. As opposed to driving my car towards the sunshine.

I'm joined by more cars now, the odd truck and bus. I have to grip the wheel tight and regain control from myself. Of course, people have to look into my eyes. It's one of my skills. Eye contact. You can't sell and hustle and win and close things without those unblinking, unbroken moments. With smiles, of course. And words. Assurance. *Trust me, my whole demeanour, but especially my eyes*. That's what mine say to the other person's eyes. The buyer's eyes. *I'm the only supplier you've ever needed. The only friend, too. And teacher, parent, sibling, lover*.

I'm fucking brilliant at all that. A winner. Constantly. Yet someone thinks I'm not functioning right. It isn't me. And someone thinks there's so much anger in me. That isn't me, either. Someone says my spirit is broken. Nope. Not me, again.

I almost snort with contempt for Neal and his *I know best* psychological shite. If he'd spent more time looking at what I've done, and what's still to come, he'd have learned something. But he chose to believe that the things he has said about me indicate the start my downfall. How dare he rip those things out of me and claim them as assumptions he can own? I know the truth and it's nothing more than an intense, unwavering, loyal normality. A skin wrapped around my pulsing, driving determination. It makes me survive and cope. No matter what. Nothing is broken. Nothing is dazzling. Nothing is too flamboyant. It's where I belong, where I've fought to be after coming from nowhere.

Was it nowhere? It exists, that place: where a father imbibed and got wild, where a sister resisted, fought back, and stayed safe, where a mother took the conflict until she snapped into pieces that could only be reassembled in another place.

<>

Dad couldn't stop himself. Steady job. Paid the rent. Never in trouble. Nobody's fool. He'd stopped drinking while I was being cooked so there was less of a cash shortfall while Mum was off work. Wanted the best for us both of them. The house where we lived had the same as all the others. Same roof and walls and garden. Same windows and doors and floors. Ours was neater than some. More tatty than others.

Mum hadn't stopped herself. When the boss took an interest in her above and beyond how well she did her job she jumped into his car and into his arms and into his bed. He said he'd shower her with gifts flowers and fine things but all he really wanted was to shower her with his watery jizz. Then he went cold on the whole idea. Said his wife had found out and Mum got sacked. She found another receptionist's job soon enough but then there was me and the job didn't last.

Leigh was happy being an only child and I think she'd have stopped me if she could. Big sisters are supposed to love baby brothers. But she wasn't pleased when I arrived. She was at school by then. Already light years ahead of me instead of just six regular years.

We couldn't stop ourselves being a family and my part in it was to smile a lot and demand gifts better than any other kids in the crescent or estate or suburb. I scored a win-rate of about 15% which would please me now but back then it was a disaster. Then I realised we had things in the house that other kids didn't. Then none of my things and none of what we had mattered any more.

Dad heard the whispers via whatever grapevine existed back then.

Always wondered about that. The way to spread dismay or hate or joy these days seems simple. Dad found out so perhaps it was simple then too? Just slower? Word of mouth took several months but it still relayed whatever malice needed preaching.

Dad found out about Mum and when I was five there was a massive fight downstairs. Leigh went down to stop it but got kicked so hard her leg went black all down the outside of her thigh. She came back upstairs and told me we might need to leave. I asked her what a bastard was and why Dad kept saying it. She said he means you. We didn't need to leave because soon Mum screamed that she was going. The door slammed. Dad came up and hugged me and told Leigh he was sorry Mum kicked her. Then he hugged her too. He said we should go to the hospital to get her leg looked at.

Mum couldn't stop away for long. She came back and it fixed things. But the repair kept splitting open every few weeks. Mum told me I wasn't a bastard. I knew what it meant now because Alice Acton told me at school. Dad never said I was to my face but every time they shouted at each other it's what he said I was. That twat's bastard. That's what he said.

Leigh was nicer now and made sure I went to school and got home all right. Made my tea. She pulled me out of fights with kids around the estate but by the time I was eight she couldn't stop me being part of a juvenile gang that did unspeakable criminal things.

Alice was lovely and we were like mates. She kissed me once and then we kissed a lot. We weren't mates any more. But we were something. Both of us clung to whatever it was. It didn't matter about being young kids.

Dad wasn't able to stop his descent into addiction. I shouldn't have known what he was up to. But I was part of that gang. I had an inside track about drugs and what smackhead meant. All the lads knew that and some of them had siblings that were. I knew why his arm looked the way it did and guessed that the occasional visit from hard men was because money was a problem. By the time I was ten I was making sure I had my own money from whatever source was easy.

Then Mum had to go. He wasn't causing physical harm. No violence or assaults. Not by him. The debts and the waste of money that was needed for basics were a terrible burden. That was a different kind of harm. Another kind of violence or assault. She slowly wilted under the strain of oppression and Mum was unable to stay. She left with no goodbyes.

Leigh brought me up from that day. Dad kicked his habit when he lost his job and spent almost all the time lying in his bed watching TV slowly converting one addiction into another. I walked in once while he was watching the porn. He didn't even bother to stop wanking. Never missed a stroke. Just told me to get out.

By now I absolutely hated him. His benefit paid the rent most weeks and Leigh spent all her wages on keeping us fed. She had no social life and no kind of relationship. I asked her once if Dad had ever tried to abuse her and she said he wouldn't dare.

Maybe that's why he disappeared. We never knew. Before I was fourteen it was just me and Leigh and we had to leave the house so she could rent somewhere smaller. One day an envelope arrived with Mum's writing on the front. I asked Leigh if she'd always been in touch with Mum. But she said no.

7:03am

Was it nowhere? Or somewhere that didn't matter? And never would.

A tractor, pulling a trailer filled with big, lumpy potatoes, makes me slow to a crawl.

You want fries with that?

<>

I hated school and by now the gang had split into factions. The fights were wild. Nothing we did was positive. There was no honour in the way we behaved. No solid unbreakable bonds were formed. Only little links we might connect up if the need arose. All I had was a sister. A bedroom. A knife. A few clothes some of which were decent thanks to thieving. Leigh couldn't stop me. We fell out.

Me and Alice were still connected and every once in a while we spent time together. She had a boyfriend she said was serious. But we still had something. She told me I was better than her boyfriend and I told her I knew. It felt like we would always find time for each other but never make it a permanent thing. My life was a bit too broken up now. Hers was better.

Mum's letter was one of several I found in a kitchen drawer. I sometimes found her writing hard to read but I got the basics. She was living in Sussex running a B&B with someone called Jason. The more I read the more I realised Leigh wasn't writing back and never had. Mum's words didn't seem to react or respond to anything that might be news about us. She just rolled out what she wanted to tell her daughter and mainly it was self pity. I didn't realise for ages that these letters were quite old.

My sister joined a weird group that disagreed with almost everything and sometimes marched up and down the Prom to make its points. More often than not another league of idiots clad in different rags and flags attacked Leigh's lot. They all said this was politics and for some sort of greater cause. But it was no different to the fights I got in. Bragging rights. Territories. Leigh came home once with her clothes torn. Scratches on her face shoulders and chest and her tights ripped. We called the police because Leigh had been raped and they more or less said she'd asked for it and shouldn't hang around with Trotskyists. It made Leigh and me close again because we knew the police wouldn't investigate it properly. That was another pointless fight.

Dad never came back.

One of Mum's letters said she might need to escape because she wasn't safe in Worthing.

Leigh and I saw two guys in town one day and she said it was them. A bit older than me but nothing special. I clocked both but she told me to forget it so I told her I would. I knew where they lived and knew they had no back up. They were brawlers. Mercenaries who jumped when the high command needed attack dogs. I lied to Leigh. One night I joined up some links. Grabbed Louie Ben and Paolo and we went and waited near where the two blokes hung out. It didn't take long. A few words. Quiet and specific. We knew they'd react. They definitely didn't like Louie and Paolo being there so sure enough one of them took a shot. When we left fifteen minutes later it was possible neither of them would have kids.

Leigh was recovering but I didn't know how to help her. We tried to talk. I didn't want her to know I'd nearly killed her attackers. I needed her to know I'd done the right thing. I doubted she would be grateful. She didn't believe in violence. Whatever it was that she believed in grated with me because her politics only seemed to create as much conflict as it wanted to prevent. The only thing we could ever agree on was getting through each day.

Alice and I had a night together then the whole of the next day. We just sat and talked then had a long walk in Stanley Park. She told me her family was moving out of town so her dad would be nearer his new job. She'd ditched the boyfriend because she didn't want any ties. I looked at her and told her I'd have done the same. We held hands and laughed at so many things and we said we'd be mates forever as we kissed each other goodbye for the last time.

Now Leigh showed me whenever a letter came from Mum and just before I was sixteen one arrived with a stamp that didn't have the queen on. She had gone to Canada. Jason had started beating her up and at one point threatened to kill her. Leigh told me it was just the two of us now.

Ben got me into the football firm. I started to go to away games in a van. We were remote from the main traveling fans and often didn't even go to the game. We just landed in places all over England and smashed up things. Beat up people and tore up the idea that everyone is basically united. We kind of won and we left a mark even if we lost.

Leigh was making progress at work and became a supervisor. She told me to work hard in my exams. I ignored her and left school with nothing. It made her mad. I was fine with what I'd done and hadn't done. That summer I went into the town and pushed for a job wherever I could get one. That's how I met Derek.

The football thing came and went in just two seasons. Ben quit too. Some of the blokes were massive fascists and were sometimes joining up with rival club firms to attack immigrants or their properties. For a while that lot were after me. Ben too. But we were hard enough to stay clear of any major trouble. The loose alliance between us two plus Louie and Paolo meant we could call up any number of troops when needed. We weren't mates or anything that sentimental. But we kept in touch. Allies.

7:37am

I pass a sign saying *Gisburn.* I have to slow down, so I decide to see if I can get some food and a brew. It's still very early but a café is open and looks good. There are two tables occupied and a small queue for takeaways. I sit and wait. The smell of cooked food and the cabinet filled with cakes are both tempting but I stick to an order of tea and toast. On an off chance I ask if it can be thick slices, and the lad serving says it can.

At the next table an old couple, maybe in their seventies, have plates of Full English. They're chatting happily about someone called Elspeth who they'll be seeing soon and who they really love. The woman keeps passing bits of food over to the man, smiling at him and saying she'll never eat all this. He doesn't object but although he smiles back, his frustrated expression confirms he can't eat it all either. Maybe once, he says, but not since the operation.

I take my phone out to check if Neal has replied. His email downloads.

> *Good decision. I'll let everyone know. You won't be disturbed. If any customers call, refer them to me. Stick an out of office reply on email and voicemail. See you in a fortnight.*

Something prickles under my skin and wells up in my chest. I feel controlled again and can't stop blinking. I stare around the café, things blurring and wobbling. This has been happening a lot. What is it?

It takes ages till I feel calm. I decide to take no notice of his instructions and suggestions. The phone goes back in my bag.

Before I've poured my second mug of tea, all the tables are full. The place has a nice vibe and I sit back in my chair to listen and learn. Then someone arrives to join the old couple and I guess it's Elspeth, because there's a lot of smiles and hugs. They really do love her. She pulls up a chair and orders a latte and they're chatting constantly, interspersed with laughs and smiles.

The queue for takeaways is almost constant. Mainly it's blokes in work gear and I'm watching the people serving, impressed that they keep up.

I butter the second piece of toast, spread some jam on it then have another look around the café. A woman at one of the other tables is watching me. I hear her ask the waiter if she can have nice thick toast too, smiles across at me like she's grateful, then goes back to making eyes at her man.

The place smells of warmth and comfort, sweet and savoury. As well as all the happy chatter, the noises of crockery and cutlery, of steam jets and frothing milk are reassuring. I don't really want to leave.

Just over an hour after I get back to my car, I park it in wet, rainy Ripon.

9:26am

From the car park I can see the building, and in no time, I'm stood outside one of its ends.

It's big.

Huge doors are open.

Welcome on board. Much love. God x.

Just beyond the huge doors, a more modern glass door slides open and I'm inside. It's all lines and curves and points. I didn't know what to expect. I don't know what to do. I'm not the only person in the building, but it feels like I'm alone. Down the left-hand side, there's a carving and then nearer the middle a raised metal stand, like something you'd give lectures from. It's got a roof, a bit like an umbrella, suspended over it. I get my phone out and search to find it's called a *pulpit*. That's from a Latin word. A dead language. I put my phone away again.

It was grey outside and I expected a gloomy interior, but the light is strong. Wherever I look, there's something that I've never seen before. Every first glance suggests complete order and... what's the word? Symmetry? But sometimes I see a line or arch that isn't quite right. An after thought. A rethink.

A statue, also made of metal, has a woman sitting clutching a dead or dying man. She's hooded. When I touch it, I expect the metal to be cold, but it isn't.

I thought the wall with its pipes and carvings was the end but, through an arch, a whole new section is filled with fancy wooden furniture, more pipes, more finery. A sign says *Service in Progress* and sitting in some of the benches towards the back of the building are people. There's also a priest in long flowing clothes. I can't go in, so I look at the wall with its carvings and the row of lights shining up at them from the stone floor. It's vaguely sci-fi.

Alongside this back room, another section has a weird set of hanging metal twists. They're like huge versions of those spinning decorations you can get to hang in your garden but much more beautiful. I stare at them. They seem out of place yet perfect, forming a screen. One that doesn't exclude or stop anyone from proceeding. You can pass through if you work out that it's safe. Beyond the decorations is the same basic stuff: stone walls and floor, wooden chairs, giant windows, another huge chest draped in heavy material with candles on it, somewhere where I think people kneel.

A voice says something and it becomes clear the service has started. The rest of my walk around the building is accompanied by this calm, unemotional voice from speakers. It's not disturbing in any way, yet it's a background noise that signals something I'm not part of.

A curved wooden staircase rises to a balcony. There's a piano with a cover, more statues, and a table with loads of candles on. Above me, the ceilings are so high I can't imagine or believe how they were made or how they stay up. Some ceilings are stone, but the big one looks wooden. How do they keep that safe?

The voice introduces someone else, another man, who is going to read something. The new voice is less calm and reassuring.

I'm standing by a table with a big cross on a long stick and, out of nowhere, a priest is next to me. She smiles, looks kind. Wears a long black outfit.

'Welcome to Ripon Cathedral.'

'Thank you.'

'Do you like our church?'

'It's amazing. I've never been in a cathedral before.'

Now her smile is wider. 'Then you chose the very best one as a debut.'

'I don't know how it stays up.'

'Well, perhaps, some would say that God keeps it standing. Or faith. But of course, those are conceptual albeit comforting, notions. Like any other construction, it relies on great foundations, the craft of its builders, physics and, especially these days, constant maintenance, and care. And love. And I'm afraid, money. Have you travelled far today?'

I tell her my journey so far, my plan and my name. She is called Lynne. Then we stand and she points at loads of things using words I've never heard. Lynne says it all with such kindness that I am drawn into the spell.

'I think your plan to visit cathedrals is excellent. It will be good for your wellbeing. Where will you go next?'

'I'm not sure, but I haven't really made any decisions. It's like I want to make it up as I go along.'

She raises her eyebrows and smiles again. 'That sounds marvellous.'

'I need to look on a map but after I'm finished here, I need to find the next place to go. Maybe something within about three hours, max. Want it to be somewhere further away from where I started, not nearer.'

'Then you have three options. Closest, and east from here, is York Minster. Then, to the north, Durham. Further to the south and east, Lincoln. All are stunning, powerfully sacred buildings.'

'Which would you go to?'

She reaches out and touches my arm just above the elbow. 'Let me turn that back to you, Joe. Maybe you should keep making it up as you go along, and decide which way to turn when you finally leave our lovely cathedral and Ripon?'

Her smile is more affectionate and kinder than I am used to. Such love for a stranger; for a guest.

A few moments later Lynne says she has to prepare for something called evensong which happens much later in the afternoon, but still needs her attention. She wishes me a safe, happy pilgrimage. When I frown, she says it means a long journey to visit, or perhaps to find, a sacred place. And, once found, to rest there.

I walk around the corridors again and again. I think Lynne called them *isles*. It is time spent looking at the writing on stone, at the organ's keys and knobs, at the screens telling me history, at the pictures in windows with their colourful scenes. I didn't know what to expect when I walked in. Now I feel that every step I take is like a lesson. I'm taught that there can be peace in places like this. Maybe happiness too?

Love?

Outside, the rain is lighter. I walk all the way round the building and find the warmth of its interior is gone. These walls and roofs with their towers and turrets seem like a fortress. Inside, affection. Outside, resistance. Scattered around the grass at one end are gravestones. Wicked faces have spouts that the rain drips or pours out of. That feels like the darkest comedy. The clock face tells me the time. Inside, the lines and arches and windows were sometimes out of reach, but they still protected whatever small space I'd stood in. Out here, I feel excluded.

Lost?

It's too wet to really enjoy the streets. I walk aimlessly around a big square with a tall monument. The pubs and cafés and shops are busy, but I can't get a feeling for what this place is. I keep walking. The rain is cold and my waterproof jacket means I've got wet patches all around the tops of my jeans. At one café, I go in. I order tea and toast, but the waitress tells me the scones are home made so I try one.

It's peaceful here. Like a café should be. People eating meals. People talking. People who are happy.

My homemade scone is amazing, as good as any toast would have been.

I end up thinking that the thing that matters most to me here in Ripon is that cathedral. Not the shops. Not the people. Not the businesses. Not the traffic. Maybe the scone, but that's all gone. And, because it now really matters to me, I want to make the outside seem as good as the inside. When I get back there, I decide to sit on one of the benches facing the huge end and its entrance door.

I just look at it.

All the things Lynne told me have kind of gone straight out of my head and I think I might look online later if I can remember any of the big words that she told me. But not now.

Slowly I find this view less troublesome. The outside isn't so bad.

<>

Leigh met someone and it wasn't long before we were back to me being the little brother she never wanted. It wasn't nice being in the small flat with just the two of us but we'd managed most of the time. But once Pete was there two or three nights a week I started to go out and crash wherever I could scab a night on the sofa.

Derek ran a small stall on the prom selling what he called Knick Knacks. He paid me next to nothing unless I sold stuff. There was enough pay eventually. Got a cheap mobile. Bits of food. A night out. Rent to Leigh. I'd stopped thieving and mainly didn't get involved in trouble unless it was unstoppable. None of that mattered.

I realised I would need my own place soon. Everything revolved around those few key principles. Work. Earn. Be good. Be honest. Get domestic.

Alice came by one day with her Mum and we smiled at each other but couldn't talk. She was still gorgeous but looked terrible. That didn't change how much that smile meant. It hadn't been forever after all. A week later she was back and asked if we could have a brew together and Derek was pleased with how much I'd sold that morning so he said I could have an extra fifteen minutes for dinner.

Leigh and Pete said they were getting married. They were in love. It didn't change anything. The flat was still my home. Leigh meant that. Pete's eyes said different.

I passed my driving test first time. It meant I could start doing more things for Derek. Once he realised that I could be trusted with his vans and cars he joined me up to other people who needed a driver. It ended up with me having a regular job every Friday and Monday. It was a bit more money too.

The flat was changing because Pete had moved in some of his stuff and Leigh had a bit more pay so started buying bits and pieces. A lamp. Cushions. New plates. I got a double bed. Leigh didn't ask me for more towards the rent. I told her I'd give her extra.

One day I had to drop things out at Lytham then Freckleton. I rang Alice to see if she was around. Her mum answered and said Alice was at college. Her mum wasn't happy about the phone call. That Saturday we had another brew in town. Alice asked me why I'd called and seemed quite emotional when I said it was just to see her. She reached out her hand and touched mine then left it there.

Every Friday I had to pick up Carolyn Harrison from her college and take her and a bag to her dad's house in Longton. On Mondays I had to be there to bring her back and drop her at college. She sat in the front seat and hardly spoke a word to me while tapping away on her mobile phone.

Mum's letters had dried up. The last one said she was living in a town called Vancouver and for the first time in her life felt happy. Leigh tore the letter up after I'd read it. I'd never seen Leigh so mad. She kept saying Mum had never once asked how either of us was or felt. She'd never once offered help or guidance. What made Leigh really angry was that Mum had never suggested meeting up or invited us to go and visit her.

The weekends got so I couldn't stay in the flat because it just wasn't right listening to Leigh and Pete having sex. I couldn't go anywhere too far away because of work but Paolo was living in a shared house in Fulwood now. I stayed there more and more. That's when the nights out in Preston started. One night I saw Carolyn Harrison with a few others in the clubs and she was still spending a lot of time doing whatever she did on her phone. The next Monday she actually spent time talking to me.

Derek sometimes left me in charge and one day he asked how I felt about running the stall. Him and Jean were planning a holiday. I told him I'd be fine. He said he knew I would. He said he wouldn't have asked otherwise. Derek said he trusted me.

Alice called me in tears one day because her dad had died. Straight after work I jumped on a bus and headed over to Warton. It took ages and I felt mad at Derek for not letting me borrow his van. When I got there Alice was waiting at the pub. She looked bleak and hardly spoke. I just sat and joined the silence. Then she stood and came round the table to sit next to me put her arm through mine and held my hand. She put her head on my shoulder. Then she started crying and told me all the things she loved about her dad.

11:39am

The man asks me if it's all right to share the bench and I say it is. They sit down after he wipes the slats with his hands, and he waits for her to sit before he does. They seem happy, like me, to just sit and admire the way all those stones are shaped into something powerful and strong. They don't say much at all until they decide to have a drink. He takes out a flask and they share the cup. She turns to me and apologises that they couldn't offer me any, but I say I don't drink coffee anymore so it's fine. Then he takes out a packet of biscuits, crunch creams, and offers me one. I say I live where the biscuits are made.

'Take two, then,' he says.

I reply, 'That would be greedy.'

She says, 'I thought it was a Lancashire accent.'

I'd never really thought about my accent before and suddenly wonder if it's strong. Something defining. While she keeps talking about how they live in Thirsk and come to Ripon every week, I realise her accent is soft, but still has sounds and undulations that make it different to mine, and to most people I know.

'What brings you to Ripon?'

'I wanted to see a cathedral.'

'Well, you chose a good one. We never tire of it.'

'I'm going to see some more these next few days. Got some time off work.'

He says to her, 'Have you ever seen any other cathedrals?'

She tells him, 'I've seen a few on business trips but never went inside or looked at them like we're looking at this one.'

I say, 'Maybe that's the same for me. I visit places for a specific reason but don't take notice of what the place really is.'

She and I have this in common, it seems.

'There are people, sometimes quite vocal on social media and so on, who see this lovely building as pointless. Think it should be ripped down to create space for houses or shops or a car park.'

They ask what I do, and I keep it brief. They do too. She's a contracts manager, he's a teacher. They've a son in his first year at university in Leicester. Then they tell me they're Annie and Phil, so I say I'm Joe.

'We used to go to Blackpool a few times every year. We lived in Skipton when we first met, and it was an easy day trip. Phil loved the Big One, didn't you? And we'd go to a show if there was a matinée. Not sure why we stopped, to be honest.'

'Life got in the way.'

They ask me if I'm married, and I answer with evasion. Annie follows it up by asking if there's anyone on the horizon and I say there isn't. She changes the subject.

'Are you staying here overnight? Ripon has some lovely hotels dotted around. Much better than the chains. And a few good places to eat, too. *Del Duero* is brilliant if you like tapas.'

I don't like tapas, but I don't tell them. Instead, I say I'm not planning to stay. Not sure what I'm planning, really. I've got almost unlimited options, and this makes me smile.

Phil's smiling too. 'Of course, you have! You're in Yorkshire.' Annie laughs. Then so do I. There's something homely and comforting about this simple conversation between strangers. Any number of things could make us avoid one another but some tiny strands help us to sit like this and be comfortable. It seems easy because that's exactly what it is. They don't give me their number in case I'm ever in the area. I don't say they should get back to Blackpool and call in for a brew when they do. No one is desperate for this to be converted into lifelong friendship, with stones lifted to check what lies beneath. When they stand to leave, I stand too, and we shake hands.

I sit back down, taking another ten minutes to gaze, my head leaning to one side, at the great walls in front of me.

<>

Before leaving Ripon, I call into a couple of shops and buy clothes for a night out. Strange assumption for me to make since I don't know what happens next. But some smart things, shoes, trousers, tops, a jacket mean I won't get barred.

I get petrol before I reach the motorway which has next to no traffic. It's dinner time.

Place names crop up on signs and I feel reassured of my direction. I know these places. Some are big cities I could visit.

I pass them by to keep moving south.

<>

Carolyn Harrison gave me her mate's number and told me she would be perfect for me and for a while that's how it was. The Friday and Monday taxi service was still a feature and Carolyn Harrison always wanted news of how I was getting on with Chloë.

Derek sometimes watched me working the customers and one day took me to one side. He told me he was amazed at how I got people to buy stuff. He said all the worthless crap we sold sounded like the crown jewels thanks to the ways I pitched it. He wished he could bottle what I had. I told him it just happened. I had no idea what he meant about bottles. That night I asked Chloë what Derek might be getting at and whether he might be setting me up to fall. She told me he wasn't and that I was lucky to have a boss who cared.

Ben Louie Paolo and I started to have trips away. It started with nights out in Manchester but someone - I think it was Louie - said that was fun but he wanted less of the same old scenes. Ben picked us all up one Friday evening and we drove up the M6. Found a B&B in Coniston and had a couple of days just being somewhere that was busy as fuck but wasn't all houses and roads and cars and noise.

The flat wasn't my home anymore. It wasn't about being unwelcome. It just seemed like my presence was alien to Leigh and Pete. The TV shows were what they wanted to watch. Music was chosen by them. Once Leigh asked me why I'd eaten something from the fridge. We had a row about it. I bought a replacement pack of ham to make up for it.

In a club Chloë and I got chatting to Carolyn Harrison and her mates then another couple joined us. They were older but no one seemed to mind. We all looked great as if we had the world at our feet. I got chatting to the guy Mark. He was doing pretty well and said he was going to ask Liz to marry him. It seemed strange he would tell me that like twenty-five minutes after we'd met. But he moved on to another subject and I saw that's how he was. He just flipped up the next headline about him or about him and Liz or about something he owned. Later after Chloë and I fucked each other senseless on one of the sofas at the shared house in Preston and she told me Liz was exactly the same as Mark.

The next time I saw Alice she looked like she was ill. All thin and pale. It upset me. She told me her dad's death had left the whole family in a mess with no obvious way out of it. Her mum was thinking of moving back to Derbyshire. Alice Grace and Kieran didn't want that. She said I looked happy and perhaps I was in love. I told her I was more worried about her than me. She said if I was in love then it made her happier than she'd been for weeks. That almost made me cry.

Derek decided to open another stall up in Cleveleys and he left me in charge of things while he sorted that. I asked him if it made sense given that things were doing all right at the main pitch. Was there really any new type of customer up the coast? He said there was no better time to be selling cheap shit to keep people believing they had something to cling to. Keep selling he said.

Louie got a job at Liverpool Airport. He moved to a place near there and we had a final trip away to the countryside as well as some proper mad nights out. He was all embarrassed when a gang of us showed up at Blackpool North to wave him goodbye but then he was gone. We never saw him again.

Leigh and Pete got married and I gave her away. It made me feel good and she told me I'd been brilliant. There was nothing grand after the ceremony. A few people came over to the pub and we had some drinks and a few sandwiches. Back at the flat Chloë and I made them a meal with candles on the table and a nice bottle of wine. Then we left them to it and headed out for the night. Chloë's parents were away so we had a weekend together and we told each other we should think about moving into a place for more times like this.

Mark called me one day. Said Liz got my number from Carolyn Harrison. Wondered if it was true. Was I looking for a place to live?

Derek's second pitch didn't work. It was soon back to being just him and me hustling on the prom. Then it was down to just him because he'd run up debts and couldn't afford my pay. He still chucked me work doing driving. Fetching and carrying but that wasn't enough money. Just bits and pieces work like the gig with Carolyn Harrison.

Chloë said she didn't mind and would help me find a job so we could carry out our plan to live together.

Carolyn Harrison said she'd help me find a job because she didn't want anyone but me doing the taxi runs.

Leigh and Pete said they'd help me find a job and they knew I'd find something soon.

Alice sat me down and looked through the papers at jobs. Then she walked with me to the agencies and job centre to see what was out there. She picked me up in her mum's car one day and we drove over to Preston then Blackburn then Wigan to check stuff there too. She said it made her feel good to help me and even though nothing came of it. It made me feel good too. Alice held my hand and told me to believe something would come up. But I mustn't be complacent.

12:56pm

I haven't eaten since my scone. When I park, the motorway services seem quiet. I head into the building to find something to eat.

What a horrible mess these places are. Stuff that is over-priced and over-rated at the best of times, but much worse here, for all these captive consumers. It really is quiet, which makes it more pointless. A building with a car park. A building where nothing happens except spending and expending.

The toilets are clean and smell sickly sweet. It's just me and a series of robots. One flushes water through the urinal as soon as I step away. Another spurts foam and water on to my hands when I wave them under the spout. Another blasts air so strong it moves my skin around.

There's no robot doing toast.

I buy a sandwich, a drink and a cake at the coffee outlet and it costs a fortune despite being called a *deal*. I stand outside to eat the sandwich and see a few cars pull in. Then a bloke, older than me, better dressed, is in my face. 'Are you Doncaster?' I tell him I'm eating a sandwich before continuing my journey.

I know what this is. This was my game once.

'Are you fucking Doncaster?' I feel like telling him I'm not fucking anything at the moment. He looks like he might hit or butt me. A distant shout makes him run off, nearly falling down the steps. More cars arrive and speed into the car park to be dumped randomly. A total of nine carloads of blokes, all ages, are suddenly fighting like they'll kill each other. No scarves, no shirts, nothing to identify them or their crews. They're well away from the main building, over by the hotel to my left, but I can see it all. I'm in a higher place.

The couple who'd been behind me in the queue for food come out, saying their car's parked close to the fighting. They look scared and I suggest they go back inside. I have a feeling these maniacs will soon be done. One of them has a baseball bat, another has one of those tools you use to cut turf. The violence is escalating and they're screaming at each other. Two are jumping on the head of an opponent, whose mates have smashed another guy's face through a car door window.

Someone asks me if I want to come inside, as they're planning to lock the doors so that lot can't get in. They've called the police. I say I'm fine and hear the door being locked. I put my sandwich box in the bin. The bottle of smoothie is tiny, two mouthfuls top. I laugh as I think about how I'm having my dessert and it's a piece of millionaire's shortbread no bigger than two of my fingers. A three-course meal of indulgent excellence, while forty or so pricks try to kill each other. In fact, I think the one whose head was getting stamped on might be dead. He'd been fitting but gets another kick and stops moving.

It looks like one side has started to edge it and another carload of lads is in retreat, driving at maximum revs, veering towards one of the winners who jumps clear. As the car howls away, the bloke who wanted to know if I was Doncaster glares out at me. I mouth - *I'm Blackpool*.

Two police cars race up and, shortly, a van arrives with reinforcements. Then more cars and another van. Now the fighting is between police and citizens. The former has the upper hand. They've got tasers. Another car of lads tries to scarper, and I notice a police car blocking the exit. Then a helicopter is hovering, blades battering the airwaves. This all means I might be stuck here for a while but, slowly, order is restored. Sure enough, one of the police runs up and asks me what I'm doing. I tell him I was enjoying a sandwich when the fighting started, and he looks like he might get difficult with me. The door opens behind us and a woman in a trouser suit and Hi-Viz jacket tells the bizzie I am an innocent bystander. He looks like he has other ideas but gets called over to help with renewed violence. I thank the woman for her support. She's terrified but furious too. She's the service station manager and this happens almost every week. I don't really want to know. Then two bizzies are back asking her how they get hold of her

CCTV. They also tell me I have to give them a statement.

Straightaway I tell them, 'Nine carloads of men sped into the car park, they jumped out and tried to kill each other.'

Neither of them likes irony, but one has to go back to the front. The other says, 'Let's keep it factual, sir.' I feel like arguing that my statement was 100% factual, then button it and answer his questions. Now ambulances have arrived, and the paramedics are tending to the wounded and dying. Some of the blokes scream abuse at the paramedics for trying to fix those Yorkshire cunts.

My answers. I couldn't tell who instigated the fighting. It looked like it was pre-arranged. I didn't see who attacked the bloke lying motionless on the floor. There was a lad here before the others because he accosted me. Yes, I could identify him. I guess he was some sort of advance party, and I think he just got away in that Merc. No, I didn't get the registration. I give my name, address, and phone number. It's the first time the bizzie looks like he believes me. No, I didn't film it on my phone. Why would that be, sir? None of my business, officer. He looks like he wants to give me some grief, perhaps accuse me of being involved. Instead, he rolls on into a script about notifying any change of contact details, and how I might get a local officer calling round, and how I might need to appear as a witness in court. I shrug and tell him I'll do whatever.

I don't tell him I won't be back there for a while, but I ask when I can leave. He wants to know where I'm parked, what's my registration and where am I headed. I point at my car, parked over near the fuel station. He's had enough of me and tells me I can go.

The traffic is still light.

When I leave the motorway it's also clear on the A road, so I drive too fast and love that buzz I get from danger.

<>

I found out Chloë was seeing someone else and when I told her I knew she didn't try to hide it. We'd been pretty good together. But I wasn't prepared to be some sort of substitute. It wasn't a particularly unpleasant break up. We just broke all the links.

Derek went out of business and him and Jean ended up in court with all sorts of problems.

Leigh and Pete were patient. But I was in the way. I knew I was. We all agreed I couldn't move until I had a job. I earned my bed and board by managing the house. Cleaning. Ironing. Washing up. Cooking. Sorting out paperwork for Leigh and generally being a good brother. I also used time alone in the flat to watch telly and tried to learn stuff.

Derek somehow still had his cars and vans. I was still a taxi service for Carolyn Harrison but not during school holidays obviously. One Friday evening she told me how sad she was that me and Chloë had split up. Then her hands were all over me and we parked up down a lane somewhere out near Weeton and we had a hell of a fuck in the back of the car. She said she didn't want us to be a couple and didn't want sex anywhere else. She wanted it like we did it that evening. So that's what we did. Every Friday evening and once on the return trip on a Monday morning.

The job Alice helped me find worked out well and I bought her flowers. She said it was almost definite they were moving to Derbyshire and her Mum insisted they all had to go. I told her I didn't want her to go. We both got really upset.

Ben and Paolo picked me up after my first week in the new job and we went up the M6 again. It was late when we reached Keswick. It was buzzing and we all got lucky. I spent the night with Jodie who was gorgeous. We kept in touch and for a few weeks I went back up there to meet her at weekends. It wasn't a great journey. Quick at first then fucking ages on a bus from Penrith.

When my job didn't work out after all I didn't have Alice to help me. She'd gone. Jodie couldn't help me either mainly because I didn't have the money to get to see her. Ben drove me up there one time. Jodie wasn't around even though she'd said she would be. Ben got really pissed off with me about the waste of petrol.

Mark called me out of the blue and asked if I was still looking for somewhere to live. When I told him I was but was unemployed. He asked me where I was. Came and picked me up. He drove us to a Maccies. We sat inside to eat and talk. He had two problems. I could probably help him with both.

Carolyn Harrison fucked me even harder now I was unemployed. We never said much but one time she gasped you fucking horrible working class prick in my ear just before she came. I dropped her off and she said she'd heard about me meeting Mark. Told me that I should listen hard to whatever he was offering.

Leigh seemed suspicious when I told her what was happening and soon dragged Pete into the discussion. He didn't care and she got mad at him for not backing her up. Then she got mad at me and started telling me to get out. Pete came in and supported me saying she was being unreasonable.

Paolo got badly beaten up by racists in Preston. Ben and me went over to see if he knew who they were but he said they weren't local. They'd stopped to talk to him. Friendly at first but when he told them he had an Italian name they called him all sorts then jumped on him.

Jodie phoned me in tears apologising for messing me around and how she was sitting in A&E. I talked for a bit and got the feeling something wasn't right. I killed the call. It sounded like she was more trouble than I needed.

Alice was living near Buxton now. She phoned me and we laughed together for nearly an hour. She told me I should come and stay some time. I told her all about what Mark was offering. She said it sounded perfect and I should do it.

Mark had this house that he rented out and two of the three tenants had disappeared. The remaining one was working at the big DWP site in Lytham as some sort of consultant and he didn't want to lose her rent. Mark also needed a dogsbody to do stuff at the company he ran with his brother in Kirkham. More fetching and carrying. Anything from driving people to the airport to cleaning to making brews to going out with the engineers or labourers to help with jobs.

Carolyn Harrison's dad came out one time and started chatting to me about where Derek was. I told him I hadn't seen D for months. He said why was I using one of Derek's cars if I hadn't seen him. I told him I collected it and delivered it to a lock up near Layton station. Derek was never there. Never had been when I collected a car. Carolyn Harrison's dad handed me a roll of notes and told me he needed to know where Derek was. He'd give me another two hundred if I gave him a nod.

I caught the train to Preston then headed to Manchester and on to Buxton. Alice was waiting at the end of the platform. We hugged each other like lovers. When she kissed me on my cheek it seemed completely normal that we should kiss properly so we did. Buxton was nice and we spent the day talking and remembering all we'd ever known together. She looked better now. Her smile was back to how it was all those times. This time when I left it wasn't forever.

Leigh and Pete helped me move my stuff to the house at Newton and Leigh got all tearful when they left. She came back twice to tell me she loved me. I told her I was less than ten miles away and would see her every weekend.

The deal with Mark was that I would pay half the rent for six months so long as I worked all the hours he needed. It seemed fine to me that way. Then Helen the other tenant told me she knew someone who was joining her at the DWP site and would probably take up the other room. When Mark heard that he told me I could have the half rent deal for nine months so long as I was absolutely excellent at work.

Derek got caught down near Leyland by Mr Harrison's heavies before I had the chance to say anything. It was kind of a relief. I asked Mr Harrison if he wanted his money back. He told me I'd helped. That was the last weekend I did the taxi run as Carolyn Harrison and her dad were moving down the road to live near Chorley. She wouldn't be spending any more time with her mum in Blackpool. We kept talking on the phone.

3:17pm

It's strange, yet exciting, to arrive at a place with nowhere to stay. It seems to make the town or city or whatever the fuck it is anonymous. A sign says *City Centre*, so now I know it's not a town. I drive on. Ring road, outskirts, signs, missed turns.

Directionless, I take a road towards the city then pull into a supermarket car park, wondering if the Park and Ride is an option. Then I start phoning hotels. There's one with parking, so I book it and set off again.

Check-in is quick, and the couple behind the counter are like good cop / bad cop. The bloke barely looks at me, the woman is all smiles. I don't bother to go to my room, and I head out to the streets, along past the castle and on towards the cathedral. This is a place like nowhere I've ever seen. Narrow streets, with buildings closing in on me as I pass. Quite small shops, not the usual names. Jewellery. Food. Bars. Fancy clothes. The word *artisan* seems to be in play. I keep going and pass one of the hotels I'd tried earlier. It looks rubbish.

Then I see this wall with an arched gateway, and beyond it, I can see towers. When I get the other side of the wall the cathedral is there, like a giant brooding monster. It's massive. Colossal. That's the end of my word options. But they're the only ones I need. It's bigger than anything I've ever seen up close. I reckon Ripon could fit inside it. This end that I'm looking at is all lines and arches and doorways and windows and spikes and details and, above it all, those two towers.

It's very cool indeed.

You have to pay to get in. That's weird. I don't mind, but it is weird. The woman doing my ticket says it's evensong at four and I nod, because I know about evensong now. I mean I don't really know what happens at it but I'm clear that it exists and not just at Ripon.

You can't walk around while the service is happening, she tells me, but perhaps you'd enjoy the music? Stay for that, she says, it's worth it.

I set off and do the same route as in Ripon. Up the left side aisle, and I know it's spelled like that now because I checked. The ceilings are high, and the walls have pieces of wood with drawings on. I dawdle and it takes me ages to get to the crossing. I know it's called that now because Lynne of Ripon told me.

My mouth drops open. I can't stop it.

Massive.

Colossal.

It's blowing my mind. Like at Ripon, there's a screen with big pipes. You can't walk through this screen, though and it's got tiny stone carvings all over it, figures and flowers, animals, and monsters. Away on my right, underneath a big circular window, a statue of a sitting figure. The light through the windows behind it makes the person look hooded. Up close, it's not a hood but he's got a big cape and funny-shaped hat. It's a bishop and he's waving at me. I wave back. Yo, Bish.

I find a memorial to the armed forces. One mini-church for each of them and a ship's bell in the Navy bit. I stop to look at a big book showing the names of people killed in World War two. Locals, I suppose. I see that Walter Horne was killed in action on April 18th, 1945. Something makes me check dates. Walter died 19 days before peace started. It freaks me out.

There's so much to see and I'm confused. Locked wooden doors, loads of candles spread on the floor, a room with walls covered in painted figures and animals. I pass under more and more high ceilings. It seems everything is out of reach, but you still keep looking up.

I go into a bit where people mill about putting things on the benches. I work out that it's where there'll be some sort of performance. I ask one of the people and they tell me this is where the choir sings evensong. This zone is completely different. Dark, carved wood. A big metal candelabra hangs down. Some of the benches have candles inside glass pots. The rear seats have a rectangle with words on. Gold letters on a black background, but the words are like a foreign language. I think they might be place names. I didn't get to see this stuff at Ripon, so this is a surprise and a treat. It feels like a place where there could be secrets. I think those named seats make this place like some sort of society. Or cult.

A voice says *Evensong will start soon*. I head back to the main bit and, while waiting, I read that the bit I'm sitting in is called a *nave*.

The music is magical. Sometimes it's one person singing, others it's a choir. The organ makes so much noise. It's crazy. Whoever came up with that idea was a fucking genius. In the end, I've no idea what it all meant. I think the singing was in English, but the words didn't seem to matter. It was all just an amazing mass of sound, loud or quiet.

After evensong, I go to the ticket desk and, when the woman gets back, I ask about the music. She tells me to wait, then someone else gets sent off to fetch a list showing all the services ending tomorrow, when there are events with names I've never seen. *Holy Communion*. I can more or less work that one out. But *Matins*? *Eucharist*? Some are marked with *Choral* and have what must be the music listed beneath them. It's a bit too much to take in so I fold it in half and stick it in my pocket.

Through a door, I think I'm headed outside and I kind of am. But here's another new thing. A square of grass, surrounded by corridors. One side is completely open, with benches so you can sit and look up at the main body of the building, those towers especially. The other three corridors have tiny windows with no glass so you can look at the grass and the gravestones lying flat on it. I walk slowly, clockwise, around this strange add-on to the cathedral. What is it for? Tea parties? BBQs? Sacrifices? At Ripon, I felt everything was simple. There was really just three straight lines to walk along. The sheer scale of this place makes me feel great doubt, makes me overwhelmed. I'm triggered. I have to get out.

Back at the massive end, I sit for a while just looking at what is in front of me. What on earth made all this happen? Who sat down and said this was going to be done? I'm triggered again.

Suddenly, a nagging voice in my head tells me I should think about quitting my job.

<>

Down the hill, I find a different bit of Lincoln and it's more like I'm used to. Things look the same as back home: the shops and cafés, banks and betting shops, people wandering aimlessly. The walk does me good, clears my head and makes me want to do something this evening. But not down here. Back up there in the old bit, where everything seems gentler.

All the while, the cathedral is there. Up on the hill.

7:48pm

While I change into my new going-out clothes, I keep thinking about the two bits of Lincoln. I've worked out that the main difference is history, which has been retained up here while the bit down there is more modern. This has no equivalent near where I live. There's no old and new bits in Blackpool or Preston. They just exist with one bit each. The trouble is, I don't know anything about the history of either of those local towns. I only know my part in it.

It's strange to think about that.

I find a pub that looks good, with tables outside and those heaters. I get a pint and take my phone out to check what Lincoln is.

The group of lads makes a lot of noise when they pass.

It's lonely outside, so I head into the bar area where a good atmosphere makes me decide to stay for a bit. I grab another drink then perch on a bar stool. The group of lads is still noisy but amiable and smart. Their self-assurance isn't threatening. Seems they won a match of some sort today. Their conversation clicks through its topics: rugby; next week's school; music;

books; exams in the summer; a despised teacher; a trip to a gallery; back to rugby and Samson's late winner.

One of them points out that my jacket has fallen off the back of my seat. When I say thank you, he invites me to join them. Handshakes all round. Firm ones. I learn their names, their plans for the evening and how there'll be ladies joining them. They learn I'm on holiday and what I do as a trade. One of them says he likes that I refer to my work as a *trade*.

They all have this confidence. Still at school, still capable of a descent into childish assessments of mundane things yet filled with a kind of charm I've rarely seen or known. Softly spoken. Brought together by the decisions to send them miles from home, they seem to have unbreakable unity.

When I tell them where I live and why I'm here, they're polite and deferential, never condescending, or arrogant. There's a brightness about their curiosity. Kids from the same kind of schools near me always behave like gobshites, looking down their noses, the very worst sort of snobs, incapable of integration. They become the kind of business owner I encounter at work. Big fish basking in a pond that's really just a puddle.

I wonder why these lads are so different. I like them enormously.

Then a raised voice makes one or two of the lads look resigned. I hear one say, 'Here we go again.'

'Horrible smell in here again, isn't there? Why do you let them in? Why do any of us tolerate these turds?'

I can see the bloke, standing by the bar, jabbing a finger at the staff and any tables of drinkers he wants as an audience. Now he points at the lads.

'Look at them. Strutting around like they own the place. You wankers, splashing your parents' money around like you own the place. Well, you don't. This city doesn't need you or your nasty little school.'

He's cut off by someone who's arrived behind the bar and wants to calm things down. But his authority isn't respected.

'No. No, Martin. You shouldn't let these leeches drink in here. We wouldn't be allowed to drink in their shit-infested drinking holes back in Godalming or Wilmslow or wherever the fuck they're from.'

He's told to drink up and leave so he chucks three quarters of a pint on the floor before slamming the glass on the bar. 'Fuck you, Martin. You don't deserve honest customers who do proper jobs and pay taxes while these scum and their families and all their kind just take, take, take.' He's walked towards George, one of the lads, glaring into his face. 'Don't you?' George shakes his head and maintains eye contact. The ranting man can't reciprocate.

'And who are you? Their pimp?' It was kind of inevitable he'd pick on me at some point.

'Think you need to do what the man said, pal.'

'And where the fuck are you from?' He's scanning the room again, like a politician on Question Time or in the house of commons. Someone in a soap opera. 'A nobody, passing through, who picks the worst kind of company? They don't want your kind in their lives, you dozy prick. You're just another slave to them.'

'Maybe we're both slaves, pal. Me to myself and my job. To all the problems they give me. Yeah, I'm a slave. And so are you, mainly to your stupid... fucking... pointless opinions.' He can't look into my eyes either. He exits, still ranting that the world's gone mad and the rich are going to kill us all.

'Just another Saturday night in the old town,' says George, but his face doesn't reflect the calm in his words. I look around the bar and I don't see many who would have backed up the shouter if he'd kicked off. None of them looks sorry either.

But Martin comes over to apologise. He's told not to worry. I order a round and when I get back with the drinks, the incident is forgotten. The lads are back to discussing ideas, concepts, ways to think.

<>

Time for me to go. I head off to find another bar but feel bored and tired. It's still early when I shuffle back to the hotel. It isn't good news that smiley woman is perched behind the reception desk.

'Good evening, Joe. You're back early. Didn't someone take your fancy? You look very desirable. I expect you were fighting off the ladies.'

'I had a nice time and met some good people. But I'm tired. Was up at silly o'clock this morning and need some sleep.'

She actually licks her lips, leans forward, and nibbles the end of a pen. 'Maybe I should come and tuck you in? Would you like that?'

It takes massive self-control to stop myself telling her to fuck off. Instead, I say it isn't necessary. Her eyelids flicker into a squint as she looks up and down my legs and torso. She's got a filthy smile on her.

This is impossible, but I persevere. 'I really need to catch up on some sleep. Goodnight.'

The smile fades and she throws the pen on the floor before storming off.

I stand inside my room with the lights out and my back to the door. The safety chain is looped into place. There's no noise seeping in.

I am quite desperately tired now and lie on the bed.

But I genuinely don't want to fall asleep in case she lets herself in with a pass key.

I've got the list they gave me at the cathedral, and I open Safari to type *Matins*. When I've learned what that means, I search *Eucharist*. These things calm me down, dilute my anxiety.

I keep going and learn that G.V. Stanford was a composer. So was Henry Purcell. Both have pieces being sung tomorrow. The one by Purcell is in Latin. The translation means *Jehovah, how many are my enemies?* I find a link to a performance of it on You Tube and what I hear sounds like a declaration of war.

Nothing like what I heard at evensong. Who knew they sang this kind of stuff in church? Maybe that's why they use that dead language?

In the *Eucharist*, there will be something called 'Missa Brevis' by another composer, called Palestrina. More Latin, written by an Italian. I'm blinking with incomprehension.

A noise at the door makes me shrivel up again, anxious, heart pounding. Something has been pushed under the door. I look at the envelope, which has my room number written on it.

It's my bill and I'm pleased to see I can pay it online.

I'll be out of here before seven.

Now I'm doing a search on the word *paranoid*.

I don't think I am. I don't have extreme and irrational fear of others.

I've never feared anyone.

Distrust, though.

SUNDAY

06:30

I've slept but nowhere near enough. A series of decisions is needed and none of them is getting the right level of attention.

The bed is comfortable. The quilt is too small. I seem to be half in and out, no matter how I lie. There isn't a plug near the bed, so my phone is charging over the other side of the room. The last time I looked at it, there was nothing to trouble me other than my worries that I should be on it, spending time planning which cathedral to see next and what route I'd take to get there. Checking and rechecking what might be wrong with me.

I shut my eyes and try to get more sleep.

<>

Mark kept me busy. I was getting pretty well paid for doing just about anything. I think he liked that I never asked questions. The house in Newton was also busy because Helen was like a maniac socially. There were always people there in the evening. I could tell they were puzzled about me being there. I kept out of their way and sat watching telly while they bitched and moaned in the kitchen. Occasionally I heard them say stuff that sounded confidential. All the rest of it was technical and really boring.

Ben and Paolo came to the house once with pizza and a few beers. We saw each other less by then and nights out were rare. That evening we had a laugh and agreed we were mates and should be better at keeping in touch. Ben was working at the pleasure beach on security. He was in a pretty long-term thing with Freya. Paolo was doing really well working for PNE and said he might be getting married soon because he really loved Silvana.

Carolyn Harrison phoned me every couple of weeks usually when I was busy. She told me her dad had a new partner who was only a few months older than her. I asked how she felt about that. She said it was hilarious. Sometimes we met up in Preston on nights out. But she wasn't there as much. I asked her where she went out now and she told me Manchester was too close to ignore.

7:39am

It's no good; I can't sleep so I get out of bed and open the curtains. My phone has fully charged, and I start making decisions, resolving my questions, problems and worries. I'm going to go to Matins because I like the sound of all those enemies. I'm going to leave Lincoln before lunch and drive to the coast, destination TBD. After an evening there, I'm going to go west and look at Coventry cathedral, because it looks so weird.

It's also time to get up and out of this hopeless place. I shave. I shower. I realise I might need new clothes, especially underwear. I add a section in my plan and the map shows a shopping centre on the outskirts of the city. When I leave the hotel, there are still ninety minutes before Matins. I try to find if a Starbucks, or whatever, is open. All I do is wander the streets.

<>

Leigh and Pete came to see me at the house every weekend because Helen went home on Friday afternoons and didn't come back until Monday evenings. There was space. Sometimes Leigh stayed over but Pete never did. I asked her a few times if everything was all right and she always said it was. Pete was perfectly okay and happy around me. I just had a sense there was tension between them two. One weekend I told Leigh and Pete they couldn't come because Alice was visiting.

I met her at Preston Station that Saturday morning. She ran along the platform to hug me. I took her bag. We stayed on platform 1 to wait for the Kirkham train which was late like always. But we had loads of time and we just sat and talked and kissed a lot. The taxi was waiting at Kirkham and got us to the house. We went straight to bed and spent the whole of the rest of the day there.

Mark took me out on a job once where the customer was one of the local celebrity millionaires over near Great Ecc. There was seven of us on the job because in Mark's words there was no option for Mr and Mrs Fuck Up to be visiting this contract. The house wasn't that big. The bloke's head was fucking massive. He was an absolutely horrible cunt of a man. Spoke to us all like we were peasants and called Mark the chief bitch. It was already a bad start. It meant the job went badly.

Alice came to stay several times and we were close. I told her I loved her eventually and she smiled like it was all she'd ever wanted me to say. Then she said she loved me too like she had since school though I think I knew there was a but coming.

Helen's colleague from her company moved into the third room at the house. I'd never known or seen anyone like him. He constantly had his laptop in front of him doing something. One day I asked him what kept him so busy. He just said numbers. He was called Brendan and seemed completely detached from the gang Helen brought back of an evening. Brendan would sit with me in the lounge with his laptop and his numbers on his knees. I watched absolutely solid gold shite all evening and he would just be locked away in that place. When he occasionally looked up his eyes were blank.

Millionaire Man was making life hard for Mark and his brother and the whole company. They were told to get out to the house one day and they asked me to drive them over. Mark and Chris were in suits and looked like they were shitting themselves. I wore my usual. They climbed into the back of their company's old Beemer. I drove them along the road. They told me to come into the house with them and be ready to do any tasks that needed completing to keep the customer satisfied. Millionaire Man was all smiles like he had won the lottery and grown five inches on his dick. Said he wanted to find a way to solve the problem on good terms. Said he'd been out of order before. I didn't think he looked honest. His charm didn't last long. He was soon screaming abuse. At one point he looked at me and asked them why they'd brought the oily rag. I got up and knocked him down. Mark actually whimpered like a kicked dog. Millionaire Man was laughing. At last! he said. Someone in your shit little company with some bollocks. He held out his hand and I helped him up.

10:05am

The coffee chains are all shut, and I've walked miles to prove it. Like Sundays are sacred and God doesn't want us to drink beverages before 1030. We might get unholy ideas.

I head back to the cathedral and go inside. *Matins* starts in twenty minutes, so I just go and sit three rows back from the front and wait, scrolling through stuff online about all the different bits of cathedrals. Transepts. The Choir. The Altar. Prebendary stalls. The Nave has filled with dressed-up people. There's total calm.

By the end of *Matins,* I've heard prayers, readings, a man talking from what I now know is called a pulpit and this unreal music. Even singing a dead language, the singers were amazing, and it was still hard to believe that a load of kids and some men, plus that organ playing, could make so much noise. The whole thing, the setting and the sounds and the echoing made me quiet, listening hard to the Latin song. I was wrong about it being a declaration of war. It's much more like resistance. At one point, one of the men sings solo and his voice is like those famous people on the telly.

When we all walk out the priests stand wishing us well and one of them welcomes me, saying he hasn't seen me before. I say I've never been before and it's only the third time I've been in a cathedral. He laughs and tells me it's the fourth service he's attended today. He hopes I come back soon. I think he means it.

The people around me are chatting. It's like a social club or institute, except here everyone actually likes each other. A couple smile at me and beckon me to join them, saying they heard me tell Canon Shaw I'm a stranger. Would I like to come along for coffee or tea and biscuits?

Later, I want to go back in the cathedral to wander around and try to get over how much it troubled me yesterday. I want to get the kind of understanding I got in the one at Ripon. But another service has started so I have to go and sit on a stone bench outside. I read about the cathedral's history and all it has been through. Nearly 900 years ago it was more or less destroyed by a fire, then an earthquake. An earthquake, for fuck's sake. For hundreds of years, things either got added or fell down. It got smashed up by the roundheads, who sound a bit like skinheads. It has a bell called Great Tom. When I look up at the giant end wall it still looks like something permanent. Yet, for centuries, it's been constantly fighting with itself and its enemies. Like in the Latin song.

I also take time to look on a map and find somewhere by the sea. The coast isn't far away in one direction, but I don't like the look of the places there. Further afield, I've heard of Great Yarmouth and think that's the answer because I could call in at Norwich to see their cathedral. Then I remember a trip there with the football crew and change my mind. I don't want to revisit anywhere. These places need to be new to me.

The resort I fancy is less than two hours away so I can be there by three if I make my shopping trip quick.

<>

Pete arrived one evening in a state. He'd never taken any time to talk with me one to one and something felt wrong about him doing it. Helen and Brendan were there so me and Pete walked out past the school across the main road and round the narrow lanes in a loop. He told me he thinks Leigh is seeing someone else and it's tearing him up.

Carolyn Harrison was in Preston one time. We spent the evening talking which seemed to piss off two of her friends. She said her dad and his new girlfriend had gone to Lanzarote so there was a load of her friends staying at the house. We all went back there. They were doing a lot of drugs watching porn and skinny dipping. Me and Carolyn Harrison kept talking deep into the night and it seems she was thinking of leaving home. Her dad didn't like the idea. I told her to come and stay at my place any time she needed a break. We ended up in bed. But nothing happened.

Mark told me I needed to sort out the Millionaire Man myself because I was the only one who didn't get abuse from him. I headed over there every other day for a few weeks and resolved the work and listened to him ranting about the immigrants and the gays and the women. It's depressing how anyone could be that angry about things that made no difference to his life or money or existence. Not one bit. He never once considered that he might be the problem. He never asked me what I think. He just told me his opinions as if they're facts. He didn't even realise that I never nodded or smiled or said anything to him about his bullshit.

Carolyn Harrison got a nice car. She arrived in it one day. It had a personalised plate. CH44 CHA which was meaningless. She laughed about it constantly. Her dad thought it said ChaCha like that weird dance word. I told her I was calling her ChaCha now and she said don't. The car and registration plate were a bribe from her dad to stay living at home. Her plan was to get a further bribe in the shape of a flat in Manchester so she could go there to stay but still technically live with her dad. She reckoned he'd go for it because Mr Harrison could use it too. We went along the road to Lytham and spent an afternoon there. She bought me a set of mugs for the house. We went back to drink from them.

Leigh and Pete started coming to the house just once a month instead of weekly. One time they both stayed which had never happened before. In the morning Leigh came down on her own and showed me a letter from mum saying she knew where dad was living. It left both of us a bit lost. Leigh wanted to write and ask mum to come back to England and help us get dad so we could try to find some sort of togetherness. I didn't think this would work.

Alice started sending me letters. Proper hand-written ones on nice paper and I read them slowly. It was as if she's speaking the words. One time she asked me why I don't write back so I bought a post card and wrote that I wished she lived close so we could see each other every day. It looked a bit personal to send as a public card. I put it in an envelope and posted it.

Me and Ben and Paolo didn't really stay connected like we planned. We had the odd beer midweek. But weekends were busy. Ben suggested going up to the Lakes again for old times' sake and we did that one Sunday. Walked up near Wast Water and got soaked but it was an amazing day. We sat and ate some snacks we'd brought and drank tea and agreed we shouldn't be down about not seeing each other. Paolo said we were all still around and ready if anything happened. Ben said we just couldn't be what we'd been. I said we should check what Louie was up to. Paolo said he'd moved on again. Lived down south working at Gatwick and living in Brighton. The rest of the walk was full of memories about what we'd all done. It didn't seem like any of it had ever mattered.

Millionaire Man told Mark and Chris he was happy now the work was sorted by me. Then he took weeks to pay the bill and I got sent over to ask if there's a problem. Millionaire Man was headed out when I got there and tried to drive off. I blocked him in and jumped in the front seat next to him. He called me all sorts. I called him all sorts back and eventually he laughed and said he still liked me. He said his people would get the payment sorted the next day and I asked him who they were and how I could get hold of them. He touched the screen between us. It dialled a number. Millionaire Man told the woman to sort out the invoice for Mark's company today. I told her my number and said she had to call me when the money's been transferred. I said it all while Millionaire Man was still on the line to her.

According to mum's letter dad was living in Southampton doing something in the docks. How did she know this? It sounded made up. Maybe she told Leigh out of badness? Helen got home from her office and said I looked worried. I told her why. She nodded her head and said she might be able to help me. But not tonight because her boss was coming to stay and that meant there'd be more noise than I wanted to hear and when I ask Carolyn Harrison if I could stay at her dad's she came to pick me up. Her car was too small for a fuck in the back. We stopped in Cuerden Park and had one against a tree.

1:10pm

Some of the place names I see on signs are unlike anything I've seen before. Except, now I think about it, near me are Grimsargh and Goosnargh. That's not so different to Ashby de la Launde, or Quadring Eaudyke. I decide everywhere can be as weird as anywhere else when it comes to names that make no sense.

Does my name make sense? Joe. Joseph. Joseph Thompson. Joe Tom. Joe Le Taxi, more than once.

My shopping had to include a big bag to carry all the new clothes I've picked up since Saturday. I was quite thorough. Bought enough underwear for the week ahead and a load of cheap tops, plus a pair of jeans, some smart shoes and some pumps. Finally, a hoodie and joggers for travelling in.

I've drunk too much tea and water, so I have to keep stopping. It's ages before I reach King's Lynn.

<>

Brendan didn't stay in the house for long and it was back to just me and Helen for a bit plus her boss when he didn't feel like going home to his wife. Then Helen told Mark her contract would be finished soon. He got quite anxious and told me he might have to sell the house. But then Helen said she'd told a few of the civil servants she worked with. They were interested. Trouble was they wanted all three bedrooms.

Mum's next letter said there was no way she'd ever come back to Britain. Leigh and I weren't surprised, but it hurt. Still no invitation to go and stay with her which actually hurt more. There was a repeat comment that Dad is in Southampton and has met a woman who he'd had kids with. Leigh thought mum was making it up.

2:39pm

As I drive the last few miles into Hunstanton, I realise I made another decision without a plan and haven't arranged somewhere to stay. I could be screwed. It's well past 2pm on a Sunday afternoon. I pull over and start looking on the map, then the Internet.

I needn't have worried because the third one I try has a room and they offer it cheap as they'd not expected it to be occupied this late. The hotel is away from the seafront but it's lovely, with smiling people and a nice welcome. They offer me a table for tea, but I can't decide and tell them I need some fresh air and a walk.

It takes me less than half an hour to reach the sea and even on a gloomy Sunday, there's cars parked up with people strolling. It's like a smaller, hillier countryside version of Blackpool. No trams and grass instead of concrete. The sea is grey to match the sky. The houses looking out across the water are grander. I like it. Another place with a different kind of history.

I walk along the grassy path until the place turns into something more familiar. The garden areas are replaced by mini golf, a promenade with cafés, an amusement arcade and funfair. It's busy and noisy.

Down on the beach, the sand has wooden posts running from the prom down to the sea. I climb down to walk on the sand. The posts form lines every fifty metres or so and I can't work out why they're here or what they do.

The beach is shallow, but the sea wall suggests it might get wild.

It's getting late. Away across the water, between the sea and those grey clouds, a small band of blue sky is lurking. The sun slowly drops down out of the grey and into the blue, turning everything all kinds of colours. The dark sky turns purple. Like an old bruise. The strip of blue soon has a big ball of orange and I watch the sun sink into the ground, making even more crazy colours as it goes.

I've walked quite a long way now and haven't really noticed that the tide is coming in. A small surge of seawater wets my feet and makes me rush back up onto the promenade footpath then head back to the lights.

Back then, I never thought of Blackpool as my home by the sea. Waves came in and out, like the visitors did in their thousands. I just let it happen and took no notice. It was part of my life while I was working for Derek, selling things to use in the water, or near it: inflatables; towels; bat and ball sets.

My walk has become an aimless shuffle in which I've lost track of time.

<>

Helen asked me what my dad's name was and said she'd see if she could help. I didn't understand how but I didn't ask. It sounded dodgy. That evening she handed me a piece of paper that told me there was no trace of my dad. Her face confirmed I shouldn't ask. The people she asked to the house the week before she left got pissed and fucked in and around the house. One of her colleagues was called Tola. She was tall and beautiful with gorgeous long arms and legs and a smile that could melt steel. She was bored and guessed I was too. We grabbed a beer each and went to sit in the garden and she told me ridiculous stories about how the company she and Helen worked for was screwing the taxpayer. Tola listened to my description of my job and told me I should keep going because it sounded real. She kissed me and it was like an explosion of passion but we both decided not to take it further. She didn't stay much longer but gave me a business card. No one had ever done that before.

Alice wrote to me every week and I tried my best to write back. She said she understood that I wasn't as good at it as her. Sometimes what she wrote was sad and open. Other times it was difficult to understand.

Mark made me do a lot more work facing his customers and making the company look good. Some of the lads who did the jobs didn't like it. One of them took a punch at me pissed off because he thought he was better than me and I was just an oily rag. That phrase again. Mark fired him. Then the lad came for me in town one time. It ended with a really bad fight in the street. The bizzies calmed me down quick enough but used a taser on the lad and he got done for assault. Mark got his lawyer involved and I didn't get any kind of charges.

ChaCha invited me to go with her to Manchester to look at the flat her dad was thinking of getting. It was in the centre and close to all the shops and bars and restaurants. It wasn't that big but even without anything in it I could tell it was worth a bit. Then her friends Roisin and Dexter arrived. We went out and hit the bars. Dexter was off his face on coke before seven and Roisin went off in a temper. ChaCha said she would have to sort Dexter out. I caught the train back to Preston. It was ugly on there. Football fans. Afternoon drinkers. People headed to Blackpool. Fight after fight and the train stopped for ages at Bolton so the police could arrest people or just chuck them off the train.

Leigh said she was worried mum had stopped writing. There'd been nothing for months and she got upset when she told me mum might be dead and we'd never know. I said we probably needed to forget mum had ever existed. She made no difference to what either me or Leigh had become. Leigh shook her head and started really crying. I asked if anything else was wrong and she said she was having an affair behind Pete's back. That's what she said. I wasn't in a mood for this and got angry with her asking if it was possible to have an affair right in front of his eyes. I didn't tell her that Pete suspected it. Maybe I should have.

9:58pm

It's dark and cold. I'm sitting on Hunstanton sea front staring out across the sea. I can't see the water because of a string of glaring lights above me that mess up my vision. But the sound of the waves means I know the sea is there.

I've bought pretty decent fish and chips but I'm eating so slowly they're going cold.

By the time I go to bed I feel like I'm a million miles from any kind of home.

MONDAY

9:17am

I'm not angry as a rule, rarely lose it. When I see people suffering from rage it's usually because they are weak. Something or someone has caused them to see a hole in their life or beliefs and they don't have the ability to stop and think that the hole might be their own problem. They just lash out at the cause and fix nothing, least of all the hole. This is why I don't understand how Neal and all the others think I'm somehow a problem. Is it all the others? Do the owners and Josie and anyone else senior think I need more anger management.

I don't. Not there. Not at work. Neal's wrong.

But this journey *is* making me mad. Every 10 miles feels like 200. The traffic is like a disease, slowing everyone down, going nowhere. Today's trip is no distance at all, but the traffic makes it like a series of tiny journeys, each without progress or destination. Why does anyone bother?

<>

Helen left me a nice gift when she moved out. A piece of curved glass. Colourful with layers like frozen oils. No one ever gave me gifts. All the toys and games I chased as a kid didn't come with me when me and Leigh moved out. After that presents became things like a cuddle with Alice or a bit extra from Derek if I worked specially hard. It seemed strange and beautiful that a much older housemate would see me as worthy of this thing. I left it wrapped in its tissue paper and box until there was a place for gifts to be.

Mark said I could stay in the house on my own without paying more rent. But he was honest about the fact it couldn't be for long. I started looking for something different even though he said he'd sort something. It was nice having the place to myself. I moved into the big bedroom. I had my own shower. I made changes by moving furniture.

Leigh and Pete could come midweek now and I saw more of them. It was impossible. Knowing she was seeing someone. Knowing he knew. Knowing it was headed down the toilet. One time Leigh stormed out when we were having tea and Pete cried. I knew no way to try to be the peacemaker. I was just her kid brother.

Mark gave me more stuff to do in the office and it didn't make sense. He said I had potential and he put me at a desk with a phone and computer and told me to spend more time helping customers. When I asked him what help they needed he told me to talk to Kirsten and Andi. Those two knew everything. To cover the house situation Mark also gave me stuff to do late in the day. Driving. Trips to the airport. Collecting him or the other execs from nights out. I was kind of doing three jobs.

I went to Manchester more because ChaCha and her crowd went almost every weekend. She had a regular boyfriend now. The nights down there were amazing but sometimes got badly out of hand. ChaCha's man was like a magnet for trouble and a few times we ended up fighting with people Frank provoked.

Andi was more helpful than Kirsten although she was better at the job than him. The idea she told me was not to let customers forget us. The idea he told me was to have a plan. Andi stuck to a kind of tick list of actions. Kirsten did whatever she liked. The computer wasn't any use at all. But I sat and worked it every day to make sure I didn't get left behind. I found my own ways to use technology. Just for me. I learnt how to control people when they telephoned. Most of them had no idea how to communicate.

I kept calling Tola and we talked about me visiting. She met me at London Euston and held my hand while we walked to the underground station then all through the journey to Putney Bridge. Her flat was in a basement down near the river and she'd made me something to eat before we went out. She talked constantly. Pointed at things she loved. We'd stop all the time so she could look in a window or browse through things on a stall. We went to a pub late in the afternoon and by the time we got there I felt like I'd lived in London my whole life. We stayed until closing time. Now she stopped talking and listened to what I was doing at work and in my life.

10:23am

When the crawling cars, buses and trucks push me to the place where I can't find my lost temper, I turn off the main road for a break in a town that looks nice. The café is cosy, and I have a pot of tea for two and toast for three. It's a nice place but some of the customers are shocking. The ones doing business are so full of shit, treating the place like it's their office and no one else should be there. One of them keeps tutting at a woman playing with her kid. I nearly go and tell him to shut up.

It reminds me to see if there's anything from Neal, or anyone, at work.

<>

Alice sent me a letter and it wasn't what I wanted to read. We were probably never going to be a couple. Yet it still hurt me that she was going to marry someone. Her letter broke the news right at the start and I didn't read the rest. The next time we talked I got upset and told her I didn't want to go to her wedding.

I was in Blackpool one day and saw Pete. He was talking to a couple and having a proper argument with the bloke. The woman was the one shouting back. People were crossing the street to avoid them. Pete must have said something bad because the bloke suddenly took a swing at him. The woman held him back. Then Pete was laughing at them.

ChaCha called me and said her dad wanted to see me. She picked me up in her TT and we drove down to Manchester where Mr Harrison took us for some food. He asked me lots of questions about Mark's firm and what I did there. I asked why he was asking but he didn't say much except don't worry.

The civil servants came a couple of times to see the house and seemed to take ages to decide whether to move in. I wasn't there whenever they came but Mark told me there were three of them and if they decided to take on the house I'd have to move. I started looking again and decided whatever Mark might offer wasn't worth considering.

Tola invited me a few times and I got to enjoy being in London. One weekend I went Thursday night and stayed till Tuesday morning and in between all the sight-seeing and a show plus all the drinking and eating out she fucked me a lot. It was amazing how she just took over and I almost felt hypnotised by her. She told me it was nothing and I agreed. We just did this if the time was available.

But I thought about her a lot when I was back in Lancashire.

ChaCha's dad picked me up himself one day and we drove along to Lytham where his mate had a company and needed young people to do selling. We met in the posh hotel on the promenade and Mr Harrison left me with three people in one of the rooms. One did all the talking and said she was HR manager. She was called Olivia but said call me Liv. The other two just watched me. Mr and Mrs Cartwright were the owners. Liv said they met everyone like this and then explained they weren't interested in people with a fancy CV and experience. Hunger. Drive. Energy. That's what they wanted. Did I have that?

12:15pm

I get to the outskirts of Coventry. I think about just fucking this all off and doing something else. Go back. Start again. I don't make my mind up quickly enough and then my phone rings. It's Glenn from Caddy-Hill with a query about the new contract. I answer his questions and we have a more general chat. We'd always hit it off one to one. When he says it's not a great connection, I say I'm driving, and my Bluetooth isn't great in the car. I tell him I'm on holiday and we should talk later when I'm not in the car. I always want to be free to take his calls. He told me I should've said and says it can wait till I'm back.

I call Neal straightaway, but he doesn't pick up. I leave a voicemail about Glenn's queries.

Without knowing how, I've made it to the city centre and parked. When I get to the cathedral, I'm really happy I didn't change my plan.

It's extraordinary.

Coventry Cathedral has no huge wall at the end, with tiny doors that are somehow closed. Instead, it has a massive window with dozens of figures engraved on the glass. It means light is thrown into the building and, just inside, several rows of words form a statement. Gold letters on black tiles.

Ahead of me there is space. Masses of it. The ceiling is curved, gently, with grids of squares in segments. No big pillars, just thin grey columns. In place of arches, I see straight lines and angles. There is light, constant light, but also plenty of shadows. Those are intriguing, not a threat.

I just stand, staring at something I can't understand yet feel drawn to. Something about its lines and stark shocks of newness are comforting. I start my clockwise exploration. I should be triggered, already, by the lack of aisles and the certainty of a structure. The crossing. The tower. The transepts. But I'm not. Those things were boundaries. Rules. Here, there is something simpler and more infinite.

In a section called the *Chapel of Unity,* plunging lines of grey stone have slits of light slashing through them. Some of the slits are pure sunlight; others are caused by the sun shining through multi-coloured glass. It's more like something out of a futuristic film than a chapel. I can't stop staring at this, either.

All down the left side of the building I walk past big stone slabs with words on. A sign tells me these are called *Tablets of the Word,* but some also have pictures. I think they must be from the bible. Across the other side of the nave there are more tablets. The thing that's most amazing is something I couldn't see from the main entrance. Not just me. Anyone. As I walk towards the far end, each angled wall reveals ceiling to floor windows, multi-coloured and dazzling, especially since it's sunny. These shed light across the space I walk through.

Like a giant puzzle, all the organ pipes are stacked up high. They look a bit like those fancy radiators people have when they do kitchen makeovers. Every few steps lead to something surprising, colourful, illuminated. Windows, like paintings. A cross of charred wood. Signs, telling me stuff. Maybe there were signs in Lichfield and Ripon, but I missed them.

One sign tells me I'm at *The Lady Chapel*. It's got these big black bars like a cage and a vast canvas with figures on. Animals, a huge person - God, I suppose. And underneath God, it must be Jesus hanging on a kind of cross, but it's not like the crosses people have round their necks or the ones on altars. Nothing like it. I read the sign, and it tells me *The Lady Chapel* is where there is joy and sadness, fears and hopes, endings and beginnings. The canvas is called a tapestry. It represents love. I go back and look at the tapestry, and blink at it.

I love it.

For most of the next fifteen minutes I'm in a bit of a daze. More rooms, one with a huge, winged figure holding a big goblet. Another with a curved array of windows, the sunshine casting bars of light across the floor and its lettering. More windows with weird lines and multi-coloured glass. Candles. Crosses. Something that looks like it might be a meteorite, fallen from the sky but the sign says it's the font.

And a gigantic wall; or is it a window? Like everything else, it's floor to ceiling. It's curved. I walk away from it to look at its effect and it has this central bit that looks like the sun with blues and reds and greens all around it. My mouth drops open. I walk back to it and a sign tells me it's called *The Baptistry Window*. Up close, it's really not that powerful. Up close, all that's in reach is maybe five or six of the individual windows. Up close, it's quite simple. Move away, just twenty steps, and it's this wall of light. A mirage. Complex and hypnotic. Hopeful.

Now I walk up between the rows of seats in the nave till I reach the choir. There are two big golden pulpits either side with carved figures. The choir stalls have what look like flocks of birds over them. Here, everything is made of wood. Simple. Except the altar, which is another massive piece of stone and beyond it is the tapestry. It's like an illusion. When I was stood looking at the *Lady Chapel,* I felt I was cut off from the rest of the cathedral. Here, there seems to be an unbroken view of the massive green and pale-yellow picture. I don't get it, yet I love it. I love it all.

When I turn and look at the huge window, it looks strangely fragile: a thin grid of rectangles. Light. Space. Love. I walk back there.

Those massive letters by the entrance spell out a message that this cathedral is relatively new. Outside, opposite the towering glass arch, there is a ruin.

It is a silent shell, despite the people strolling around. In one end there's a kind of bay window. A stone altar with another charred wooden cross sits there. It says *Father Forgive* on the wall behind it. The glassless windows seem strong, still show there is a world outside, still shed light on the inside. At the opposite end, a tower rises up to a pointed spire but between me and that structure there is nothing but a stone floor and the remains of pillars. I can't see any evidence that this building was ever in the shape of a cross, like I've seen before. I walk, seeing statues and sculptures. It's eerie, but not threatening. I need to know what happened.

It was bombed.

The whole city was bombed, killing hundreds, destroying homes and factories. And the cathedral. Those charred crosses are formed from burnt timbers found in the wreckage. They built the new one and left this old skeleton as a memory. A link showing they'd created one place, not two.

I'd begun to feel quite calm, more than I've felt for months. But the shock of this destruction is powerful, much more than the shock of the new that I'd felt when I walked through that glass screen.

I just sit and soak in all that I can see. Ahead of me the giant canopy that bridges between the two structures seems to give comfort to the ruins, holding them up, keeping them strong. The whole thing has this powerful visual impact. What I saw at Ripon and Lincoln was impressive, solid, and bold, but also traditional and somehow unyielding.

Here, in this place, I feel as if for the first time in my life I've seen and felt great certainty.

I take out my phone. Standing under that giant canopy, I take a picture of the old spire, walls, and windows alongside the fresh new stonework. Blue sky and green trees. A cross. Dazzling sunshine.

None of the photos I'd seen on the internet looked like mine. I've captured the essence of that beauty and certainty.

<>

I spend some time in the city. It's end of school time so lots of kids and teens are roaming. It makes everything seem alive. I sit outside at a coffee place and watch them all. The older ones trying to look cool and hard. The young ones talking about things that seem exciting and new. Boys and Girls, some of them together, others in their own groups. The scenes don't last long and when they dwindle, except for a few stragglers, the shoppers and business bodies take over again.

Across the square is a statue of a woman on a horse. That makes a change from the usual statues. I decide that I like Coventry more and more, with every minute I spend here.

But my tea isn't great, and the toast is limp, so I look on my phone for places to go. I can't decide. I eat up and head back to the car. I check my phone and find some work emails. Neal saying he'll sort the client out. Glenn thanking me for taking his call and wishing me a happy break. Also, a text from Carly:

Hope ur ok hun. Neal said ur on holiday x

I reply that I'm having fun then head out of the city with no idea where I'm going.

<>

I asked Tola's advice about the company when it was clear they might be offering me a job. We talked about how I should handle the situation with Mark too. She told me I must be honest with everyone especially myself. She said if I want the job take it. Explain to Mark that I'm grateful for all he's done but it's time to move on.

Alice sent me a formal invitation to her wedding. It's over where they both live near Buxton. I still don't want to go so don't reply.

The last weekend I'm in the house Leigh called in to help me move my stuff. I hired a small van as I really didn't have much. We talked about how letters from mum had dried up and perhaps that's a good thing. Not knowing makes it easier not to care. Same as it's always been with dad. Leigh said I'm all she has now. I asked her what's happening between her and Pete. She said it's all fine but he's avoiding her.

Helen kept in touch for a bit. I wondered why. Told me her manager had left his wife to be with her. But it wasn't what she wanted. I mentioned I had to move out of the house. We spent a while chatting about how weird it had been living there like we had.

Mark got a bit angry with me when I told him I was leaving and kicked off about all the rent I owed. It made me a bit mad inside. Something made me keep calm and I told him I'd stopped all the shit from Millionaire Man and that calmed him down too. Later that day he picked me up in a brand new Range Rover. Took me for a bite to eat and said no hard feelings. We agreed I'd work a month's notice then he'd pay me a month for holidays.

Tola came to visit. We booked into the big hotel in Lytham and had two nights messing up the sheets. On the morning she was leaving we walked out to head to the station to catch the Preston train and a couple driving past shouted nigger lover at me. First her then him. Then the woman said fuck off back to the jungle and take Tarzan with you. Tola laughed and told me she'd always hated this bit of England.

The rent on the flat wasn't too bad and I'd saved a bit in case I needed stuff. Leigh came over with a box of things. She asked how I'd manage without the occasional use of a car. I told her I was near the station and reckoned I'd be fine. The landlady was all right most of the time and fixed some things I'd complained about. The flat next door was empty. The one underneath had someone in. She seemed quiet. Everyone in the block was nice. I put Helen's gift near a lamp and so it was lit up.

I started for the company and spent a week learning about the products and services they do. Then I worked on the phones. Liv was always around but I never saw the Cartwrights. The woman in charge sometimes called herself the CEO but she had Managing Director on her door. Her name was Josie Parkinson. She was in the office before everyone and never left until the place was empty. Every single day. Lots of the others were nasty about her… I didn't understand that.

Pete came to the flat one day and sorted a few things the landlady kept ignoring. Then we went back to theirs and Leigh had made some food with a bottle of wine. It was a celebration they said because I'd got my job but also for them settling their differences and being happy again.

2:45pm

I've been driving round in a circle without realising. I'm stuck just outside Coventry and still no idea where I'm going or what to do. The phone rings but I ignore it. Then it pings messages at me, so I have to pull over to check. It's the fucking utilities company chasing me about that new boiler. One tiny expression of interest by me, they convert it into a deal. What the fuck is it with these companies?

I ignore it, like all the other things I should be doing that I keep ignoring. None of that matters. It can all wait. Till whenever.

Back on the main road I look at the signs with no real idea where any of the places are. Near? Or far? How much longer do I want to be doing this? The next stop isn't listed in my head. This is not what I want to do any more.

<>

The new job soon became just the job. One day I got there and Josie the MD's car wasn't outside. I said a little yessss that I'm first in. She was there in her office. A light shone on a writing pad to her left and she was looking at the big screen and sometimes typing. I'd been at my desk fifteen minutes and was still the only other one in. Josie asked me if I wanted a brew. We went to the kitchen. I always like the look and smell of the coffee machine. But I make tea.

She used the last of the coffee so she cleaned it all out then set it off to make another pot cleaning up as she went. Josie asked questions. I answered that I was glad I joined and felt I'm ready to do more. Josie asked more questions. I answered that I don't mind travelling or staying away. Josie asked more questions. I answered that I would feel I'd succeeded when she didn't need to ask me any more questions. She laughed. When we walked back to the main office, we were still the only people there.

Alice called me and told me she understood how I felt and invited me to go and see her and meet Jonny…I hated hearing his name. When I got to Buxton station she was there on her own and she ran up to hug me and kissed my cheek. In that hug she still felt like she always had except she was someone else's and that's torn off a little strip from my heart. I stayed over and the next morning Alice introduced me to Jonny. I thought he was a prick. It killed me that she wanted him and couldn't see what I saw and won't see me instead.

Each weekend I bought something nice for the flat. One time I got a plant. Another some beer glasses. Another a thing for holding candles. One morning at 6:15 I was sat with my tea looking at the candles on my table and laughing that all this was like I was going to throw dinner parties with guests dressed in their finest and talking shite about current affairs and paintings. I wondered if my toast would be enough of a meal.

ChaCha dropped in to see me and we had a laugh. She told me her dad had been ditched by Geri and was in a really bad mood. Someone might get killed she told me. We got in her car and drove off with nowhere to go. Just chatting about stuff. Taking the piss out of couples in other cars who weren't talking. ChaCha got her window down. She shouted talk to your husband you crazy bitch. Stop looking at your fucking phone. We booked into a hotel in Leeds then had a night on the lash. It was wild. It was the next morning when she told me Frank had asked her to go and live with him and she wasn't sure. I told her she shouldn't do it because she wasn't sure. I saw her phone buzzing about messages when she was in the shower. I didn't look but knew it was Frank.

Alice really pushed for an answer about her wedding because the numbers were tight and said she needed to know if I was going. I asked if I could bring someone which was a stupid bit of emotional blackmail because really who would have gone with me? Alice said she couldn't wait to meet the lucky lady and I could see her smiling happily down the phone at me and felt like a massive twat. I said I'd go and let her know later who with.

Josie took three of us to a meeting in Southport. All the way there she was telling us about the client and how we're going to win the business. I was in the back with Lee. Orla was in the front. Those two were obviously messaging each other and it made me uncomfortable... but I kept listening to Josie as she mapped out the plan for today. At the client's office we sat along one side of a table and this guy sat opposite looking like he runs an empire. Why'd you bring back up Jos? Are these the best you've got? Am I supposed to be scared? He said that stuff like he was in charge and some sort of celebrity. But Josie started on him and he was soon on the back foot. At one point he told her he wanted the three of us to leave and she refused. Told him her team was part of the deal. Take it or leave it.

3:17pm

I take a turn off that says Warwick but don't think that's where I'll go. Tonight, it's just about somewhere to stay, not to visit. The phone keeps ringing and at one point I feel like throwing it out of the car. It's never anyone I want to talk to. I should call someone, perhaps to break this cycle of poor communications. Who can I call? My car has no fancy system that stores my contacts, so I have to stop to decide. Then I see the *Recents* on my phone's call log and it's either just numbers or business names. Unknown customers, actual customers, but no one I really know. It is *The Unsolicited*. It makes me scroll through my contacts to look at the names that are at least acquaintances or, at best, friends. None of them has called me lately. And I've not called them. Why is that? What's going on? The last person in that category that I spoke to was Carolyn Harrison and it was ten days ago.

Something's wrong. But is it with me or with them?

I'm passing Warwick. One sign says *Historic Warwick* which makes me giggle.

I feel like I'm stuck on the road to nowhere else.

<>

I liked my flat and started to feel like I'd made a home at last. Simple things made it feel better every time I added something or even if I did little bits of decorating. People came to see me there and it was nice to welcome them. Lee and Orla from work dropped me off one night after a couple of drinks in Lytham when I missed the last train. They came in and Lee said she didn't feel too good and went to be sick. Orla kind of rolled her eyes and we weren't sure it was a good idea for Lee to travel any more. So all I could do was let Lee stay and Orla went and helped her get undressed and into bed. I had to sleep on the sofa. Orla drove home. I ended up sleeping on the floor and got cold.

I didn't like routine. But it seemed necessary to have one. Up at 5:45. Showered. Dressed. Fed. Walked to the station for the first train and it took 17 minutes. The train was usually on time. Then I had a walk along to the office. I was in at 7:20 latest. Josie was first. I was second. Every day. It was in reverse later. Josie was the one left behind when I closed up at 7. Walked. Trained. Walked. Home well before 8. Bed just after 10.

Lee wasn't good through the night and pretty ashamed the next morning. She had to get back to near Preston. I told her she couldn't leave looking like that. She went back to bed. I washed her sick-stained things and dried them. The football was on the radio and when she got up it was half time and she looked nice in my dressing gown. I made her tea and some toast. She said it was delicious. Lee told me Orla was going to leave because she thought Josie was going to sack her. I shrugged. Lee told me everyone thought I was fucking Josie. I told her that was ridiculous. She shrugged. Her boyfriend called and I could hear him shouting even when she went in the other room. I walked her to the station then went for a stroll around the town.

Leigh and Pete really did seem to have kissed and made up. They called round twice a week whatever night for just a quick chat then always on Sundays for breakfast. They brought the stuff to cook. It was nice and lasted a couple of hours. If it was a fine day we walked somewhere. Perhaps out to Treales and back. Maybe once every month I went to theirs on a Saturday and we went into Blackpool for a bit then back to the flat for a takeaway. If we were done by 10 I got the train home. If not, I stayed. We had breakfast somewhere in town. Leigh said she was worried I didn't have anyone steady.

After the time in Leeds ChaCha told me she's moving in with Frank but still wanted to see me. I didn't mind that but said I wasn't going to be messed around. She raised her eyebrows at me and told me I'm the best she's had so why would she mess me around? It's just loose. So that's how it stayed.

Lee's boyfriend broke in the main entrance and tried to kick my door in to get at me. We had a pretty serious fight and it ended with me taking him out with a table. Next thing he was laughing and told me that was evens. The table made a massive bruise on his back. He seemed okay about it. We went to the Stanley and got a pint. He asked what happened between me and Lee. I told him straight. He said she'd slept with loads. He was sick of her. I told him not this time pal. She was so ill I couldn't stand the smell. He laughed. We ended up having a few and he had to leave his car.

One day at work there was shouting in Josie's office and Orla came out looking like she was ready to pop. She stayed the rest of the day but when she went at 5 she said goodbye to a few. It was nice working with you. Liv sent out a companywide email warning people about inappropriate use of company property and IT. Word went round that Orla was caught saying bad stuff about the company and the owners and managers. Maybe somebody snitched.

I went to see Tola and it was the last time. She was going to work in Switzerland and wouldn't be in London for more than a year. She was offered the work because she was doing so well. We talked about how you need to be ready to go if the company needs it. We had a lot of fun and no sadness that weekend. She gave me a gift voucher to buy something for my flat. It was worth a couple of hundred. Tola came back to London Euston with me and held my hand all the way and while we stood in the concourse kissed for so long it made us laugh.

Alice and Jonny got married and I went on my own. She looked beautiful and I couldn't stop staring at her. I was on a table with people my age and only two of them were a couple. I chatted to Richard from Stockport and Heather from Derby and both of them were really funny. They went off when the dancing started. Heather didn't come back. Richard sat opposite me to talk to someone else. It was a nice day and for about twenty minutes Alice spent time talking to me about our lives and how much it all meant to her and would keep meaning to her. I told her to be happy. But I didn't mention that I didn't think she was.

Josie took me into Preston one day and we met a client who was very serious and stiff. She kept saying our costs were high for such a simple job. Josie was struggling. I told the client all the facts about the figures. Broke down the price into people costs. Products. Travel. What our margin was. Finished by saying it was a fair price. She said she wanted a better discount. Made it clear she'd go somewhere else. I said she should go somewhere else then. Josie took me to a place for some food and told me I shouldn't have been so open about the numbers.

I used Tola's voucher to buy a set of pictures I liked and got them framed. Pete came over and he made a nice job of getting them level on the wall.

Orla messaged me wanting to know if I'd be a witness for her as she was taking the company to court. I didn't reply for nearly a day. She sent another message saying it must have been me who snitched on her. I replied straight away saying I didn't know what she was on about and if she was innocent what was there to snitch? I never heard from her again. Lee said Orla tried the same with her. It wasn't long before Lee also left the company.

ChaCha sent me a message saying she was on the train coming to see me. Something was wrong. She never went on the train. I met her at the station. She said Frank had smashed her car up and she was pissed off with him. But she was happy to see me. We went to the flat and dropped off her bag. She showed me her new tattoo. It was really simple like a string of leaves running down from her belly button to her pussy ending with a tiny blue flower. We went to Morrisons where she bought some stuff then made me a meal. She stayed a third night and told me how her dad had Derek beaten up for pretending he was bankrupt.

Josie called me into her office and told me to shut the door and sit down. She said the serious stiff woman in Preston had agreed to give us the contract. Josie shook her head and smiled then apologised that she'd bollocked me that day. Seemed I'd done the job. Then Liv came in and told me I was getting extra in my salary as a bonus.

3:50pm

When I get to Stratford I decide to stay there. One of the chain hotels is on the outskirts so I wander in, and they give me a room. I close the door and lie on the bed listening to my phone buzzing every once in a while, which makes me think there are things left undone.

I thought all this was a good idea on Saturday. It maybe wasn't. The hotel is noisy and, nearby, there's a telly on too loud. I can hear people talking and kids laughing. I don't know where to go next.

A pub is linked to the hotel, and I conclude that's the place to eat as it's an easy decision. But I feel worried that my hand is shaking when the bar guy gives me my drink. I put the glass down and try the other hand but it's the same. When I get to my table, I worry that the chair won't be able to support me as I feel like I weigh tons.

The food they do is what? Good for me? Bad for me? Eating out is the thing, and don't we all love it? I can sit here pretending a pile of nachos has a fucking rosette on it and it will be fine dining. So that's good.

I choose the cheesy garlic bread and the lasagne, then get another glass of fizzy apple juice and fiddle with a beer mat while the chef and team prepare my meal. All around me there is space. Empty tables. I decide that if the next person that comes in doesn't say *hello* I will leave. I've pulled the beer mat to pieces.

The food is okay. The third, fourth and fifth fizzy apple juices are okay. The missed calls and popup reminders on my phone are okay. Not going home is okay. Having nowhere to go is okay.

Being okay is not okay.

Back on the bed, I wonder where I am.

<>

That work routine stayed the same except I walked quicker to and from the stations. I also added time on to the day. I spent some of the bonus they gave me on a gym membership at the place near the office and started going there straight after work and doing an hour. I arrived home later but that was fine. I still went to bed at 10. It was like a chain of gyms so I could use the one near my place at weekends. I sometimes thought I'd like a bike but there was nowhere to keep it safe.

Leigh and Pete went away on a holiday that was supposed to be the final part of their reunion and togetherness. They left me a key so I could check in on their place and I dropped by twice. It felt like I was intruding. The second time when I picked up the post and sorted through all the junk mail there was an envelope from Canada.

Without really wanting to I joined Facebook but kept my stuff low key. There was a kind of creeping pressure all around me to be on there and sometimes I wished I hadn't caved in. I didn't spend too much time on it but not long after I joined people at work tried to connect. I looked for Alice and Tola and Helen. But they weren't on it. ChaCha wasn't either. I found Leigh. Orla. Lee and loads from work. Paolo had like a joint account with Silvana. That freaked me out a bit. Leigh hardly seemed to get through a day without posting something. Signs with a quote or encouraging words.

Mark called me one day and asked me if I'd consider moving to a house he was renting out. No strings. Not much rent. I told him I was happy where I was. He said things were going well for his company and it sounded like he was dropping hints. But nothing came of it.

Lee's boyfriend invited me on a night out. One of those ones with a meal and a speaker. It was men only. He'd split up with Lee and said she was out of work since leaving the company. I didn't like the sound of the event anyway and there was something that didn't sound right in his voice. I made up a story about being away that weekend.

Tola sent me post cards from places she went to work. She said it was something real not a text or email. But that was all I could send back. We slipped away into nothing.

No more cards. No more texts. The framed pictures were left for me to know she had been around.

The Cartwrights showed up at the office one day and there was a lot of fuss. They spent time in with Josie then strolled around the office chatting to us. The question he asked me was pretty wild. Are you making waves? I said I'm a tsunami and it made Mrs Cartwright laugh. After they went a load of trays arrived with food and everyone got stuck in. Liv and Josie gave a bottle of champagne to Ben Tiler and told everyone it's really for the whole team. We all knew he wouldn't share it. A few of us went out into Lytham after work that night. Siobhan said she'd heard the Cartwrights were selling.

ChaCha got arrested with Frank because they'd been dealing cocaine. She said it was just him when she called me. Told me her dad would get her off. She didn't even take the stuff. I thought I believed her because I'd never seen her take anything when we were together all those times. It was the end for her and Frank.

Josie and Liv took me along to the Caffè Nero early one afternoon and I joined the queue for drinks. It was busy. The woman in front of me had headphones in and seemed impatient with the guy behind the bar. Then she got her drink and turned round quickly. Half of her drink went over me. It caused quite a lot of fuss and I saw Josie and Liv laughing. The woman was in a rush she said but seemed she meant her apology. Then she laughed at the big wet patch all around the front of my trousers.

Leigh and Pete got back. They'd brought me a packet of the spices you need to make a rice dish they liked in Spain. She didn't mention anything about the letter from Canada.

Alice sent me a card and said it's from Jonny too from the place they went on their first anniversary. It said and then there were three with loads of hearts and smiley faces drawn underneath.

The gym was making me feel better and a lot of people said I was looking good. I felt great.

The nights out after work became more frequent. There was six of us that went. Me plus five. We didn't always all go out. There was a hardcore of three. Then two came along 75% of the time. Anita was the lightweight. Three women. Three men but it was never three couples. There was no stuff going on between us. Gemma was married and Darren had Harry who he loved. We just all got on and looked out for each other. Siobhan was gorgeous and often went off with people who chatted her up. Me and Fred got on great and often ended up talking quite seriously about work. Not bitching or moaning. Just about how we could be better and make the company better.

Leigh told me she'd had the letter from Mum. It said she had cancer. I went to see her and Pete one night. He was out so me and Leigh spent the evening chatting about what we should do. The letter was hard to read. Mum had less than three months to live it said. This might be her last letter. Leigh suddenly got furious and shouted about how we couldn't be there for mum. I said she didn't want us there or she'd have asked. We discussed whether we had to try to find dad but we both knew that couldn't and wouldn't happen.

Josie told me I would be made a team leader in sales and Liv brought me a letter to confirm it. There was an email too. The next night out everyone made a big fuss of me. I was worried they'd be shitty about it. I ended up feeling emotional about how much they said I deserved it. Fred was the only one whose enthusiasm was different. Gemma said he was doing coke and that explained it. Josie and Liv joined us. They brought a bloke who might be joining the company.

A message popped up on Facebook one day that said something weird. It said sorry I made you mess your pants. I had no idea someone could message a stranger like that.

Pete called me and said Leigh was getting more and more unhappy about mum. I went there again. Leigh looked wild. Her eyes were red. She kept looking around as if someone was going to attack her. In the car on the way back to mine Pete told me he was struggling with Leigh's behaviour and mood swings.

Jonny called to say Alice lost the baby. I asked what he meant she lost the baby. Like it was her fault. He put the phone down on me. I sent her another post card but realised it would have gone to her mum's address because I didn't know where Alice lived. I felt terrible that Alice had married this prick who was the one blaming her for something so tragic.

I asked people I knew on Facebook if they knew who Natasha Pavlovic was. No one has heard of her. I ignored her messages because she'd sent more. Then one day I was in Caffè Nero again and she was behind me in the queue and tapped me on the shoulder. Don't throw a drink over me she said. It's you I said. You're a rude man for ignoring my messages she said. I'm not always good with unexpected attention from strangers I told her. I'm not a stranger. I'm your coffee monster. I like your shirt she said. It was me that bought the drinks. I wanted to know how she found me and knows my name. She pointed at my lanyard and its ID card. We sat in the window seats. I was a sucker for her smile and eyes and the way she raised her eyebrows at the end of everything she said like it was a massive challenge.

The next night out Siobhan said I must be in love. Darren said he knows I am. But I wasn't in love.

The Cartwrights were back again soon. Siobhan was wrong. They weren't selling. It's the opposite. We were expanding with the main office moving to Preston to get new business over that way and the St Anne's site remaining as sales for the Fylde.

ChaCha got off with a caution. Frank got sent to prison for dealing because he was also done for GBH. She moved back in with her dad in Chorley but then she told me her dad had met another younger woman who wanted him to move to a place south of Birmingham I'd never heard of.

I wasn't in love. It was just that Natasha was so good to be around. She was tall and had short hair that changed colour most weeks. Brown eyes and giggles that made me weak. We met for coffee then drinks then a meal. She worked for one of the shops in Lytham but only went there a few days a month. It was a chain and she had plenty to go to. She lived over near Garstang.

The work changes meant Josie and Liv were in the Preston office now and I went there two days a week. But the bloke they introduced to the team that night was now the main manager at our office. I thought he was decent. The others weren't so sure. Darren didn't trust him. Gemma soon left because she had hoped to get promoted but others got there first. Fred said he'd kicked his coke habit. Siobhan said he hadn't. We all knew he was still doing it.

I wasn't in love. It was just that Natasha invited me to dinner one night at her place and there were two other couples. She told me to get there early. I told her I'm not good with food. She said we should eat each other instead. It was quite a starter. After dinner the others left. She told me she thought I'd be a bit nervous around strangers. The fucking was supposed to be therapy. But then she said I didn't need it because despite them being posh and rich I smashed it as co-host. I stayed until Monday and when we left for work that morning. I totally was in love.

Alice wrote to me. The pain was pouring out of her words. The baby had a heart defect and might have been all right until Alice got a chest infection. The worse Alice got the worse it was for her baby. They realised the baby had no heart beat any more when she went for one of her regular scans. I cried when I read it.

I needed a car but they're really expensive. At work Darren said I should ask Josie because you never know they might give me a company car. He was joking but I gave it a go and Josie wouldn't even consider it. She told me I didn't need a car for my job. Then she said she knew someone who arranged leasing and I might get something that way.

I was in love. Natasha left some things at my flat so she could stay whenever. But more often than not we got together at hers because it was nicer and there was more to do over there. We went walking a lot and had day trips most weekends. Everything seemed to work. We never argued. There was a lot of laughter.

Being in a relationship and in love made me feel my flat was a bit small and insignificant. But it was all I could afford. Natasha liked it. She said it was cosy and liked being there with me.

Neal was made sales director. He gave me a lot of support. A few people left because of him. He took me out for lunch and told me I was the best he'd seen.

ChaCha had gone but she still sent me messages. She seemed happy and I told her I was happy too because of Natasha. She said it was probably just as well I'd met someone as she was starting to think she wanted me. I said that was nice although I knew she would never put up with me as a boyfriend. She said she knew I could never take her on.

7:44pm

I get up from the bed and sit on the sofa, then look at the map for places to go next. As I'm browsing, I make my mind up that I'll go home soon. I can't, and don't want to keep doing this for two weeks. That was the original idea. Instead, tomorrow, I will head somewhere not far from here then I'll drive north for one last cathedral. Then I need to rest.

The route I plan will take me through Shropshire where I don't think I've ever been, so I read about it and things I could do there. I look on a site that does holiday cottages and make a short list of four. Two aren't available. I pick the more expensive of the other two and soon I've got it booked from Saturday.

It feels like I've done something positive. It means I'll get some peace. A base where I can do nothing, or many things. Better than all this driving. All these thoughts. The known. The seen.

The decision ends up feeling like an island in the darkness.

<>

We never heard any more about Mum and Leigh said she was sure Mum had died. Pete said we needed to find out or it will eat her up and Leigh got upset again but I agreed with Pete. We did some work together to try to find out how you found if someone had died. We didn't get very far but then an official letter came that said Mum died from cancer. It was from a lawyer who was closing down her affairs and told us we had been identified as Mum's only surviving next of kin. We had to send proof of our identities so the solicitor could send us any money left after her costs and also a list of personal effects.

Josie and Liv arrived at our office one day and Neal grabbed me. We all had a meeting. They'd been made up about the work I did and the way I'd led my team. They told me not many people could deliver on targets as well as being good with their people. They made me head of sales and Neal shook my hand. Josie gave me a hug and Liv handed me a letter with my new pay on and what percentage bonus I got for winning contracts.

When I called Natasha to tell her about my promotion she laughed then cried and told me she was really proud of me. Later she sent me a message and it was a photo of a booking she'd made for us to go to Copenhagen for the weekend. Then she sent another photo. It was her naked after a shower and there's come and make me wetter written on it. I couldn't get away from work. We had sex on FaceTime.

Leigh and Pete came to the flat with a bottle of bubbly and some bits to eat and we had a little celebration. Then I went to the co-op and got another bottle. We got drunk and laughed a lot. Leigh looked happier than for ages and told me she was really proud of me. She said mum and dad would be too but then she said they didn't care so it wasn't worth much and she quickly got angry again then all confused. Pete said they needed to go.

Neal made Darren one team leader and Siobhan the other and they reported to me which worked well. We went out one night and talked it through about how we needed to work together now. Darren said he didn't think we could keep having social lives together. We agreed we should still go out occasionally and maybe do more eating out with partners and stuff. Siobhan had met someone. She didn't seem so keen on the idea because she liked having her man all to herself.

Natasha had booked a fancy hotel in Copenhagen. We had a really special weekend. Easy flight. Good food. A trip on a boat to see some of the sights. Laughs on the funfair in Tivoli Gardens. Street food in the place across the water. Natasha told me she had fallen in love with me. I asked why it took so long. But we had a long conversation about getting married and agreed we didn't want to. Maybe we could try living together though. She said not full time. What we have worked fine

Mum left us a bit more money than either of us expected but it wouldn't change anything. I gave half of mine to Leigh and Pete because they needed it more than I did. I used some of what was left to take Nat to Paris by train. Leigh was calmer now about mum. Pete said she was still a bit difficult some days. Leigh and I went for a brew in Blackpool one day and looked at the list of mum's things and decided we didn't want any of it. We told the solicitor to sell whatever she could or give the rest to charity.

In the first year after being promoted I won a lot of new contracts. They gave me a massive bonus. I talked the money over with Natasha. She said buy a house instead of renting. Then we would have two places to live together instead of one. I quit the flat. I lived at Natasha's full time while we searched for a house and sorted a mortgage and stuff like that. It felt natural and happy for both of us. It helped us work out that living together full-time wasn't what we wanted.

Leigh arrived at the office one afternoon and said she had to talk to me. She was worried about Pete telling people she was difficult and had bad moods and anxiety attacks. But she said he was lying. I told her Pete had told me this too and Leigh got upset because I hadn't told her. I reminded her she had made it difficult for me when I had to keep it secret about her affair. I said we should go and talk to Pete together about it. She wouldn't. Said she'd sort it with him on her own.

Alice called me one day asking why I'd ignored her letters. They'd gone to the flat and I didn't leave a forwarding address or one of those redirection things. We talked for ages. She said I sounded happy and that I'd never sounded like that before. Jonny had been made a partner at his work and they might be moving again possibly to London. They were still trying for a baby. Her voice choked a bit when she said those words. I wanted to go and see her. It couldn't happen.

Liv left the company and it felt like a wrench. But she had an offer from a really big firm over in the East Midlands. Josie did a speech at Liv's leaving do and everyone was upset. We had a night out and almost everyone came and a lot of us cried. I told Liv I'd never forgot how she'd supported me and given me the chance. She told me everyone in the company knew how good I was and one day I'd be running it.

Nat helped me move into the house and spent the first two weeks living there with me. We bought a bed and christened it. We bought sofas and christened them. Darren and Harry came over with some beers and we had a great evening. The others at work clubbed together and got a voucher so I could get a housewarming present. I got some gardening things. Josie called in one evening with a bottle of wine and we drank it with some takeaway pizza. She asked me if I knew the rumours about us fucking and I said someone had told me. She said it was hilarious.

Work got busier and busier. Sometimes I was away from home. I didn't win every deal we worked on. I did win more than anyone else including Neal. Siobhan said she thought he had some sort of hold on the owners and Josie because he was really shit but they thought he was great. Darren said similar. I told them to be careful what they said. There was lots of new people joining all the time and I felt like every day was stretched.

The weekends with Nat kept happening and we bought bikes to ride back and forth and wherever. But there were some weekdays when we didn't see each other because of work. She was busy too because her company had opened a new store in Poulton. We talked daily and sent dirty messages. We didn't see each other every day. It made the weekends special. We showed each other what we'd missed.

My new neighbours were nice. We talked over the fence in the back garden. The house the other side was empty. Nat was convinced it was haunted. I made a small area to sit out the back that wasn't overlooked and got the sun all morning and most of the afternoon.

There was a rumour about how Mark had been arrested and soon it was in the local papers and on the radio. His brother had disappeared. People were saying he'd fled to Spain.

We'd been together for a few years when me and Nat had our first really big row. It was about something I said to her mum which I didn't remember saying. It got really unpleasant. Ended up with her telling me to get out of the house and not come back.

TUESDAY

3:04am

I wake up sweating. I probably shouldn't drink the tap water from the bathroom, but I have several glasses. When I look in the mirror I still look like that sketch, and I haven't shaved since I left home so it adds to how grim I look.

I check my phone and think about all the people I could call or message, and who never call or message me. Not even Carolyn, who has been such a constant friend. I have a stack of messages, three voicemails and 38 emails. When I look at a few there's nothing I want to join in with.

The pillows are damp from all my sweat, and I have to lie on the sofa to get dry and cool. I don't think I'll sleep on there, but I do.

7:30am

The breakfasts in the linked pub look crap. You have to make your own toast in one of those strange machines with a kind of conveyor belt. I can't be doing with it and walk to a shop to get bottles of water, plus some orange juice, plus an all-day breakfast sandwich.

Back in the hotel room I sit on the bed and think about what I've done since Saturday. What the actual fuck have I done since Saturday? This journey into all kinds of dead ends. All these names, that would confuse anyone who can't keep up. *I* can't keep up. I don't know what divides me from then and now. All that past, all those mistakes and crashes, all the ways I've taken steps up. All for this present. Driving away. Seeking out something, anything, that might mean I can stop being me.

When I look in the mirror, the sketch of my face has broken lines drawn down from its eyes, blurring or erasing the charcoal.

It's no distance to Worcester. Some of the place names on the main road cheer me up. They seem truly daft.

<>

Each year I was given praise and recognition. Neal called it kudos. The team kept changing and each new joiner seemed to learn quickly. There were still occasional nights out and the old gang actually was older than the new young guns in our teams. I became the first-in-last-out inspirational one. Working in the dark.

Alice was miles away and all we could do was send infrequent messages. She had another miscarriage and one of her texts said she felt her life was worthless. I asked if we should meet. If I could help. If there was anything from our pasts that might help her become less broken. Alice thanked me. Said it was a good idea. Told me Jonny would not cope.

There were weeks and weeks of uncertainty that slowly unknotted the love between Natasha and me. I hardly noticed at first but realised something serious had started when she didn't like one of the presents I had bought for her birthday. Just one of them. Out of about ten. Another row. More raised voices. Tears on the phone after she went home. White flags waving.

I never saw or heard again from any of these people. Tola Helen Mark Liv Orla Lee Ben Paolo Louie. Nor from countless work people. Customers and colleagues whose names I forget. There were no reasons why I should see or hear them. But it was me that sent the last message. I made the last call. I tried the last connection. Everything about them was part of something outside what I had. Satellites that blinked signals for a while then took a different orbit.

My flat had been such a happy place. Those three rooms tidy and uncomplicated. I thought about it often as my house turned from being a happy home into a series of interconnected cells.

There was work to do and the people I knew there remained. Josie Siobhan Darren Neal and more recently Carly. Countless people whose names I forgot despite their place in my office life. They all made orbits around planet Joe. Constant and predictable. Demanding but giving. A two way street. Them circling me circling them.

Natasha called and said we should meet to try to see if we had any kind of fresh start available. I said I'd come over after work. She said meet me halfway. The pub was quiet. We were the youngest in there. She'd already had a coffee when I arrived. I asked if she wanted to throw it over me. It made her smile but in the wrong way. Nat spoke without a break for more than ten minutes and without actually saying it she made it clear she had never intended to find a fresh start. I asked if there was someone else and she said yes. Your fucking job Joe. She didn't actually want another man. I was what she wanted but I was imperfect and torn and committed to the wrong things.

When I got back to my house that night Natasha had been and taken all her clothes and everything she owned. She hadn't said anything about this earlier. She took nothing that wasn't hers and left anything we bought together. A suitcase and holdall with my things from her place were in the bedroom. The letter said she loved me and might always love me. She couldn't keep giving all her love to me if I gave less back. She said we should remember all the good times and never be bitter. Don't hate me she said.

Back at work I sat and wrote my resignation. Neil read it. Then we went in his car to the Preston office and spoke to Josie. After a few minutes she tore up the letter and just me and her went out to grab a brew. You're the best she said. What's wrong? I told her my work had destroyed my relationship with Natasha. Josie said she didn't understand.

At last Alice and Jonny had a baby and called him Rupert. She sent me a photo of this tiny thing and it seemed like he was healthy but how would I know? I sent Alice a card and asked where I should send flowers. She didn't reply for months.

Josie drove me home from the café and in the car talked me out of resigning. Don't stop she said. Accelerate. She came in and made me sit at the table while she cooked me some food. I stared out of the window while this amazing woman - boss leader mentor saviour - threw stuff in a pan and the place smelled so good. In the end I shut my eyes like this was pleasure. She told me to eat then kissed the top of my head and left.

ChaCha called me almost straight away when I messaged her that me and Natasha had split up. Do you want her back? I said I didn't know. Does she want you back? I said she didn't. You're well shot Joe. It was her call.

They gave me five new clients to pursue. Three local and two down in Cheshire. I was away one or two days each week and got to like being there. Except one of the clients was like Millionaire Man but with a much posher accent and several cars better than Millionaire Man had. He took me for some food and almost everyone in the restaurant was the same. Haters the lot of them. I called Josie that evening and told her I couldn't work with these people. She told me she'd get Neal to have a word.

Natasha called me twice more. Once to tell me she loved me. Once to say she couldn't believe I was ghosting her. I rang back and asked what the fuck that meant. She told me. I told her I wasn't. I told her I was too upset to even think about her. She cried. She said she loved me. That night I quit Facebook. Soon we met up at Beacon Fell and sat on a bench staring out to the coast. Nat made more or less the same speech she'd made in the Farmer's Arms that day and now it was me crying. Let's just pretend it didn't happen. Eh? Yes. Let's. A few days later I sat in the bar and told Liz it was over between Nat and me.

Two police came to the office and walked in to see Neal. A couple of minutes later they all left together. Neal sent me a message on my phone saying I needed to come out to the car park. Everyone had watched them leave. Now they all watched me.

Alice wrote to me and said Jonny had been offered a job down south and they were moving. She wanted to see me because she might never see me again. I called her but she never answered. I wrote back saying I wanted to see her too and later that week she called and said if we waited another few days Jonny would have gone to Southampton and it would be easier for a meeting.

ChaCha called me three or four times a week and just talked. She said nothing that was advice or judgement or criticism. She just talked about me and her and Mr Harrison and his new squeeze. And all the times we spent driving around in Derek's old Toyota and what the fuck she ever saw in Frank. And we agreed that it was ridiculous for me to still be calling her ChaCha.

I saw Alice get off the train at Manchester Piccadilly. She looked like she had that day after her dad died. Except now she was thin and haggard as well as pale and drawn. We sat in a bar in the back streets. She told me all the things she'd never told anyone. About her beautiful child who was demanding beyond words and how she couldn't cope. About the stillborn baby. Her miscarriage. Her mum's illness. Her fears that Jonny wanted to try for a second child. She resisted because she didn't love Jonny. Her fears that Hampshire really was so far away she'd never see me again. I said we hadn't seen each other for years. Because of Jonny she said. Yes. Because of Jonny. I told her she shouldn't go. She didn't have to go. Not because I wanted her to be with me. Because I didn't want her to be so miserable. Far away and likely to get more and more ill. We went to a hotel and booked into a room. But nothing happened. We lay on the bed and talked. We checked out the next morning and she kissed me and told me to forget her.

The police told me Leigh was dead. Pete had killed her. He had given himself up. Confessed. Told them where to find her.

9:41am

I drive into the city and at one point pass what must be the cathedral. The traffic is busy, and I can't really look. I park down near the river, and, in the sunshine, a fountain looks really cool, so I stop at the café there for a bit. The fresh air feels good. There are swans and small boats on the river. It's already warm and my lack of sleep and dehydration are still giving me problems.

Maybe I shouldn't have driven? It feels like a hangover. The kind you get from those strong lagers. Like you're schizoid. Tea and toast don't help. Nor does the realisation that my online searches show the city's hotels are either booked up or look horrible.

It takes three cups of tea for me to find a place I like, about five miles out of the city. It's in the wrong direction, but I call it a treat.

The walk along the riverbank is pleasant, shaded by trees. Soon, I get a glimpse of the cathedral, but it doesn't dominate the scene. I look over at the other riverbank and think it might be more commanding from there. On this side, it's like a tease. Am I here? Or not? I go through an arch with big iron gates before I finally get to see the building and I don't know what to make of it. It's quite striking but there's no massive west end. It's more slender. The tower is quite grand and makes the building look lean and hungry.

What I see as I walk around the north side isn't inspiring. Litter, some barriers like they use for roadworks and grass where muddy paths have been worn. It all looks unloved. The road I used earlier is about fifty metres away, constantly noisy. Just beyond that a few modern buildings - shops, offices, apartments - make it all a bit grim. Messy.

Maybe I'm just getting fussy.

Inside is better.

By the time I leave, I've seen fancy marble floors, sometimes black and white, other times more colourful with intricate patterns. I've learned that the outside corridors, like I saw at Lincoln, are called cloisters, and this one has windows and some sort of exhibition in it, plus a café and a weird room called the Chapter House. There was a crypt, which I realise I need to research. There is a King's burial place, where Robin Hood gets mentioned on a sign. Instead of one crossing, there are two and that seems greedy. There's a screen between the choir and the nave, but this one isn't solid. It's more of a fence.

On a bench overlooking the river, shaded by trees and quite cool, I sit and read about crypts and cloisters. It's as if these huge buildings are inexplicable to anyone that lacks inside knowledge, which is closely guarded by the few. Maybe it's in safe hands?

I walk back and look at the building one last time. I didn't truly dislike any of it. But the only thing I felt was special was really nothing. Lamps on the choir stalls. And maybe the crypt because it was underground.

<>

Pete had stabbed Leigh once in the heart. He said he meant it. It wasn't an accident or a crime of passion. He'd just had enough. With the carving knife in his hand. Then he killed her. While they were in Stanley Park.

Neal drove me home and said he'd stay but then Siobhan and Darren called round and they all looked after me. Neal went back to work and said he'd sort stuff. They wouldn't let me drink alcohol and sat in silence while I said nothing and ate whatever they put in front of me. Darren slept on the sofa. Shuv in the second bedroom. I lay awake. The first of about five hundred nights that I didn't sleep.

Alice never called or wrote but that flashed past me unnoticed.

Nat came to see me with her mum and dad. It seemed strange they should come too but the kindness was total.

Carolyn drove up from the west midlands and stayed with me and it seemed almost permanent. She took my calls. Answered emails and post. Went to the office to talk to Josie. She drove me to all the places I had to go to deal with Leigh's death. Mortuary. Registrar of Death. The flat.

The court hearing. Funeral Director. Priest. Police station. Inquest. Carolyn bought food and made me eat things. She slept with me and held me close squeezing the horror and pain out through my eyes. She kissed me and caressed me when I felt at my lowest. When I felt some tremors of recovery she smiled and picked me up to dance.

Pete said he wanted to see me. I went. He was in custody at Preston prison. I couldn't talk to him. Wanted to rip the head off his body. He didn't apologise. He just said he wasn't going to seek any kind of defence. In the end all I managed to do was call him a cunt.

Carolyn took me to see Josie who hugged me and told me the company was right behind me in every respect. Then the Cartwrights appeared. Mrs C gave a short speech about grief. Everyone was kind. Carolyn took me away to her car when I nearly collapsed then went back to see Josie and agreed what leave I could have.

I didn't want to be away from work. We agreed I could do stuff at home and occasionally go to the office. Neal said it was fine for me to just drop anything I was doing and leave. He didn't want me working. He was right. But I was determined to be wrong.

Leigh's face was white like the fancy cups Alice's mum had used to serve tea. My sister was beautiful. All the things she'd ever done to keep me alive and ticking and relevant were beautiful. The way she fought for what she believed in was beautiful. The way she'd clung on to the hope that our mum or dad or both might come back and love us was beautiful. The ways in which she'd been my mum and sister and every aunt and gran and cousin were beautiful. I kissed her cheek and forehead and took her face in my hands and my tears soaked her closed eyes. Carolyn took me away again.

We went to Leigh's flat and sat there talking about how it had been my home too. I didn't have a clue what to do with all the things Leigh owned. Carolyn told me she'd sort it and her dad would help.

The funeral was at the crem. I couldn't believe how many people came. Not just the ones who came for me. All the love in the world seemed to have been living around Leigh in faces and smiles and hugs and handshakes and tears that I'd never known. Nat came. Everyone from work came including the Cartwrights. Carolyn helped me get dressed in the right things and held my hand all through the entire morning and in the limousine and all through the service and while I spoke my speech. She took my head in her hands when the curtains closed. Then she told me to keep crying.

The wake started at the Pleasure Beach. We all stood in our black clothes waiting to ride the Big One and by the end of that ride there were more laughs than tears. It wasn't any kind of dying wish or request in her will. Leigh hadn't left one. She just used to go on and on about how she felt low about mum or dad or about being raped or about her affair being wrong or because I let her down. She'd tell me that she'd take four or five consecutive turns on the Big One and it made everything seem right again.

We had drinks and finger food at the Metropole. Everyone filtered away after an hour. Carolyn sorted out all the admin and drove me home and we drank tequila like it was water.

Carolyn went back home after staying with me for many more weeks being everything I needed at that time. We lay in bed on the morning she left and talked and talked.

Eventually I asked why she did it. All this help and support and love. She just said five words. You did it for me. I frowned because I didn't think I had. She cuddled up to me and didn't say any more. The last thing we did before she left was dancing. One slow and close. The second fast and manic. Music loud. Smiles and kisses to die for. And live for. Then she left. About 15 minutes later she called from her car. We spoke for the whole of her trip back home.

Pete was found guilty and given life. A strange outcome since he'd taken one.

1:35pm

I'm nearly out of the city and the traffic seems constantly busy. A sign shows the fuel is cheap at the supermarket, so I drive in and park. A few drinks and snacks for the car will come in handy and I zip round the shelves. I don't mind the queues for the checkouts. I'm two from the front of mine and they've only got a few things.

In the next queue there's a couple getting a bit full on. He's standing behind, is pushed right up against her and has his hand up her skirt at the front. Not the best place for that stuff but she doesn't seem to mind. Then she reacts in a way that suggests she does mind and, when she turns to look at him, it's really bloody obvious what's going on.

I say to the guy on my till that he should call security because someone in the next queue is being assaulted. The guy has his hand up the back of her dress now and is making a fist pump action at another guy waiting the other side of the tills. They're grinning like a couple of twats. She's trying to stop him or at least extricate herself from his attentions.

I shout, 'Leave her alone.'

The security guard is running now. I move around the back of my till's conveyor and, as I approach them, the guy pushes her out of the way and joins his mate before they sprint away. The security guard doesn't know what to do and it seems like he will chase them, but instead he comes to talk to her.

I ask him if the shop has CCTV on the tills and he says he'll fetch the manager.

The woman is blinking with incomprehension. I ask if she's okay and tell her I'm calling the police. She says don't and I tell her she's crazy. The man assaulted her. But she keeps shaking her head. We're still arguing this point when the manager arrives, introduces herself very formally as Mrs Drury and says she agrees with me about the police. Her name badge says she's Imogen.

We learn the victim's name is Louise and there's an efficiency about the way Mrs Drury gets the incident moved away from the tills. I guess they need to keep selling stuff.

Louise constantly refuses to allow anyone to call the police and seems increasingly anxious that she is somehow being kept waiting. She also seems baffled that someone has helped her. It's like these things, these moments of care and kindness, are a mystery to her. But Mrs Drury has arranged for someone to pack up Louise's shopping and it's been brought over. While other people process the payment, their manager issues curt instructions to her team about opening more till lanes, to the security guard about CCTV footage and into her walkie-talkie to whoever might be listening.

I ask Louise if she will be able to get home all right.

'Thank you, yes. I live very near here. Just outside the city. But thank you.'

'Can you drive in those shoes?'

She smiles but it's restrained, as if she doesn't want me to think it's a favour. 'No. Barefoot or trainers behind the wheel.'

'Let me get you a trolley.' Louise says she can manage. I insist.

When I get back, Mrs Drury is assuring Louise that the team will review CCTV films and notify the police if there is anything captured. Then Imogen looks at me and asks me if I can give my name and a phone number. I'm beginning to wonder how much more I will be asked to witness and testify.

While I'm writing my contact details, Louise quietly bids us goodbye and clicks off with many pairs of eyes watching. The manager is flicking her fingers at the security chap and pointing at Louise's departing figure. The guard jogs to catch up with her, says something, then follows at a discreet distance.

I pack my items in a bag for life and head to the car park. There's no obvious sign of Louise out here so I guess she's safely on her way home. The security guard is strolling near the first rank of cars. When I pass him, he moves his head in a tiny motion of acknowledgement. I mimic it but he's already looked away.

The car park is busy. Lots of cars. When I get to mine, I open a back door and put the bag behind the passenger seat.

The door is slammed against me as I'm leaning in. A voice, hissing with hate, says, 'Very fucking clever, Mr Knight in Shining Armour. What are you, gay or something? Stopping a man getting his fingers in some old slut?' The door is banged against me again. I can't lash out with either foot and both my arms are inside. I take a punch to my hip. Another voice gives stage directions about potential witnesses. He's got a strong accent that I don't know, and he suddenly says, 'All clear, mate.'

They pull me out, hitting my door against the neighbouring car in the process. I'm dragged to the floor, and they start kicking. I clench my forearms either side of my face so they can't get me in the temples or back of my head, but it means my torso is unprotected. Kicks and punches, then something metallic rattles. I feel a chain smashing repeatedly against my side. I kick back and catch one of them under his knee. He shouts in pain and backs off. 'He's done me, Harv. Cut him.'

I wait for the slash, somewhere, but an engine revving loudly gets close and a raised voice shouts, 'Stop it. Leave him alone.'

'Fuck off you slut. Next time it won't be my fingers in your dried-up pussy.'

Now I manage to get a kick on one of Harv's legs, right on the outside of the knee. He screams, which seems extravagant considering it wasn't that hard. Then the whiny voice says, 'The bitch is filming us, Harv. Kill her.'

Now I'm able to get up, but my sides and back and bollocks are really painful. I don't know if I can do much. Then another voice, then more. Customers. Next up, it's the security guard: I know it's him; I've heard him before. He's shouting that the police have been called. The two thugs yell abuse at him, then run off after Harv kicks the chain under my car. They are rushing, occasionally crashing over the bonnets of cars and I see them split up and run off in opposite directions once they reach the main road.

Then I bend double and throw up.

Voices are asking if I'm all right and why they attacked me. I hear her voice saying it's because I stopped them harassing her inside the shop. The owner of the car parked next to me is on his haunches holding out a bottle of water, telling me to take a drink. I say they might have damaged his car, but he says they haven't. With a final check that I'm all right, and his hand briefly on my shoulder, he says goodbye and take care.

The manager is back again, that Mrs Drury, and she's almost beside herself with rage that this has happened on her watch. She is looking with unconcealed anger at Louise, as if she is the root cause of every problem that has ever come to pass in this retail nirvana. She unleashes a series of statements, like the popping and flashing and random explosions from an untended box of fireworks, accidentally lit by a stray spark. The police are coming. More CCTV checks will be needed. It might be necessary to close the store. It's coming up to the busiest part of the day. Do you need an ambulance?

That bit's an afterthought.

Before Mrs Drury can spit out more of these declarations, Louise's voice says, 'Please just shut up. This man needs support, not your frustration about how bad your day might be.'

Louise asks if I can stand, and whether I feel disoriented or dizzy. Do I have pains in my stomach or sides?

'Maybe you should go to A&E?'

'I'm going to sit in my car until the police get here.'

'Do you live far away?'

'Yes. About 200 miles. But I'm staying near here this evening. I am... I was on holiday.'

She giggles. It's fleeting and tiny. She knows it's improper timing. 'A holiday in Worcester. Are you some sort of porcelain freak?'

I don't get the joke, but her giggle makes me join in, and it sends a shaft of pain searing up my side. My shake of discomfort causes her smile to fade.

'Here's the police. No sign of the ambulance and I think that's more important for you. I really need to get going but I guess I have to make some sort of statement.' When I look at her, she has an expression that I can't understand.

The process that follows takes too long, for her and me. The police are very precise, especially with Louise. Again, it's like she's at fault.

I hear her ask if she's allowed to speak to me again, to say goodbye, and they must have said *yes* because her face appears at the window to my left. She has the most perfectly oval eyes, with very little make up, so the effect is doubly perfect. The pupils are pale green and hypnotic, but I break the spell because I can't stay turned sideways due to the pain it causes. Louise thanks me for stopping the man in the shop, then apologises repeatedly for the fact I've been beaten up. Her voice is soft, diction good, an accent I can't place. I'm learning I don't really know accents.

'It isn't your fault that two nut jobs decided to assault you, then attack me. You didn't tell the bizzies what they did to you, did you?'

'No. Did you?'

'I said I broke up a disagreement between you and one of them inside the store. I felt that was what you would want me to say.'

Louise raises an eyebrow, then pats my forearm and nods. She has quite terrifying long nails. 'Yes. Thank you. That was good of you. But it may have been wasted if security and Cruella contradict you.'

Another giggle and now a smile. Then she says sorry twice more, then thank you, pats my arm again but leaves her hand this time before giving the tiniest stroke and, in its wake, the hairs on my arm bristle up. Then she says she needs to go. 'Here's the ambulance. I hope everything goes all right at the hospital, Joe. Thank you. I'm so sorry.'

The paramedic asks me to get out of the car so he can examine me. Lots of questions about my chest and ribs, using big words that end in what sounds like Thor Axe. I say he had a hammer, didn't he? They put me right about how it's spelled. We laugh about that, but I wince, and they ask where I hurt. I say everywhere from the neck down and knees up. They look at my side and tell me there could be a risk to my liver and kidneys. In the end they tell me I have to go to A&E because they're worried about the pains in my sides and lower back. I don't want to go, it's just a kicking after all, but they insist and the bizzies back them up. So, I shrug and say okay.

As the ambulance glides away, one paramedic sits in the back with me still checking and asking questions about pain.

I am wondering if, and when, I told Louise my name.

The hospital had intel from the paramedic, so they know what to expect. I'm able to walk in without assistance. A quick question and answer session follows, then they examine my injuries and ask about pain. The nurse, who's called Meg, says she'll take some blood for tests that will show up any problems. She says pain relief is also needed and I'm going to get a scan.

It takes a while and, in the end, nothing is broken. No internal damage.

Eventually, the doctor says she's okay for me to leave but I shouldn't drive and need to see my GP when I get home to check on any further problems. She has a last look at the big striped wounds on the side of my chest and tells me to watch out for breathing difficulties. When I put my shirt back on it smells of dirt, oil and sweat.

Then I'm released into the wild.

I don't feel bad enough to take any notice of the advice about driving. I collect my prescription from the hospital pharmacy and wait for my taxi. When it drops me at the supermarket entrance, I walk to my car and take one of the tablets, washed down with Irn Bru. I'm pretty sure it's right that I shouldn't be driving but I'm truly past caring.

<>

When I check-in to what turns out to be an ultra-posh hotel, I am surveyed in a way that suggests I'm not welcome. The receptionist can barely swallow his snobbery, and my voice seems to grate with him. I have no credentials that he can approve, no place in this oasis. My battered exterior isn't the only thing he dislikes. I tell him I'm planning to eat in the restaurant later and he reserves a table with a kind of dismay. It's as if I couldn't possibly enjoy the brilliance of whatever feasts might be offered on the menu.

At the spa I spend time in the sauna and steam room then get a massage. The guy doing it says he's a bit worried about being too strenuous as the bruising and abrasions on my torso look really serious. I tell him to do his best. By the time I've had all that, swum a few lengths and made myself wrinkled in one of the hot tubs, I take a final thirty minutes in the relaxation zone and feel like I'm in less pain.

Over tea, I think long and hard about what happened at the supermarket. Louise might have her reasons for not wanting to report the assault. I can't understand it but, fact is, it's her call. The two lads, Harv and his mate, get me wondering. They were young, early 20s I reckon. It might be that Louise was a chance encounter. Why would they be tooled up if their main priority was feeling up women in supermarkets? Hmmm. I decide they were more likely looking for someone to mug in the car park, and Louise distracted them. The horrible, disgusting little cunts.

I go to favourites on my phone. Really, it's singular. Favourite. That's all.

I send Carolyn a message. It's the first for weeks. She replies quickly and we chat for a bit. News about all she is doing and her new man. When I tell her where I am she tells me she's less than 25 miles away, and why didn't I tell her. I write *it's complicated* and she replies *as usual*. She asks if I'm alone. When I say yes, as usual, she tells me to come and see her tomorrow. We agree to meet for breakfast.

The food is nice, and I feel I deserved this slap-up treat after these few days on the road and all the shocking pub and takeaway food. Perhaps it even made that kicking worthwhile. Whatever, it's cheered me up. Usually, posh food does nothing for me.

While I'm waiting for my pudding, I send another message to Carolyn.

<>

A stroll around the town would have been nice, but I'm too sore and decide to go and spend an hour in the lounge. There's me, a couple who aren't talking English, and two other people sitting alone, one noisily reading the paper. He rustles it especially loudly every time the couple say something too loudly. Eventually, he stands up and chucks the paper down and storms out muttering *bloody French...* I think he expects me to join in with his scorn.

The other guest wanders over and asks if she can join me, introduces herself as Tricia Phillips and we spend a while chatting.

'What brings you to Malvern, Joe?'

'Pleasure. Just a single night.'

'Jesus. At the rates this place charge, one night is about enough. Thankfully, my company picks up the tab, or I'd be at the Journeyman Inn.' She goes on to explain she works for a company that specialises in railway signalling systems, then explains in some detail how they work. 'I hope I'm not boring you. It bores the fuck out of me.'

Her laugh is somehow strained and false.

'It wasn't boring. I'm interested in what people do.'

'And what do you do?'

'My company sells geo-thermal systems, and I sell almost all of them. We're based near Lytham St Anne's on the Fylde.'

'The what?'

'The Fylde? Fylde Coast?' Her face has the perfect expression for the phrase *What the Fuck*? I thought everyone knew about the Fylde. Maybe it's just a local thing?

'It's in Lancashire. The bit of land west of Preston, between there and the sea.'

'Right. I'd never heard that before.'

I carry on explaining about the company, and how I'm head of sales and some of the deals done recently. Her eye contact is unnerving. Then I realise it's also a bit contrived. I've seen this before. It's what people do when they want to seem interested, perhaps because it's written down that that's what you do. Her eye contact masks the fact she isn't listening. I close down the conversation quickly and ask if she wants more coffee because I'm grabbing more tea. She says yes to a second cup. Why not? It's free.

'Not having a night cap? You're on holiday, after all.'

'No. I never drink during the week. But I'm also on medication.'

'Oh, right. What for?' She looks bored, as if people on medication are some sort of risk to her world view.

I end up giving a shortened version of the events in a supermarket car park and the subsequent findings at hospital. She seems impressed, now, as if something lawless is terribly cool and attractive.

When her phone rings, she says it's her husband calling so she can say goodnight to their kids. It's clear she's going to do this sitting in front of me, so I wave, and mouth *good night* then stroll stiffly away. I'm really sore now and pretty sure that nothing, not even those pale green eyes, had made the kicking worthwhile. I wash down another tablet, switch off my phone and roll myself up in the duvet.

WEDNESDAY

7.55am

The drugs make me sleep well, or maybe it was the fresh air and that terrible night before. Was it the pampering session, and all those essential oils? Or a combination. Yes, that will be it.

I just lie there, trying to remember the last time I felt this comfortable. I hate that I sleep alone, unknown, and isolated, but somehow this comfort is a fair exchange. When I turn to one side to get my phone, I nearly hit the ceiling with the pain from my lower back and ribs and chest.

My phone starts up and alerts me to more messages and mails. Carolyn has sent details of the place we're meeting, and I work out it's less than 45 minutes away. After all the usual stuff I find a small mystery. A missed call from a number I don't know. Whoever it is left a voicemail. It's several minutes long.

If it's work, I'd know the number. Unless it's a new client. It can't be spam because of the voicemail. And it was left at 2am.

What?

At first, I think the message is blank, then an intake of breath happens and a soft voice with a lilting accent and good diction starts speaking.

'Hello, Joe. It's Louise. Forgive the anti-social timing but I took a guess you might be asleep, so safe to leave a message. Sorry if that's wrong. Anyway. What you did at the shop yesterday was a decent, kind thing to do. I feel terrible that you took a beating on my account from those monsters. That's not good English, is it? But you get my drift. I spent the rest of the afternoon and evening reflecting that it's a difficult thing to act with honour and dignity these days. I never encounter it. So, what you did was special. And perhaps it was also for no reason because I ended up brushing aside your good deed. But thank you. I won't ever forget it.'

There's a long pause but I can see more than a minute left on the message timer.

'What I meant about calling while you're asleep... It isn't because I don't actually want to talk to you. I just wasn't sure a long chat would be right. Although it probably is much easier to leave a message. Which I suppose I could have done by text. In fact, it's more that I get time to think in the early hours because... well, I don't get that much sleep. Long story. Too much info. Oh fuck, sorry Joe. And I didn't mean to swear.'

Another pause, breathing.

'But listen, thank you so much. You're a good man and I'm sorry about what happened to you. Hope they patched you up well and you're not in pain. Okay... that's me finished. Thank you, Joe. I really am sorry I missed you, but it was by design. Oh God. Bye.'

There are several seconds of silence, in which I have a sense that more words will come. But she says nothing and the message ends.

What a completely, utterly weird thing to do.

<>

It takes me ages to get dressed because the pain is so intense. Just putting a tee shirt on hurts like fuck and I can barely bend down properly to pull up my pants and jeans. Socks and shoes take forever. I have to be in a really strange shape to get all this done. I consider the possibility that I might need to just drive home in my pants and flip-flops. But I need to see Carolyn, so I crack on through the pain barrier.

What did Louise mean about me ignoring her? Why would anyone take a call from a number they don't know at two in the morning? What was she really trying to achieve? There was something strange in her voice, and sometimes the pauses and breathing sounded like she was scared. Why? Scared of me? Or some sort of danger? Or simply not scared at all? Just my imagination.

Driving hurts a bit but the drugs kick in and I don't notice the pain once I've skirted around Worcester and reached the motorway. Driving in a straight line, with no manoeuvring and gear changes, makes the soreness go away and gives me time to think.

About Louise.

How did she get my number? And my name. I'm so triggered by this that I drift into the fast lane, and someone beeps repeatedly and gives me a finger when she's level.

Perhaps the police told her my name. Or the manager. I smile about calling her *Cruella*, then chuckle.

It gets slow on the motorway and I'm thinking about what happened in the shop and how those filthy little fuckers behaved as if they had the right to touch Louise. Or anyone. Or even go near her while she's doing her shopping. Maybe they had worse things planned. To attack her again at her car. I'm grinding my teeth thinking about the harm they might have done. They didn't hesitate to beat me up, so was that next for her? Or rape? Fucking hell.

And I don't understand why she didn't react or want to call the police. It makes no sense. I wonder if she was really filming when they were kicking me. Or was it a fake? Does it matter?

She missed me *by design*. What? I mean that's just a stupid thing to say. Or too clever.

9:17am

The Starbucks is strangely quiet and none of the five cars has Carolyn's private plate. I'm still thinking about Louise and yesterday's events. Don't reply to her, is my instinct. Potentially, a lot of things about this make it best to just walk away and avoid. In fact, she didn't really suggest I should reply. It was a one-way message. Thanks. Stop.

Carolyn arrives looking very elegant and she says I'm worth it. Laughing hurts too much and I tell her to stop joking. She looks worried when I tell her about the beating and why it happened.

'Hence your message', she says. 'Understood. Daddy is on the case but wanted to know about their accents.'

I try to mimic it and she nods, then messages someone - her dad, she says. I tell her one was called Harv, and she messages some more.

Then she tells me that chivalry is cool and I'm the king of it.

I ask her why someone would avoid reporting sexual assault to the police. I tell Carolyn how Harv had his hands all over Louise. How she seemed to be accepting, at first, then tried to resist him but without really making any fuss. As if she was sweeping it under a carpet.

Carolyn says it doesn't sound right, but maybe Louise is very fucked up and both wants and hates the attention. Her conclusion is that it's not my problem and making it my problem might make me fucked up too. When I try to say more, she closes me down by smiling at me and asking how come I know this fucked up woman's name.

Before long all that is history. We talk about what Carolyn's been up to and how her love life is blossoming, specifically because he lives miles away and therefore there's something special about when they get together. Like every meeting and kiss and fuck is the first.

She asks me about work and why I'm on holiday. I tell her I've pissed them off. She says that seems unlikely. Then she asks if it's because of how I feel. Asks if it's still raw.

Yes, I tell her. All of it, nearly two years on.

She looks at me like she always has through all our days: part care; part sorrow; part determination; part despair. Determination's the biggest part. Then she asks what the fuck I'm doing on this bizarre road trip and its associated obsession with cathedrals. We have another brew and I confirm that I can't explain it. It's just me being elsewhere and picking towns and cities to visit based on something that isn't about nightlife or places to eat or house prices or aspirations or deals. It's made me worried about how little I understand history. Carolyn says history is dead, like truth.

I must look hurt, because she puts her hand on mine and says I maybe shouldn't be doing all these things alone. I'd have come with you if you'd said, she says, even if I am crazy about my new man.

Maybe I needed to just do this alone, I say. Carolyn tuts loudly and I've never seen her look so frustrated. No, she says. You need company. You're miles from home and even the remotest links to someone there.

But I shake my head and she backs off. We sit talking for another hour and, before she leaves, she gives me a hug that hurts so much I cry out loud. Call me when you get to wherever you're headed, she says. I remind her it's Chester.

11:21am

I head back to the nearby town then set off across country. I don't really know where I'm going. After an hour driving, I realise I've taken the wrong direction. I decide to have a break and, while I eat, I decide I should reply to Louise. At least to acknowledge her message.

Typing,

> *Hi, Louise, was good to get your message and really it was easy to step in and stop what was*

happening. It was wrong. They are bad people. They have no right. And thanks for asking about injuries. I'm OK. Nothing major. Got some pain relief.

I hit send. Then I think it looks a bit shit, so I add,

Take care of yourself. J.

Now I think it's even shitter.

The place I've reached is Ludlow and it's nice, especially the castle. I'm not up to walking much so I just look at it. The good news is that it's not far from where I'm staying next week, so I have a little smile that I've finally made a great decision. When I walk back to my car, I stumble off the kerb and it sends a surge of massive pain through my hip and side. I take two tablets to make it stop.

Maybe it was a mistake to drink tea and water with my food, or maybe it's the tabs, but I need to keep stopping to piss. It's a slow road too and I end up going down the side roads to find places where I can just go behind a hedge.

I listen to her voicemail again and, even with the dodgy Bluetooth connection, her voice fills my car with its even tones and careful words. The silences, with their steady breathing, feel a bit scary. The words that sound most special are *I won't ever forget it,* because when she said them, it sounded like the only words in her whole speech that might have been made with a smile on her face.

Carolyn phones me and says she hopes I didn't travel on the A49.

I tell her I'm on the A49.

She laughs and tells me to read a good book while I'm driving. I tell her she knows I don't read books.

While we're talking, a message tone sounds on my phone, and I assume it's just Carolyn fooling around.

Anyway, I can't look due to the road and traffic. Next stop is the first time I get to read it.

From Louise,

You still in Worcester?

Makes me frown. I start typing a message explaining where I am, but it also looks boring, so I decide to call once I'm back on the road.

I get voicemail. Her message says: 'Louise McAdams here. I hate that I missed you, but we'll talk soon. Bye.'

'Hi Louise. It's Joe. I'm no longer in Worcester. I really was only visiting for a day. This might sound weird but I'm just randomly visiting places with cathedrals. Been to Ripon, then Lincoln and Coventry. Worcester was yesterday and I'm headed to Chester. I realise this might not seem too sexy and I can't really explain why I'm doing it. I set off without a plan and have made it up as I drove. So, I guess it's just something I needed to do. Anyway, I've just passed a place call Great Ness and I think maybe I'd like to live there. It's where I belong. I'm not carrying on with my cathedrals plan. After Chester I'm going home, then coming straight back this way for a week in the countryside.'

I run out of things to say but don't want to stop.

'I didn't understand your line about porcelain.'

Another pause I don't know how to fill.

'I'm in the car for maybe another hour. You could call back.'

I'm on a dual carriageway and realise that I've sped up to nearly 100mph and there's a roundabout ahead. The hard braking makes me say, 'Jesus. Fuck!' then, 'Sorry. I'm so sorry Louise, that was nothing to do with our conversation. I better go. Bye.'

A truck driver blasts his horn at me because I pull in late, then have to swerve and slide through a roundabout. I'm still going too fast when I reach a stretch with a speed camera and I'm sure it's captured me, although I wasn't aware of any flash. Something feels very wrong, and my chest has tightened into palpitations. Maybe strained, rather than wrong. I decide it's because I've left a really rambling, ridiculous message for a complete stranger I'll never see again. I can't explain to myself why that stranger makes me nervous. I don't like not knowing why I feel this.

Louise calls back. 'Joe, I'm glad you answered. Your sudden swearing made me worried. That maybe you'd had an accident.'

I explain what happened.

'You had no business driving that fast while your reactions are probably poor because of your injuries. Have you slowed down?'

I tell her I'm doing 55 in a 60 and think I got nicked for speeding.

She giggles. I can hear birdsong. 'Maybe you can claim you were running away from those bastards. And a crazed harpy with her talons.'

I look down at my forearm and the hair bristles up in a line where she stroked it. I say, 'Are you okay after what they did?'

She sighs. 'I am. Thank you. Have the police contacted you? I've heard nothing and I know I never will. Those two are probably back in whatever hole they crawled from.'

I tell her I've also heard nothing and don't expect to. But I don't mention Mr Harrison.

'Tell me how it went at A&E.'

'After you deserted me at Sainsbury's...'

'I didn't desert you, Joe.'

'It was meant to be funny.'

'I'm rubbish with irony.'

'Is that what it was? Well once you'd departed the crime scene...' She laughs now, loudly. The car feels like a new place with that sound cascading through its speakers. '... the paramedics and police ganged up on me to make me go to hospital.'

'I'd have ganged up with them. You had to go.'

'They took some blood and gave me a scan.'

'MRI? Or CT?'

'The latter. The doctor was great and explained there was no evidence of internal damage. Told me to take it easy and gave me a prescription for pain relief.'

She asks me what tablets I've been given, and I pick up the box to look but can't really pronounce the brand name. She says it back to me and it sounds right.

'So, you took it easy by driving a couple of hundred miles.'

'It's not that far.'

'Me and geography are total strangers. But you shouldn't have driven last night and shouldn't be driving now. Did you stay in Worcester?'

'At a place called Malvern. It looked nice.'

I tell her about the hotel, the spa, the food, and strange behaviour of guests. She says the pampering was a good idea but doesn't know the hotel and hardly ever goes to Malvern even though it's so close to her house. When I ask, she tells me she lives in a little village about halfway between Worcester and Malvern.

She says that I live in Lancashire and a spark of concern shoots into my head. How does she know this?

'At least, your accent is Lancashire. Which doesn't necessarily mean you live there, does it?'

I want to ask how she knows my name and number. 'I do live there. Between Preston and Blackpool...'

'Don't forget, I'm geography blind.'

Our laughter fills the car. 'Okay then, yes, I live in Lancashire. It's in the same country as you.'

'That's exactly the kind of context I need.' She's still talking when my phone signal drops. By the time it returns, Louise has called back and left a voicemail. 'Was I boring you?'

I call her back and it goes to voicemail. 'The opposite. I was enjoying your company. Need to ask you something though.'

She calls me back and without introduction says, 'Go right ahead and ask.'

'Just puzzled about how you know my name and number.'

'That isn't a question, Joe.'

That should have pissed me off, but instead makes me smile.

'Louise, do you mind telling me how you know my name and number? Please?'

'Sarcasm is so special. Excellent. There's nothing to worry about. I watched you scribble your name on a piece of paper to give to Cruella and her team. You wrote *Joseph*. Very formal. Then, when the police interviewed you, I overheard you tell them your name and number.'

'But not my address?'

'No. I missed that bit. But I was too busy memorising the phone number and tapping it into my phone. If it's a problem I did that, please say.'

I had thought it was a problem until now. But her explanation sounds honest and uncomplicated. I ask Louise what she intended to do with my name and number, and she tells me it's this; getting in touch, saying thank you, wishing me well. She hopes that's okay.

I'm still smiling. I'm too used to people with agendas and games and subtexts. Suspicion comes naturally to me. But not in this case.

'It absolutely is okay. I hope you don't mind that I wanted to know.'

'You had a very good reason ask. I'm sorry if I made you worried, and glad we cleared it up.'

'I've got another question.'

'Joseph! You're so demanding. What is a girl to think?'

No one alive has ever called me Joseph. Me excepted.

'Can I ask my question now?'

'Oh, that's an easy one to answer. No, you can't.' The laughter is longer and louder. I have to cut through it.

'What did you mean about *missing me by design*?'

'Did I say that?'

'Yes, Louise. It's a matter of record.'

She breathes in deeply. 'Okay. Umm. I guess I meant that I wanted to let you know I was grateful. I didn't want to message you, as it might have seemed cold. But I think if you had actually answered I might have hung up.'

'Why call me at two in the morning?'

'Ask another question. That one's too complicated.'

'Oh. Okay. Well, no more questions about that then. My phone was switched off anyway.'

'Please don't worry about this, Joe.' I hear a loud burst of birdsong. 'I'm not in an aviary, by the way.'

'A what?'

'An aviary. A birdhouse.'

'Where are you, then?'

'Right now, I'm walking around the curve of a river. Soon I will cross fields, walk through some woods and head back to my house. I won't ask where you are, because of the geography thing.'

More laughter.

'Do you know the name of the river, or is that also a mysterious blank?'

'It's the River Severn, downstream from the bit you would have seen during your time in Worcester.'

As I start to tell her about the time I spent in the cathedral, the signal drops again. I've no idea where I've reached. The road signs had kept me honest before Louise called but now her problem with maps seems to have transferred itself through the microwaves into my own head.

When she calls back there's the sound of footsteps, on gravel or similar. She says it's because she's almost back at her house.

'How far have you walked?'

'Maybe four miles. I walk most afternoons. Tell me what you're listening to in the car, while I'm not interrupting you.'

'Nothing. I don't really listen to music.'

After a short pause she says, 'Well that really *is* weird. So, you just drive in silence?'

'Until I set off on this trip I've never driven all that much. Except odd work trips, and then I'm more likely to be on the phone, doing deals. For local journeys I mostly use the train. For this trip, I've been thinking about things. Music, or the radio, would have been distracting.'

'You must have a lot to think about. Maybe you can tell me one day.'

'Maybe.'

'You said you're headed back this way next week. Where will you be?'

'If I tell you, will it actually mean anything?'

'Good point. But nearest big town?'

'Shrewsbury, I think. Maybe Hereford.'

'I've been to both. Once upon a time. And you're staying in a cottage?'

I tell her the details and why I decided to do it. I miss out all the background stuff about work and stress. She says the holiday will do me good. She's right.

'Louise, the road is getting really busy, and I think I need to concentrate.'

'You beat me to it. I've reached the garden gate.'

She sounds like that makes her sad.

'It was nice talking.'

'It is lovely, Joe. I'm glad I got this time with you. Maybe you don't speak enough.'

'Only to myself.'

'That's sad. We should fix it.'

'I think we have.'

Her giggle is so charming. I want to think of things to say to make it happen again. But, as I'm trying to come up with something, she says her signal has gone. It drops and we say nothing else.

2:45pm

I'm on a fast road again. Then another, and then on the final couple of miles towards Chester and my hotel.

At the first lights I message Louise to thank her for her company on a boring car ride.

While I'm in the queue to check in at the hotel, I message Louise again.

I can't face another night, stuck in a hotel with no one to talk to. By the time I'm waiting for the taxi that will take me into town, I've sent two further messages to Louise, and she hasn't replied. It makes me feel down, maybe because I hadn't realised our phone calls had made me feel very up.

6:29pm

I really like central Chester, so I decide to stay two nights. I'm nearly back home, aren't I? Plenty of time on Friday to get back, get the house sorted, get out on the bike, get packed. Then, on Saturday, get on the road for my holiday.

When I call the hotel, they say a second night is fine and I won't need to change rooms. I can't be arsed trying to get a discount on the room rate. Who needs that shit? Not me. Definitely not the happy receptionist who couldn't have been more helpful.

Instead, I roam the streets, grab some food in a pasta and pizza place, feel the steady onset of discomfort in my back and hips. Maybe a beer would help, but I really don't want to drink alcohol, mainly because it's midweek but also because of the meds. That could end up being a very bad look indeed. Convinced there must be other strangers here, other aimless travellers, I go into a bar. Almost everyone seems to be under twenty. I get a sparkling water and sit at one of the raised tables. It's boring as fuck and I leave in less than ten minutes.

I've convinced myself every other pub will be the same.

This whole mood isn't good. I'm back to being easily rattled, easily distracted. Back to seeing nothing of value. I'm already unsure I want more of this. It's just before eight and the streets are busy. There has to be somewhere that isn't problematic. I can't go back to the hotel.

A smiling, chatty couple walks past. I turn and follow them into the pub they choose, where there is endless smiling chatter. The sparkling water tastes the same, but the clientele is safe. At the bar, I get talking to a couple who are both called Chris. You couldn't make it up, they say. Chris 1 works for one of the banks and has nothing good to say about her employer. Chris 2 works at a local micro-brewery, has a big loud laugh and a massive belly. He says the beer served here is piss, so he sticks to the vino.

The evening suddenly seems normal. I'm back to being part of something. My journey is no longer a waste of time and a solitary, aimless indulgence. We chat and laugh, become friendly, and the joy is extended when the Chris's are joined by their friends, Rich and Sue.

The whole distraction of being in a city, with good people and plenty to say, has made me forget that Louise has stopped communicating, just 24 hours after she started.

Back at the hotel, I sit on the side of my bed looking at my unanswered, unread messages. Something runs through me.

I think it's failure.

THURSDAY

6:19am

The green phone button has a white 2 in a red circle.

Here we go again.

The missed call was just after 2.50am, the voicemail is nearly seven minutes. I seriously think about deleting it. She isn't in my contacts yet, so it's just the number, no name. Raw. Untamed.

Several minutes go by and I'm still staring at the screen. During these blank, indecisive moments, a spam email notification pops up and my banking app tells me a standing order got paid. Neither event completes me.

Not drinking last night was good, the right thing, but I feel like I've got a hangover. A mild one. The zones of pain remain. Worst, where the chain got used. Next worst, the soft spot above my left hip. The least painful, bollocks, unless I touch them. Even if I wanted to, I don't.

Progress.

More drugs and, when I look at the bubble strip, I can't be sure I've taken the right quantity. *One to be taken twice a day with food.* Eight empty bubbles. Should've had four.

I open Safari and read about the drug. Okay, there are side effects and it's not good to take too many so I might be in danger. I take a ninth tablet and decide that's it till Saturday. Pain or no pain.

I'm glad I didn't delete the voicemail.

'Joe, we had such a lovely long talk, didn't we? When the signal dropped it was nice that we persisted. Laughing felt good too. Short supply. Sorry. Ignore that.

I've been thinking about what you're doing, all the driving and looking at the cathedrals. You said it's not normal and you can't explain it. That you made it up. It's made me wonder what you're looking for. It isn't a pilgrimage, is it? It's like you've chosen something, completely by chance, that has strength and purpose. New to you, but strange to you too. Ancient and enduring. I wonder what you've learned.'

She laughs. It's a small sound compared to what was booming in my car yesterday. Controlled. But still with enough fun.

'Listen to me, analysing like a TV academic unravelling some great anomaly for an audience. Sorry.

You said you didn't understand about porcelain. Here's some reverse mansplaining. Worcester is home to a brand of porcelain. Tableware. The old china. World famous, although maybe that notion is crushed by you not knowing. So, there you go. Facts.

I hope the pain relief is doing its job but be careful with that drug. It's not good to get stuck on it, and definitely a bad idea to take too much.

Did you have a good time in Chester? What's it like? I've never been. Will you be heading home today? I hardly ever seem to travel any more. No business trips. No holidays. Sorry. I'm rambling, and what's more, I'm rambling in a morose, uninteresting manner. You deserve better.

It's nice talking to you while you're asleep. I hope I didn't wake you. And I hope Thursday is wonderful. Take care, Joe. Bye.'

I listen to it again. I've no idea what *mansplaining* means and, when I look online, it still doesn't make sense. Another made-up word to suit the inside knowledge of people who made it up.

The bathroom has a really powerful, really hot shower and it makes me feel good. My brain is filtering through the things Louise said, as well as why she always phones me in the middle of the night. Except she doesn't. She's only done it twice. We spoke in the middle of the afternoon yesterday. But after that, with a load of times to choose, she waits until 3am to call. I wonder what would have happened if I'd answered but rule out the option to sit up through the night just to test this.

It was nice that we persisted. True. I felt that.

Short supply. To be ignored. Supply of laughter? Is what I think she means?

A pilgrimage. How does she know what it is or isn't? What have I told her, what have I said? How does she know me? Who else mentioned a pilgrimage? Lynne of Ripon, wasn't it? Not Louise of nowhere.

Strength and purpose. I keep coming back to those. I keep thinking she might have a point.

Unravelling. Anomaly. Not my kind of words. They sounded natural and commonplace in her speech and voice. Was it a challenge?

She laughed and giggled many times. Almost like that was why she called. Leaving me the message was the outlet she needed to top up the short supply. Yet so many apologies. What's that about?

The old china. It's rhyming slang, I think. For what? China cup - pup? China bowl - soul? China teapot - er... teapot. I laugh aloud. China plate - mate. That's it. It must be that. Another small laugh. Decoding her message has made me laugh with Louise.

Be careful. Not good to get stuck. Don't take too much. That's right though. Nothing is worth getting addicted to. Except work? Yes. Keep mainlining the day job. It pays the bills and buys the things that show the day job is worth doing. The drug of work/life, so they blur into one. Relief.

Business trips. Rambling. Morose. Uninteresting. She's low, isn't she, despite the giggles and laughter? Louise is drawn to my pointless adventure because it's moderately less sad and lonely than her own.

I deserve better. Than what? Than all this? Than the world I see through my hazy, black, and white lenses? I fear she means that I deserve something that isn't Louise, in her morose, uninteresting state.

What's the opposite of *opposites attract*?

Similarities repel? Is what she means? Or what I think she means? She and I might be similar. But I'm not sure how anyone, especially Louise, could reach that conclusion after a strange meeting, some texting, and a few phone calls.

Talking while I'm asleep. I have a sudden, crystal-clear vision of me lying still; eyes closed; breathing deeply; head immersed between the two ends of a plumped-up pillow. I can't see Louise's perfect green eyes, gazing down at me, half caring, half questioning. *You look peaceful Joe. Why won't you wake up, Joe?*

She's right. I really do need to wake up and take care.

9am

The park and ride bus stop is near my hotel so I go into Chester by bus. Nice and cheap. Public transport is best, I'm sure of it. The road into the city is a bit humdrum but there's a couple of sights I like. Old buildings, some with black and white timbers. A steam mill. Little surprises of individuality in amongst the usual retail suspects.

From the bus station it's a short distance to the city walls so I set off walking along them. It's still quite early and, in places, very quiet. The walls take me past the cathedral, above the streets then down to the river Dee. It's got a big weir and a stone bridge. Then, after an old arched gatehouse, or similar, the walls disappear, and I feel let down. It's been brilliant walking along the top of something that has defended things all this time.

I look at the river flowing away and think it must have been part of the defences too. I wonder where it goes next. The sea probably. When I look on my phone's map, I see it's not that far until it becomes all straight, like a canal, before it empties into Liverpool Bay.

I like this city. There is something homely about it. The pedestrianised streets that I saw from the walls seemed calm. Soon I'm walking along those streets and some of them have raised walkways.

This activity has caused pain to return and it's pissing me off. I don't want to spend the whole time looking for the next bench or café. I left my drugs back in the hotel, which might have been a bit stupid. But I've no choice other than to sit down and buy something to drink.

It's well past noon when I get to the cathedral, which is a funny looking place from the outside. Not as massive as Lincoln, as cold as Worcester, as solid as Ripon and nothing at all like Coventry. Am I becoming an expert? Strength and purpose?

Maybe.

I go in through a funny little entrance, then a shopping bit. A sign says you have to pay. Instead of following the signs to the main building, I turn left and walk out into a garden with a statue in a pond. It's peaceful and the statue is like two mermaids that have had their tails bonded together. Their bodies form a circle.

In the cloister, a small, blindfolded head makes me stand and look at it for ages. It's hypnotic, made from metal I think, and it's the colour of coal. It's called *Pity of War* and the head has no mouth. There's something beautiful and troubling about it, all in one place.

I walk into the main building and head up the left aisle. It's the last use of my routine.

The floors are a muddy red colour, and the walls would be too except they have a grey tint. There are mosaics showing scenes, perhaps from the Bible? It takes me ages to reach the far end of this side because I stop to look at many things. Organ pipes. A weird metallic sculpture of the birth of Jesus with one of the wise men on a camel. A big cabinet, the size of a wardrobe, with a set of crosses and a big stick with a curly metal top. They look valuable. They must be valuable or why are they locked away?

I look back down this aisle and it seems like the place I walked in is miles away.

When I get into the choir, I really like it, especially all the wood. The lighting makes it seem really brittle. The seats have little carved statues. A tiled floor has yellow and blue colours, lines, and squares. My really favourite bit is the metal plaques on the prebendary stalls. Those people own these seats.

The ceiling in the tower is like gold and people are up there looking down.

There are colourful side windows and a big wooden door with a smaller door set into it. It's bolted shut, like it's never meant to be used but must have been once. Right at the end of the south aisle is a strange little room, with a big wooden table, a throne of some sort with a canopy over it and wooden benches all around the table. Up on the wall, a weird-looking crest has strange symbols on it, a letter *S*, a letter *P* and *1775*. A metal light fitting is hanging down on a big, long chain and it's got a couple of bulbs not working. Is it a court? Is this a trial? Am I innocent?

On the way in I'd spotted the café, so I head there now to rest. My legs and back are sore again.

It's absolutely packed. But everywhere has a table for one, don't they? My whole life is a fucking queue of tables for one.

I get my phone out and read about this building, Saint Welburgh, Saint Anselm, and the rest. The tea isn't great. Weak. But the toasted tea cake is top, almost better than toast. The bread of Christ.

Where did I hear that?

Why does anyone call a stranger at two in the morning? It's bugging me. It feels weird.

When I walk back into the nave, the storm that's been brewing has bubbled up and overflowed. It's made the interior dramatic because floodlights up in the arches create a lot of light, but deep shadows. I see this building through new eyes.

More people have come in seeking shelter and they make a lot of noise. I feel that's disrespectful. What I've learned in all these cathedrals is how it is the silence that matters. These newcomers are laughing and joking so much I don't hear my phone.

I don't find out that it's Louise until I stop to take a photo.

Do you use WhatsApp?

I say I don't. I also start typing about social media and what it does to me, but then delete it.

That's a shame. But texting is fine. Did you get my voicemail?

I did. Thank you. I had to do quite a lot of research to understand some of the words.

A laugh out loud face pops up. I've never used those. I didn't even know how to or what any of them really mean. Turns out it's the first of a million emojis.

Was worried you were ignoring me. Or I'd offended you with my kitchen sink psychoanalysis.

I wasn't. You didn't. I've been walking around the city and this cathedral.

Oh yes! Your travelogue. You should be writing a book to accompany it.

Way beyond my ability.

I'd read it.

I probably wouldn't.

Really? Why?

I don't read books.

No music. No books. You're fascinating. In a slightly dangerous way. I have challenging work to do.

I'm easily led.

But not astray. Tell me about reading.

I'm walking quite slowly again, phone in hand, trying to form what I should say to Louise. A really loud crash of thunder seems to make the windows rattle. But it also shuts people up. I stand in front of a wooden screen and point my phone at the big colourful window at the far end of the building, then take a photo.

There's more lightning. I kind of wish I'd captured it on my snap.

I tell her I just never got shown how or what to read. It's ages till she replies that she's sorry and had a meeting. Tells me she wants to call, but too busy.

Would I be able to answer? Stood in a cathedral? It makes me anxious when Louise keeps saying she's going to call. I think about switching my phone off. She says she wants to hear my voice but has too much to do.

I'm looking at my phone trying to find how I send an emoji. I've no idea which one I'd send to indicate I'm slightly offended, but in an ironic way.

I feel panic. Why don't I know? When I ask her, Louise tells me to look underneath the keypad on my screen, bottom left. A smiley face. When I touch it, it shows emojis.

She sends one with a winking face, blowing a kiss. So now I know.

Are you going to charge me for this service.

There's another long break.

You bastard. I laughed at that and dropped my phone in my soup.

Is it OK?

Yes. The soup's fucking horrible though.

What flavour?

iPhone.

Delicious.

A hint of apple.

Well played.

I've sat down on a seat facing the altar in the Lady Chapel. It's really dark here, and the two suspended lights don't make much difference. I'm a bit mesmerised by the patterns on the floor. It's colourful but every section is a series of lines and boxes. A puzzle I can't solve. But the plus side of sitting here is that all the noisy lot are down in the nave, basically just waiting to head outside again once the rain stops.

Which words did you have to research?

Mansplaining.

Oh yes. I hate that word. I also hate that I used it to try to be funny. Which fell flat.

It did. I also looked at the Royal Worcester site.

Buy anything?

Ordered you some new soup bowls.

Now it's you playing well. That's funny. And sharp.

I don't know what to write.

Sorry Joe. I'll be slow to reply for a bit. Got to be a grown-up next hour or so.

I'll pray for you.

Ten LOL emojis. But I can't hear her laughter. I kind of want to.

I've walked back to the west end. The floor slopes up to the big window with a glass door under it. It isn't used to get in and out. All it lets in is light, and all it lets out is the gazes of people wondering when the rain will stop. I sit and look back up the nave wondering why so much control is exerted on people who want to get in. So many locked, boarded up doors. Does God know?

It's ages before Louise gets back to me. She is apparently very busy so I tell her she shouldn't let me distract her.

*Am I distracting *you*, Joe?*

You're not. Sometimes you make me puzzled.

How? Why?

Easier to talk about that.

Maybe later. When I'm walking.

*What does it mean when you put * either side of a word?*

You really are so innocent about basic on-line stuff, aren't you?

I've never thought so. Innocent in what way?

You seem so savvy about what you want and need from being online. But you don't know the basics that everyone uses. Why is that?

I suppose it's because they're not my basics. I prefer dealing with people in the real world.

Ouch. I'll consider my ample ass well and truly smacked.

It isn't. But tell me about the asterisk thing.

Louise explains it, and other things in the rule book of being cool on social media.

I'm still curious.

What are the benefits of WhatsApp?

I've literally no idea.

I'll have a look.

It's ok, really. I'm sorry I asked. iMessage is fine.

I've opened a page explaining about WhatsApp. It seems like any other way of messaging. Encryption is some sort of selling point. Not sure why, or who needs it. I'm not sure I even know what it is. Cathedrals have crypts. Is there a connection?

You ok?

I am. Was researching.

You like research.

It's about the only thing I do online.

Don't you ever use it to engage with someone, or people?

Not really. I go online for knowledge. It's a feed for my internal benefit.

Have you researched me?

Why would I do that?

To see if I'm real.

Have you been researching me?

I know you're real. But tell me what I'd find.

Not much. My LinkedIn profile.

I'm not going to look. I'd rather research you direct. Not work through a catalogue of possibilities.

Fire away.

No. Not now. When we can talk. Here's another interruption, sorry. Back in a bit.

I'm hungry now and my injuries are hurting more than I want them to. Maybe I could get some over-the-counter drugs as a filler?

I have one last look at the garden and around the cloister, wondering why cloisters are different depending on the cathedral. There wasn't one at Ripon. Nor Coventry. What I saw at Lincoln and Worcester was different to Chester's, which seems discreet from the main building, here for a different purpose. Natural and self-contained.

Thinking about those other cathedrals now, I realise this fifth one is also my last. I begin to try to assess them, to understand them and rank them. But I'm in pain and need to get that fixed.

<>

The man in the pharmacy says anything he gives me over the counter would not be a good mix with what the hospital gave me. He more or less refuses to sell me anything, and I decide he's being sensible but cruel.

I eat a burger instead and it's a pale substitute for analgesia. Until I spoke to Louise, I'd never heard that word. Probably couldn't say it. But now I'm cool. I can pronounce the name of the tabs too.

I'm hurting, occasionally badly. I've no choice other than to go back to my hotel room and keep my dose over the stated amount. The bus gets held up in traffic and it takes ages to get to the hotel. While I'm sat there, listening to the chat and laughter round me, I download WhatsApp and set it up.

She sticks with standard messaging before I can try my new app.

> *Tell me what you meant about never being shown how and what to read.*

> > *It's how I grew up. School books were school, and I hated school. Didn't have anyone encouraging me to read for pleasure.*

> *Teachers let you down, maybe. What did your parents read?*

> > *Nothing.*

> *Siblings? Do you have any?*

> > *No.*

> *I feel like I'm on dangerous ground. You're suddenly monosyllabic.*

> > *Not at all.*

> *Smartarse.*

> > *Books just don't interest me. It's a hole in my makeup.*

> *I've got plenty of those.*

> > *I thought your make up looked really lovely.*

There's a long break.

Thank you. But maybe your memory is defective.

My memory is excellent. Too much so.

That's a sad message.

I suppose so.

Have I upset you?

You haven't. I'm not easily upset.

Explains why you came to rescue me. My guardian angel.

Harv and his wanky little mate called me a Knight in Shining Armour.

This time yesterday I was driving and we were talking. and I wonder if, by now, Louise is out walking and we can talk soon. She stops that thought in its tracks.

Sorry for long gap. Had a big problem to fix and it's kept me working when I should be out walking and talking with you.

A shame. But work comes first.

Really? Not in my world it doesn't?

I hear Nat's voice about my fucking job.
Careful. I need to be careful.

So, we won't be talking today.

'fraid not. I'm disappointed.

Back in my room, I put Louise's number in my contacts so I can message her on WhatsApp. It feels like some sort of step forward when I send this.

I went ahead and got this app.

You really didn't need to.

It's strange using a new way of communicating. I think maybe there'll only be me and Louise chatting on it, but as I wonder what to say next the word *online* disappears under her name. Like she's ignoring me. I don't get it. Soon the blank space is filled by news of the time she was last seen.

So, I try to make her come back.

Well, it's there as an option. I thought it's what you wanted.

It sits there. It's now many minutes since Louise was last online. It's strange. Makes me feel defeated. But it doesn't stop me falling asleep. And I stay like that. No dreams. No subliminal tags. Just deep, untroubled sleep.

When I wake up, Louise has left a message and it hadn't disturbed me.

It isn't vital we use WA, but some things might be easier. Like this.

She's copied a link to a song. It's on an app I can't use and, when I tell her, it causes rolling eyes. Louise says it was inconsiderate of her to assume I used the music app.

Then a link to a YouTube video of the same song appears. It's called 'Livewire' and I've never heard it or of the band, Oh Wonder. I blink at it.

Will I be able to play it on my phone?

Have you got the YT app? Because if you don't, you're going to need it.

I need to get it then.

She writes,

Good lad. But listen to it later. Let me know if you like it. It's not that new. But I hope you like it. I need to start getting you to listen to music. Because music is all I have.

Then,

That's more TMI. Sorry Joe. And also, sorry that I need to drop off now.

Louise must be able to type so quickly. I ask how she does it. She says she dictates, and I've got no idea where to start with that.

Dictate how?

Work it out, Joe.

A gif pops up, of Tom the cat spanking Jerry the mouse.
I reply,

I feel like I've been told off.

> *You've been dictated too. I really have to go. Sorry. Was lovely chatting today. Listen to the song. Enjoy your evening.*

Before I can reply, *online* disappears again. So, I stop typing.

While I'm drying after my shower, my phone does a tone I've never heard before. The screen shows Louise has left a message. When I open the app there's no words, just what looks like a recording with a *play* arrow. Something else I need to work out. Her voice is quiet.

'Joe, I feel bad that I sounded impatient and worse that maybe it felt like I cut you off. So, I'm sorry about both. Really sorry. And I'll be even more sorry if I've made you feel bad.'

She pauses and I hear the sound of running water.

'Evenings are difficult, okay? Don't let that be a problem. Please, Joe. Bye.'

Her voice and message sound sincere. Am I reassured? Do I need to be? Is this all just too difficult? That word, difficult. Is it difficult? Evenings are difficult. Just evenings. That's all right then. I mean difficulties are difficult, aren't they?

I decide that, although it's still a school night, I will have a drink or two. Driving tomorrow but doesn't need to be early. So maybe a beer, or a cocktail? But plenty of water between times.

8pm

When the taxi drops me, I head straight for the bar where I met Chris 1 and 2. I liked it there and feel like I will just stay all evening. They might be here again but if they aren't it's the kind of place where similar folks will be.

It's nice again.

The music is loud enough to be fun but not to be a nuisance. Club style. The beer looks boring, so I choose a cocktail I know and get a sparkling water to have with it. It's busy and, in the time, I'm ordering my drinks, it seems to fill up by about 25%. It's okay though. Relaxed, nice blend of ages, couples and singles. Some tables with people eating. Mainly it's a big mass of *us*, just stood about, waiting to be whatever the evening demands.

I listen to Louise's voicemails and her voice clip. Against the background of music and laughter her words seem out of place. Would she be happy here? I'll probably never know.

After half the water I start drinking my cocktail. It's nice, and I wonder if I'm taking a massive risk drinking anything at all when I'm on meds. Fuck it, though. It feels like a good thing.

So does a voice.

'Your drink looks good. What is it? I might get one.'

She's one of a group of five women. My age, maybe just a little more.

'It's called a negroni.' I don't tell her it was Natasha's favourite and she got me hooked.

'I've never heard of it. What's in it?'

'Gin, red vermouth, Campari. Twist of orange zest.'

'Sounds brilliant. And dangerous.'

She turns back to her mates and asks if any of them has ever had a negroni. Seems not.

'You're an influencer. I'm trying one. Can I get you another? We can trend together.'

Something vaguely responsible kicks in. 'I'll have one more. But these are not a sensible all-nighter.'

'What is, these days?' She has the ability to arch her eyebrows so perfectly and smile so broadly. It's a treat. She's stunning.

Her friends don't seem interested. The four of them are chatting noisily. While she's getting the drinks, I finish my water.

'Here you go. Chin chin.' I've no idea what that means. She drinks about a third of the glass in one and her eyes flash. 'Oh my GOD, that's amazing.' She turns to her mates and tells them they have to have one.

Turns out she's called Claire. Her mates are Fliss, Martha, Anj, and Debs. When I tell her my name, she turns and introduces me to them, and I feel like she's a gameshow host. Her audience looks sceptical. I might not get past round one.

'What brings you to Chester, Joe?'

'Sightseeing. It's lovely.'

'It is. Where do you live?'

I tell her all about the places I inhabit, house, office, and gym. She lives somewhere called Frodsham and works in IT, at Daresbury. Claire talks about both places as if they are the centre of a universe and seems shocked that I've never heard of either. But that doesn't spoil things.

Her friends are buying bottles of Prosecco and drinking one between them pretty much every twenty-five minutes. One of them, I think it's Fliss, has become the centre of attention for two blokes and it's clear she'd happily fuck either of them.

'Shall we try a different cocktail. You're right about these. Dangerous. Not good for stamina.' The eyebrows and lips and teeth confirm that's a matter of some importance. 'Why don't you choose something for us to try, Joe?'

I get mojitos. She's never had one of those either.

'How long will it take you to get home this evening?'

I tell her I'm staying and wonder who the fuck would come here from Kirkham for a night out, and then go home. We talk for a while longer and I think she's never more than a sentence away from saying we should go back to my hotel. It's a bit shallow. Then Martha says, quite loudly, 'What are the fucking odds?'

They all rush away to the toilet. It's some sort of conference, I suppose.

Claire comes out first. She walks past me to a group of lads and kisses one of them. Slowly, out come the other four, two together and two on their own. Within ten minutes, they've gone. My drinking pal's smile and perfect arched eyebrows are someone else's.

I message Carolyn to tell her what's happened, and she chats with me for a bit. She thinks it's hilarious that I got sucked into an encounter with off-the-hook marrieds.

Louise hasn't been online since 18:25.

I drink two mojitos and decide to mind my own business for the rest of the evening. More water. A couple of different rum cocktails.

The hotel reception area is crammed with people when I get back just after 1am. The atmosphere is dreadful and eventually something kicks off. I can't get to the stairs. I'm only up one floor and I hate lifts. The police arrive just as seven blokes and four women start battering the shite out of each other. Maybe it's a wedding?

2:51am

I know that the tone I'd never heard before is what I now call WA. It's Louise. I check my watch. She's early.

Na-night you.

I'm learning. I send a hug.

You're awake!

Just got back. There's a riot in the hotel reception.

Be careful.

If it reaches my room, I'll get my lance out.

I wish I could call but not poss.

I'm sad.

Have you been drinking?

Why?

Answer the question, Joe.

I've had two negronis, three mojitos and two rum punches. And a lot of water.

That's so stupid.

Me too.

Not funny. You're on powerful pain relief and it's in your system and alcohol was a really stupid fucking idea.

I don't know what to say. No one has ever, ever disciplined me.

When are you driving tomorrow?

Not before ten.

When was your last drink?

I feel a small prickle of annoyance. Is this caring? Or domination? Why is either needed?

I left the bar at 1230.

Don't drive before noon. Drink a lot of water. Don't take more tablets.

I don't reply.

Please Joe.

Several moments pass until she sends kisses.
She cares. And maybe dominates. She thinks both are needed. So, it matters.

OK skipper.

A smile lands. WA makes emojis big when they're on their own. It makes me keep going.

*If I told you that I wish you'd been here, would it be ok? And when I was having my fourth drink, I was a bit pissed and wished it more and more and wanted to hear you laughing. Talk to you. Learn things. Make me immune to the glances and smiles and raised eyebrows pursuing me. Just wanted your eyes to look at me and say * I won't ever forget this. **

Nothing happens, then *online* disappears. I am too drunk to worry. Then the message receives its two blue ticks and she's back.

You're a bad man, Joseph. You made me cry.

I write, * *sends tissues*.
But after I hit send, I've mis-typed and it's gone as * *sends tossies*.
It isn't even a word. Why the fuck did the software make it a word?

Within a moment or two, a voice clip lands. Louise tells me she can't laugh or cry as loudly as she wants, but feels we've found the very essence of our evolving charms.

Tossies.

FRIDAY

8:15am

By the time all my stuff is packed I've listened to her recorded message more than ten times. Then the shower hits me hard in many places. Then the taste of tea made from crap tea bags and processed milk doesn't stop me having two cups before I look in the mirror and tell myself it's time to go.

Based on Louise's instructions I shouldn't leave yet. There's no reply to my early morning greeting. She hasn't been seen since 03:05.

I can't stay in this room.

Like I said. Time to go.

The reception desk has a smashed window next to it. Things seem to have escalated. The receptionist is cool and smiley when I mention the broken glass. Says it was a minor disagreement. I like her style.

Wondering if the fight ended well for someone, I drive away.

The house will be there when I turn into my road in about two hours. Piles of vomit by the gatepost. More litter in the garden. Repointing needed. Curly dog shit lurking. Badly fitted windows moaning and wailing like a haunted house when the wind is in the wrong direction. Rooms like I left them: empty. Places to sit in silence wondering about the things I should do and how to put them off. Change that light shade. Redecorate. Dust, especially where the spiders have been. Shopping. Trim the hedge. Dust. So much dust to clear. Handfuls of it.

Louise is further away from me with every mile. When the roadworks and queues make me slow down and stop, I glance at my phone to see there's still nothing from her. So, I send nothing, even though in my head I have so much to send.

One motorway becomes another, then another. The signs show me familiar places.

I'm back.

The house has a very bad smell. It's the bin and, even with the back door open, it's a while before it's less stinky. I head to the One Stop shop for milk. I make tea and it's much better than I've had at any point since last Saturday. I drink it, stood in the kitchen, looking through the window at the wheelie bins, wondering which ones should have been out while I was away. Will miss next weeks', too. That's two collections without my contribution to the world of waste.

I take a tablet and notice I hurt less. Were those cocktails more effective than actual medicine?

She still hasn't replied. This carries on. *No reply* is a situation that people at work would call *ongoing*. Status equals *work in progress*. My fingers and thumbs twitch over the letters, waiting to type more hopes and wishes. Last night's messages glare back at me, daring me not to add more. I switch off the phone, plug in its charger and get my cycling gear on.

The bike is just about my only luxury, and it sometimes pisses me off that I ride it less and less these days. Today, I ride miles and miles. Up into the hills, back to the coast then down the lanes to here, all the while feeling the soreness in my body getting worse from the effort, especially in my hips.

I soak in the bath. I take another tablet and eat a plate of pasta with chilli and garlic. I should be more tired than this. But I'm a live wire.

When I finally get there, my own bed feels good. Cosy enough to sleep.

SATURDAY

I pack two bags with my favourite clothes. The old ones, comfortable and everyday things, plus stuff I can use to walk in. I may not do any actual walking. I plan to fail.

Louise hasn't replied. She isn't interested. I should delete all the chats and stop using WA. It was only on my phone for her to reach me. She's stopped reaching me.

I send Neal an email asking if everything is okay at work. I send a message to Carolyn telling her where I'm going. I drink tea. I've no bread for toast, so I eat porridge with honey. I put the bags in the car and switch off what's on in the house. The Maps app tells me I'll be there in 3h25m and I can't check in till 2pm. If I leave now, I can drive slowly and stop somewhere nice to eat. Or rush and get there early to explore. Or both.

Do both.

Neal's reply says nothing to worry about, no need to check in, hope you're okay. I frown, puzzled at how formal it looks.

Carolyn says she might pop over to see me one afternoon, as where I'm headed is quite close. Depends on how needy her man is.

As I set the alarm, ready to lock the door and leave this house, I wonder where all the memories have gone.

Part 2

Brand New Day

2.1

The roads are full of weird shit. Every few minutes provides something I feel I've never seen before. Hills. Roadworks. People sat in their cars, vans, buses, looking like all kinds of things. Sunshine, in occasional bursts. Speeding. Crawling. An accident. Gestures. Hand signals. Glares and snarls. Another accident. Different sounds coming up through my wheels. Roars. Hisses. Pulses. Hums. Overhead signs with messages, strident and glaring, out of date. I wish I could switch some music on.

Should I have brought my bike? How could have done that?

Thoughts of Louise are hard to drive away. How we met, the ways in which we've communicated and not communicated since that checkout encounter. These seem important. And in their way so do the silences. They aren't silences. There is no contract between us to send and receive. It's a zero hours and minutes commitment. But her voice keeps using words I'm drawn to. *Our evolving charms* - those are my current favourite three. She has told me something I need to know. We are evolving. One of us has charms.

Something kicks in. All the things I've been shown and given, all the instincts, all that I've become, that evolution. These tell me to act. Don't accept silence, or *no*, or *maybe*. Since there are charms, I should feed them, weave new spells around them and watch them create something real, not an illusion.

Call? Or message? Or one of those voice clips? Which would she like?

There was that song. *So, hold me when I fall away from the lines*.

All three. She'd like all three.

I pull into a lay-by. I type,

Headed back your way. J x

Then I wait a few moments and take a mouthful of water. Louise remains offline.

I press the microphone symbol and say, 'I didn't mean to make you cry.'

Then I set off again and, once I'm cruising, call her number. She's still Louise McAdams and still hates that she missed me. 'Hi Louise. I guess you're working. And I'm driving but wanted to talk. Or maybe say stuff. In the car for about another ninety minutes so call if you can? Your company would make it seem like thirty.'

I'm staring at dials, as if the numbers and pointers will provide the next thing for me to say.

'Umm, take care. Louise. Please.'

I go a different way than I travelled yesterday. It's no quicker but I see new things. I end up in Wales for a bit and the slowness means I arrive late enough to check-in.

I'm in the middle of nowhere and it feels perfect.

When I connect to the cottage Wi-Fi, a load of messages pop up. It's Louise, and no one else.

Are you there yet?

Sorry - realise you can't see messages driving.

You better not be looking x

You better not be ignoring me.

I tell her I'm in and it's a nice place, surrounded by nice places. With no phone signal. She replies with a voice clip,

'It sounds perfect Joe. Send photos soon. Please.'

I send a photo looking out across rolling hills. She says she loves it. And so do I.

Limited time now, Joe. Got to be somewhere soon. A return to our fateful meeting place.

Please be careful. Get Cruella out of her office to be your bodyguard.

It's OK. I've got you as back up. Everyone will know you're waiting to pounce on anyone that tries to molest me.

Then she reverts to voice.

'Which reminds me. Absolutely nothing from the police. Typical. But it's fine. I didn't want them to do anything, and knew they wouldn't, unless it was to blame me. Got to go. Bye Joe. Hope you settle in nicely.'

Bye Louise.

There's a patio with sunshine, so I head out there and soak it all up. I'm surrounded by something I've never really known before. It's not silence, but it's like silence. No traffic noises. No sirens or church bells. No garden machinery, or builders using angle grinders. No shouting and screaming. No over-tuned car engines making the windows shake. No voices wanting my approval or opinion.

Instead, there are animal noises. Trees, rustling. Birds, tweeting. It makes me doze off.

No problems in the shop. Thought I'd let you know. Got you a treat. How is the cottage?

More photos, inside and out. I tell her I've been asleep in the sun.

I'm not surprised. You've had an arduous week. Maybe get an early night? Sorry. That's not an instruction.

I intend to. What are you up to?

Shopping to unpack. Then I'll eat your treat. Off for dinner later with friends. Will be a late one.

Will we talk in the morning?

Maybe. Sorry. Don't be worried if we don't, OK?

It makes me worried, but she doesn't give me time to express it.

What are your plans for tomorrow?

Going places. Tourism.

I bet it's lovely all around there. Of course you must send me pics.

Shall I send a selfie now? Instead, I just type,

You'll see everything I see.

She hasn't replied and, when I go to bed just after nine, Louise has weaved no more charms.

2.2

I rush out of the cottage early because I've no food and need something to eat. I want to go west, and see stuff that way, but there's a Greggs in a place along the road called Craven Arms, which is added to my list of crazy place names.

No overnight voicemail and no messages. The whole thing about the long gaps between messages is slowly becoming okay for me, so long as I don't dwell on it. In my head, I've made it something I should deal with. Louise is probably going to get bored soon. I've no right to expect anything.

Also, I still think it all seems weird. And, partially, I am prepared to wait because all my life the people I've wanted to be linked with have been distant. Or non-existent. We, they, and me, us, we just did things when it mattered and were easy. So maybe that's what Louise will end up being. And if she's something more than weird, like dangerous or something, then I'm far enough away to be safe. She isn't though. I don't want that to be true.

I need to check why she didn't want the police involved. Part of me understands it. Why involve them in anything? They never help. Is she some sort of villain? The needle edges towards *dangerous*. Then back towards *weird, but intriguing*.

To comply with her wishes, I take a photo of my bacon sandwich and send it with *Morning* written under it.

<>

By the time I get home from today's tour, I've sent more than 20 photos without reply. Then, while I'm making some tea, Louise does reply to one of them. It's the photo of an old Iron Bridge.

That's an amazing pic Joe.

I look at it, wondering why it's amazing. I just pointed my phone at it and clicked. The more I stare, the more I see.

Underneath the single arch of the bridge, moving towards me, is a swan and it's looking to its left dismissively. It's the hardest swan in the hood. The little town had been really busy, people pointing and looking at the history lessons, learning. Yet, in the moment I took the picture, there was no one standing on any bit of the bridge. It means that, above and on the slow, still river water, an oval is formed by the bridge and its own reflection. And through this oval, a distant, single, quite small white cloud is framed; the only one in the sky.

Is that what Louise saw, too?

I ask her. I give this description of all I that I see when I look properly at my photo.

She replies,

That's exactly why it's amazing Joe.

Perhaps five minutes later, during which I'm looking at the photo on its app and wondering what the *Edit* function does, she sends,

> *And you shared it with me. So, I felt like I was there with you. That would have made it doubly amazing.*

Night night, you xx

2.3

I lie-in late after sleeping for more than ten hours. The tiredness isn't unwelcome but I'm a bit phased by it. Louise was right, I guess. I drove something like 750 miles in a week and I usually wouldn't do that in three months plus stress, and not knowing where I was going, plus tension, plus being beaten up, plus things about Leigh and Nat and everyone and everything, plus the sense I keep getting that something is wrong with me. Plus drugs.

And what about Louise?

She hasn't called or messaged but I don't worry. What does worry me is work because it's Monday. Without hesitation I start an email to Neal then decide it's better to call. He'll be done with the Start the Week Sales Huddle by now. It's past ten.

It goes to his voicemail. He doesn't call back. Just over an hour later, his email arrives.

> *You're on holiday, Joe. There's nothing to discuss. See you next Monday.*

I blink several times at this message. I say *Fuck You* loudly, then repeat it twice. He's always made me regard him as a lightweight. But for the first time ever he's made me really angry.

Louise says she doesn't understand why I called work. We're talking again, while she's doing her afternoon walk.

'I recommend no further contact with him or anyone you work with. Talk to me instead.'

'He's easier to get hold of.'

She laughs. 'Touché. I'm sorry. I have many moments when I can't be available. For you, I mean. But it's not about you.'

'I'm learning. But maybe, you could give me a clue when those moments will begin?'

'I'll try. Joe, please don't ever take my silence or absence as a bad thing. It's just necessary. Maybe once you're back at work, you'll be the same.'

She's right.

'I will try to let you know when time-outs start. Promise. In fact, I'll tell you right now that, from around six this evening, I won't be chatting or anything. Okay?'

'Aye aye, skipper.'

'Good boy. Acceptance, with neither challenge nor difficult questions. Have a gold star.'

Almost as soon as she says it, a gold star pops up in the window. I reply, 'You can pin that on me some day.'

'You can bank on it. It's lovely here. Nice to have the sun. Is it warm there?'

'I'm on a lounger in my shorts.'

'Oh, Joe. Be still, my beating heart.'

She sends a gif of a woman pouring water over herself.

'They're a bit tatty, to be honest.'

'Even better.'

'Tell me about your walks. How come you have this time every day?'

'It's kind of work-related. My days start very early, because of time zones. By the time most sensible people are finishing their lunch break, I've worked more than eight hours. So, I take a long break, then usually have another spell with people in different time zones. The walks are also about getting exercise and fresh air. And a break from the house.'

'What do you do?'

'Boring question. Maybe for another time. Try another.'

Words that could be a slap down, but she says them in a tone that makes them fun and kind. She prefers to tell me different things.

'Then tell me about your accent. I realised over the last few days that I don't really know about them. Yours is lovely.'

'Lovely how?'

'Like you're concealing it a little, but not completely; because you're quite proud of it. Secretly proud of it.'

The accent is suddenly stronger. 'I was born in Newcastle, bonny lad. And if you catch me in the wrong mood, you'll get sworn and shouted at in this voice.'

She said it *shooted*.

Louise reverts. 'I am massively proud of my accent and heritage, but when the family moved from the northeast to this part of the world, I was only eight. So it slowly got suppressed. My folks kept me clinging on to it. Their accents never left them till the day they died.'

'How long since they died, Louise?'

'This is one of your charms, Joe. You don't dance around handbags. Keep doing that, please. Promise me. It's five years since Mam died and seven since Dad. He had a massive coronary. After deciding to take early retirement at 60, he enjoyed less than a year of that freedom. Mam's heart broke too, but in a different way. She never recovered from Dad's death. Her despair turned to anxiety and then depression. She took an overdose.'

'Louise, I'm so sorry. That's awful.'

She had sounded level and calm but when she starts again her voice wobbles. 'It's cruel. I miss them. And I blamed myself for not seeing how bad Mam had become.' The wobble becomes a sob. I stay silent. It doesn't seem like words are needed.

Louise fills the silence. 'Maybe you could send over some tossies.' Laughter makes the tension snap, briefly.

'It must have been a terrible shock to lose them so young.'

'It was.' She sighs. 'Mam would have loved you, by the way. Placed great faith in men being gentlemen. Rescuing me in the supermarket would have earned you super double points for gallantry.'

'Do you still feel that blame?'

'Not so much.' Another deep sigh. 'What about you? Tell me your family news.'

'I don't have a great deal to tell.'

'Oh yes, you went all monosyllabic on me about siblings. We don't need to discuss it.'

'It's fine. I feel comfortable, now. My sister, Leigh, was more or less my parent when she was a teenager, and I wasn't yet ten. Mum walked out on Dad's drug habit and debts, then one day he went too. They'd been proper parents - as a couple - for less than ten years of my life. Then they just seemed to crash and burn. We never saw or heard from Dad again. Mum sent letters from wherever she'd ended up. She died from lung cancer in 2014.'

'And what about Leigh?'

When I don't speak for a few seconds, Louise breaks in. 'This is a raw nerve for you, isn't it? Let's change the subject.'

'It is raw. Leigh's husband murdered her. Went for a nice, married couple walk in the park. Then he pulled out a carving knife and stabbed her once, through the heart.'

'Fucking hell, Joe.'

The renewed silence makes me wonder if Louise has some built-in knowledge about my feelings. She somehow knows I've got tears in my eyes and need time. How can she tell?

'Joe? Talk to me.'

'That's the first time, for ages and ages, that I've said this out loud.'

'How come?'

Now my tears are joined by snuffles and my voice comes in short bursts. It's almost like I'm barking.

'No one else has asked. About Leigh, I mean. Mum and Dad were different. Them leaving. So long ago... just a statistic. Mum's death wasn't news, because anyone who knew me, and Leigh, had no idea who or what Mum was. Dad, well, he wasn't even real by the time I was sixteen. I'm sorry. That probably all sounded like a really bad answer.'

'It didn't. But friends, work colleagues, lovers?'

I've recovered a bit. 'Not many of those. When Leigh was killed, the people I needed to tell got told. People knew. It was part of the deal if you happened to know Joe Thompson.'

'Fuck, Joe. This makes you seem and sound terribly alone. Filled with guilt and blame.'

'I feel all those things. Yes.'

'Not many friends. Why?'

'With two exceptions, I don't seem to make real friends. At school I made a few, lads mainly, but those didn't last. We never fell out, but we fell apart. I was working the instant I left school and I've never stopped. Some people I work with are great, and never fail to support me. But they don't know me. They don't need to know me. Just care for me. Which they do. And have.'

'But there are two exceptions?'

I tell her all about Alice. Her breathing says *keep going*.

I tell her all about Carolyn.

'Are you and Carolyn lovers?'

'No. She and I, we've done all the things that might make us that, but two things mean we aren't. We love each other too much. We don't want to be a couple. Neither of us has ever once seen ourselves as the future.'

Louise makes a small exhalation, part laugh, part annoyance. 'The future never ends up as a worthwhile present.'

'Well, this was fun.'

She laughs so loudly I have to move the handset away from my ear. Then she swears repeatedly and profoundly. Louise has lost one of her headphones. She says she'll call back but after nearly half an hour she hasn't. A message says she found the lost Air Pod. Another says I make her laugh. Another says she's trying to call but getting voicemail. It's me that calls.

'How was the dinner party on Saturday?'

'It was perfectly all right. And it was late. The others got very drunk. I watched them and felt smug.'

'Is that a big thing for you? Not drinking?'

'I'm not tee-total. I'm just not interested in getting drunk.'

Before I can say anything, she adds, 'But don't worry, I'm not self-righteous about it. You can drink all you like when we're together.'

'I'll try not to. You expect we'll meet again?'

'I hope so. No idea when, but I'd like to feel this doesn't just peter out. What you did last week, the incident in the supermarket, deserves more than just my thanks and gratitude. You showed me unbelievable kindness and integrity. Kindness like I haven't known for years, possibly decades.'

'But Saturday. Your friends, dinner, late night. That was kind, wasn't it?'

'Wrong kind of friends. Different sort of kindness.'

'And integrity?'

'I suppose. After a fashion. The fluttering topics of conversation at safe, middle-class dinner parties rarely step outside the bounds of decency. But your integrity was honourable. I think maybe you believe in doing the right thing.'

'I'm not perfect.'

'That's why you are good at doing the right thing.'

I can hear how her footsteps have begun to cause that different sound and soon we won't be talking.

'It's been lovely talking, Louise. I know you're nearly home.'

'How? Oh, wait, yes. The crunching. It's true. Here's the garden gate, the drawbridge to this castle. What are you up to this evening?'

'I'm going to plan tomorrow's day trip, perhaps drink a beer and make a meal.'

'Is there a pub or anything nearby?'

'Yes, but not for tonight. I want an early night.'

'Time to go, Joe.'

'Hope you've got your keys, Louise?'

'You're funny. Have a good evening and sleep well. I've loved this conversation, even the sad bits.'

'Me too. Bye.'

'Bye.' She breathes in as if she'll say more, but the line drops.

<>

The late afternoon sunshine is warm, and I lie back on the lounger, wondering if I can handle an evening and night without Louise telling and asking me things. I can still frame her face from last week's incident. Her eyes are still the major memory: subtly lined, alluring, but somehow sad. The shock of dark blond hair, long and wild, is next in my picture. Eyebrows full, always ready to be arched. Her nose and mouth are neat lines, and the tiny pout from that pale pink lower lip a challenge, or maybe a shield? She was tall, even without her heels. My mind's eye just keeps going back to those eyes and how they found mine.

2.4

When I wake up Louise has left a link to another song. It's by a band, or something, called *The 1975* and it's called *The Sound*. No message. Just a song. I reply,

> *Will listen in the car. I'm going to look at some dams.*

> > *Try the whole album. It's a bit old now, like lots of the music I listen to, but it's special, I think. Take lots of photos. Sorry Joe, but I'm incommunicado until much later. But let me know you're safe? Please?*

> *I will. No idea where I'm going and how long it will take.*

> > *Please be careful xxx.*

It's a sunny day. Shorts and a tee shirt are good, plus sunglasses. I stick to 50 max and piss off a few people who are desperate to rush. I like the places I see, all the hills and forests. I stop once in a while to get out and take a picture. All I seem to see are things I want to remember.

I end up quite pleased with myself for the decision to bring walking shoes and socks. The dams provide a choice of walks, so I just pick one and set off along one side of the lake and then across the wall of the dam.

Carolyn messages me to ask if she can call, but there's hardly any signal. Her messages start by telling me she spent an extra few days with her man, won't be back before the weekend and won't be coming over to see me. I say it's fine. She wants to know if I'm all right and says I looked really low when we met last week. I tell her I'm getting better. She tells me those two lads won't be around in Worcester again. I nod but the messages stop.

The mistake I made was not bringing water or food. It's warm now and I need something to drink. Some people walking towards me say hello and I ask about shops or vending machines nearby. They tell me they saw a café at the far end of the lake. One of the blokes offers me water and I'm grateful. One of the women tells me to take care.

Louise sends a message telling me she's busy but wanted to say *hi*. She also tells me we can talk this evening, but the rest of the day is looking pretty bad for her.

I go back to the cottage using the same route and stop at all the same places to take photos in the different light of late afternoon. At the cottage I unpack some things I bought to eat and drink more water. Out on the lounger I spend ages editing today's photos wondering if Louise will be bored if I send too many. There must be more than fifty.

She calls me after eight. Preamble is short. Hey. Hey. You okay? I'm okay. Tell me about your day.

'I didn't take your advice.'

'In what way?'

'Was very careful driving and took the right footwear for walking. Good start.'

'Very good. That's my boy.'

'But I didn't put any sun cream on. And I had no water. So, I ended up in a state.'

'Are you feeling okay now? Please tell me you didn't drive in that state. Have you rehydrated and put some sort of after sun on? Do you feel nausea or faint? Is your pee very yellow?'

'I bought some fancy gel with aloe vera and have smeared it all over, even on the unaffected bits.'

Louise makes a small sound. 'Joseph...'

'I have drunk almost as much water as in the dams, I don't feel sick, I am pissing clear, and I have an appetite. No. I didn't drive in that state, but I was stopping constantly.'

She tuts. 'It was stupid of you to neglect the basics like that.'

'I know. It spoiled the second half of the day. On the plus side I have a lot of photos to show you. Too many.'

'Not possible.'

'Don't want to bore you.'

'Also, not possible. But why don't you do this? After we finish talking, pick just one photo and learn more of your newfound editing skills. Then send it over. Then tell me why you chose it, why you like it and what you see. And what you think I will see.'

I smile and, if she could see it, Louise would know that my smile is a happy one.

'Shall we listen to some music together? Wait. Let me play you what's on the system here. Can you hear this?'

I realise music is playing, but quietly. Suddenly it's loud in my headphones. I've no idea what it is, who it's by, none of that. Then suddenly Louise is singing along, and her voice is absolutely on the money. In tune. In time. In the moment.

...I'll forgive and not fight all the moments I play in the dark.

'Louise?' But it's like she's not there.

...Wild and fluorescent, come home to my heart...

The song is quieter now and her singing stops.

'Louise, can you hear me?'

'I can hear you, Joe.'

'Thought you'd deserted me.'

'Just got a bit lost in the music. Can't remember the last time I turned it up that loud. Any plans to be in Worcester soon?'

'I could be there this week. But won't you be working?'

'Evenings best. Tomorrow, I have a very late finish. Thursday evening is free, always.'

The map tells me it's between 41 and 46 miles and will take me just over an hour.

'What do you have in mind for Thursday evening?'

'I'm going to see a band, like I always do. They're really good. Come and join me. If you want to.'

I tell her I want to. Then before I can ask about location and time and whether there's a dress code she just says, 'Sorry. Really sorry.'

The line drops.

After the sudden end of our call, I feel like the effort needed to send a photo makes no sense.

Why does it keep happening? Where is she? I should confront it, I'm sure. Or roll with it?

I flick back and forth through the photos I took today and can't decide which is best.

The one I choose shows the lake, divided by a bridge with loads of arches. A road crosses the bridge but from where I took the photo a path heads alongside the lake. A tower is there too, with a green roof, like a dome. The tower is partially submerged in the water.

I edit it. I filter it so it's black and white. It looks sinister.

I write,

> *I chose this one because it's how I feel right now. At a fork in the road. I like it because despite the huge power of all that water, the scene is calm and there is no danger. But the danger is there. The photo is monochrome, but what I see isn't black and white. I don't know what you'll see. If you'd been with me, maybe I wouldn't have taken this photo.*

Then I hit send. After a few minutes, a big red heart appears from Louise. Then, maybe ten minutes later,

I will explain everything. Soon.

<>

It seems I can't stop sleeping late. I wake up after eleven and am still lying in bed at noon. Over the last few days, the injuries from last week have slowly become little more than fleeting, occasional aches. The bruises have dulled. I can touch them without pain.

When I switch my phone on, there's a message but it isn't Louise.

It's Darren.

Hey Joe. I didn't know you were on WA!! Does this mean you have a guilty secret?

He sent it just after nine. I laugh at his comment.

My secrets might not be safe with you. How's Harry?

He's online straight away.

Tell!!

Can we talk?

He rings straight away.

'Harry is gorgeous, but you knew that. He says hi and he also says you have to tell me what's happened. Anyone who suddenly goes on WhatsApp has met a new lover.'

I am really not sure what to say. My instinct was to talk, because Darren has never judged me or been anything other than a good workmate and friend. But now I think about what's happened and hasn't happened with Louise, it almost seems crazy to say any of it out loud.

'I know what that breathing means, Joe. Stop thinking. Talk.'

When I dive in, full disclosure, nothing held back, he listens patiently to the end.

'And I'm lying here in bed without any more news.'

'Are you planning to go and meet her?'

'What do you think?'

'Who are you, and what have you done with Joe?'

I'm laughing and he joins in.

'Seriously, Joe, I've never known you ask advice.'

'But I'm doing it now.'

'Which suggests you are torn. Head or heart?'

'I really don't know.'

'For fuck's sake. HEAD. OR. HEART.'

'Heart says maybe.'

'Head?'

'Also, maybe.'

'Then you go. Why not?'

'I'm not used to all this.'

'If you don't go, you'll spend another few days messaging and being in doubt. Possibly regretting that you still don't know. Go and see her. She sounds fun. And mysterious. And a little dangerous. Incidentally, is everything else, okay? You disappeared at very short notice, especially after your amazing success with Caddy-Hill.'

I tell him I needed a break, and nothing is wrong. He says he's sceptical. I tell him that's nothing new and we have another five minutes reviewing how much of a cock Neal can be.

When I take some food out to sit in the sun, Darren sends another message.

> *Harry says three words. Fun. Mysterious. Dangerous.*

Sounds like I will have to go.

2.5

Before I leave, I listen again to Louise's voice clip. It arrived just after 4am.

'Joe, this might seem like a massive contradiction, but I am really looking forward to seeing you this evening. Maybe it's me that is the contradiction. Sorry. But I owe you an explanation and you will get one. I promise.'

Long pause.

'It might not be tonight. I just need you to know that all the gaps and sudden stops aren't because I don't want to talk. And now it probably sounds utterly shit when I say that I won't be around much, or at all, for most of the coming day. But we will make up for it this evening.'

She tells me the venue and the best place to park, and says I should message her when I'm outside the pub.

'The first band is on at eight. Can't wait. Bye.'

Her follow up message contains a photo showing two tickets for the evening. I'm a bit surprised it needs tickets. Must be a big band of some kind. But I've never heard of them.

My reply says,

> *I also can't wait. Will be good to meet you.*

And then I think the second sentence looks cold and distant. It's not work. So, I add,

> *Please don't feel any pressure to explain anything that is hard for you. Tell me when you can.*

It gets me another massive heart with about twenty x.

<>

My journey is slow and without clear direction. Ludlow is nice, which I already knew. Then a place called Tenbury Wells is a random stop, mainly because I took a wrong turn. It's a minor road to Worcester and the journey seems to be better because it's so slow. There are tractors and other farm vehicles, plus people doing what I'm doing.

The journey back will be quick, via main roads. In the dark. It will be fun. Dangerous. Mysterious.

2.6

I'm here. Where are you?

The security guys have been watching me and I make sure I look back.

On way.

There she is, talking to security. Pointing at me, showing them the piece of paper in her hand. She looks amazing, dressed in dark things. Her eyes show me this confused mix of attraction, worry, desire, relief, and happiness.

One of the security dudes nods his head and she reaches out her hand to pull me inside.

'You look good.' This is accompanied by a squeeze of my hand, but then she lets it go.

'Old tee shirt and jeans. Not the best.'

'I didn't mean your clothes, Joe. But you dressed right for this place.'

It isn't noisy but it's pretty full and mainly with blokes. Louise seems to attract many stares and leers. As we pass him, one bloke says I've done well. I don't get time to challenge him.

We get drinks and stand with our backs against a wall with the small stage to our left.

'I hope you like these bands. I'm sure you will. I'm still a bit astonished by how little you know about music.'

'That album you suggested was good. I listened to it twice in the car. Once in each direction. Will you send me more?'

'I will. But be curious. Take a look yourself and try things. You've got a whole world of music to tap into on your phone.'

'And what about tonight?'

'The main band are excellent. I've seen them loads. The other one is new to me.'

Someone has started doing stuff among the various pieces of kit on the stage. She switches things on and taps the microphones, each touch making a sound like someone is whispering the letter P. Louise is standing close, so we are touching at shoulder height and hips. We are of a height because of her heels. She leans in to speak to me. I feel like being alongside means it's not the same as being able to see her eyes, even in the dark.

The music starts and Louise moves constantly and sings along. The band is good and plays songs I know. Old ones, from when I was a kid. The 90s. People start dancing and, during *Killer*, Louise turns me to face her and we're dancing too. It's like she's in another place. Movements completely in time, she glides through the song with the words on her lips. Every once in a while, she watches me dance and smiles, then reaches out a hand to touch mine.

In this space, we dance to all the songs they play, and we haven't spoken at all since they started. We're just moving, watching, touching.

Then it's over. Cheers. Applause.

I want more.

'Let's get drinks and sit outside. Much more space out there. The main band won't be on for ages. Don't you want a beer or something?'

'I'd love one but driving in the dark later. Even one drink would be stupid.'

'It would. Should you have stayed over?'

'Tomorrow's my last day at the cottage so really need to have the whole day there.'

'Maybe tonight wasn't such a good idea.'

'It was a great idea.'

We sit opposite each other and there it is. Her constant, challenging gaze while we talk. Under the table, she slips off a shoe and runs her foot up my shin.

But when I reach my hand towards hers, she shakes her head, smiles, and says, 'Not here. Not yet.'

'Where does your love of music come from?'

'All sorts of places. Mam and Dad were always playing music at home. They liked all genres. My friends couldn't believe how cool they were. I had singing lessons, but I walked away from them because I was more interested in parties.'

'Your singing is great.'

'Thank you.'

'It's a shame you stopped. When you were singing just now, during that George Michael song, it was like you could have sung it instead of him.'

'It's a special song. *Looking for some affirmation*.'

As she sings the line, Louise puts her foot on the inside of my knee, so I run a finger along its instep then along the line of her toes.

'I don't regret that I stopped singing lessons. For about a year, just after university, I sang in a band. Backing vocals. A bit like the one we just saw, lots of covers. We were excellent, had bookings and everything. I thought it would be a good way to repay what my parents forked out on the lessons. But the egos were shocking and one of the guitarists was a serial misogynist and I walked away from that too. Now, I sing in the shower, sing in the car, and sing on the phone with special people.'

The eyebrows rise, part coy, part challenge. I've discovered in just one conversation that Louise makes me smile like it's a reflex. She does another movement with her foot. *Stroke me some more*, it says.

'I also sing along with bands at gigs. Live music is the thing that keeps me going, the balancing act for my work / life woes. The scene here is good. Good venues with talented bands. But I go further afield too.'

'What about bigger gigs?'

'Sometimes. I just prefer to be somewhere like this where it's right there in front of you. Smiling, or snarling, or soothing.'

'What if it's rubbish?'

Louise tilts her head.

'It's never rubbish. They all deserve a chance. What are your plans for tomorrow? Packing and a gloomy mood?'

'I travelled light, so that's fifteen minutes work. But I've got no plans. It's been a good week for me. In fact, I've had two good weeks. I'm ready to get back to work.'

'You need to go somewhere to take more of your brilliant photos. Have you always been so clever at capturing scenes?'

'Until the other day, I'd never once thought about it. I took a few last week, at the cathedrals and the seaside. I've never shown them to anyone.'

'So, I'm your audience.'

'You are. For as long as you want to be.'

'It will be forever if you always wear that cologne. You smell good enough to eat, and I meant what I said about you looking good. Last week, you seemed like you'd been hollowed out. A few carefree days in the sun have made the difference. Aside from all the grief you feel about Leigh, is anything else affecting your mental health?'

'Work has been pretty tough.'

'That's a given. But you told me all that is covered. What else?'

Something rises up inside me. It isn't upset or anything defensive. I just feel like I can't say what's wrong. All the loneliness. The isolation. The things I keep putting off because they aren't important yet, every day, grow into bigger things I still don't do. The broken lost friendships and relationships I can't fix and believe are broken because of me. The blame I pour on myself for everything that has ever gone wrong. I don't know where I am going, don't have a clue what the future holds, can't see beyond the end of my desk and the next customer. The sheer monotony of a life where nothing is truly wrong, but not one thing seems to be right. The knowledge that someone loved me without any conditions, yet I drove her away and made her incredibly unhappy.

'Joe?'

'I can't tell you. Can't explain.'

'Is it lots of things or just one big thing?'

'It's just one thing. Being me. Maybe that's not too big. It's still something.'

'From where I'm sitting or standing, watching, or listening, being you is a good thing. Why would you think otherwise? You're kind, filled with empathy. Overflowing with it. Uncomplicated, an endearing mix of innocence and streetwise. Someone who isn't glued to their phone. A fighter, a defender of people in need, an amazingly observant photographer. Handsome, a hard-working professional, desirable, smart, you do smell delicious and that doesn't even get me to the things I think might also be true about you but are, as yet, untested. So: come on; talk to me.'

'I can't. Not here.'

Her eyes narrow briefly. She nods. 'Maybe we owe each other some time to tell.'

'I think we do.'

A small speaker under the canopy where we're sitting announces that *Latin Tags* are due on stage in ten minutes. As we head back inside, a group of men at a table starts up with a crock of shit about Louise and me. Some of it is gross, especially about her. I haven't really reacted, but Louise tells me to leave it. All four of them are mainly older than me, maybe fifty? One is pretty fat, another pretty small. But the other two are in decent shape. I think about the aches and small pains around my body.

'Is it always like this for you when you're out?'

'Yes.'

'Not sure how you cope.'

'I don't.'

The main band is amazing. They play about four cover versions for every one original song and the originals are way better. We don't dance much but end up swaying along to the music, with Louise standing in front of me. I've one arm around her waist and she strokes it in time to the beat. We don't say much. It's just like this. Two people with things to say, unable to face each other, and letting the music say it instead.

She unravels herself when the lights go up, turns, strokes two nails along the line of my chin and says, 'What time do you need to go?'

'There's no rush. Let's have another exciting soft drink. If you've got time.'

'I don't. And nor do you. It's past midnight and you should be on the road. Let's walk. Come on.'

One of the blokes from the table of four is having a massive row with the bouncers and it's caused a crush we can't get past. Louise pulls me in a different direction, and we end up leaving via the fire exit, causing alarms to go off. I then get treated to Louise running in her massive heels and, by the time we've gone two streets and slowed down, all we're doing is laughing. And holding hands.

Cars are beeping their horns at us, lads shouting abuse and filth; like it's the funniest thing in their world; like they've never seen a woman before.

It's hard to talk against the backdrop of traffic. I want to tell her I think she looks gorgeous, and how much I've enjoyed seeing her. But the moments keep flying away. It feels like this evening is going to end up as nothing.

'Do you know where you're parked?'

I admit I haven't got a clue.

'Did you park where I told you to park?'

'Yes. Cattlemarket?'

'Then we're headed in the right direction. Nearly there, in fact.'

When we reach her car, Louise pulls me to a halt and kisses me. It's lovely. It lasts a long time. We're locked into it, like it was all we've ever needed, all we've ever done. And we are experts at it.

I need to know something.

'When can we do this again?'

'Kissing? For almost all of the next fifteen minutes.'

'Funny. I meant *meet*.'

'Well, you're headed back to your northern home, and I'm headed... somewhere else. What do you have in mind?'

'Maybe next weekend?'

'Maybe.'

More kissing. Louise has her hand inside my shirt and those nails scratch my back like she means me harm. What if she does?

'You, I, we... need to go, Joe. I hope you had fun, sharing my passion for music. I definitely did. It's lovely that you drove over here. How long to get back to... wherever it is?'

'No time. How about you?'

'Less than 15 minutes. I'm going to scratch you again.'

When she tears herself away and opens her car door to take off her heels, I wait for a goodbye embrace, kiss, and whatever words we can find. I don't want to say goodbye. She's slipped off her shoes, and steps out, barefoot.

'Let's keep in touch, hey? This was good.'

'It was. You're amazing.'

'I might not be. But thank you.'

A final kiss then, 'We both have things to tell each other. And I think we both need that to be face to face. But for now, I'm just going to say *goodbye*, that I loved having your arm around me, and I loved feeling this.'

She grabs the front of my trousers, and when I smile and look into her eyes, I see the pale green has darkened many shades.

I watch her drive away and just stand there for ages, hoping Louise will drive back and run away with me.

<>

It's quiet on the roads. I crack on at speeds I'm not used to and eventually realise it isn't safe going that fast. But I still concentrate hard. Not drinking was a good thing. I think that's not just about the fact I needed to drive. Perhaps I'll take a break. Would that be sensible?

It's past two in the morning when I get back and Louise's message tells me she's home safe and I have to drive carefully and let her know I'm back.

I've just got back. Hope we get to talk tomorrow.

I was getting a bit worried. Glad you're safe, honey. Have you still got that hard on?

No.

Maybe we need to do something about that.

2.7

I've tidied up the cottage by mid-morning and packed, ready to leave. Looking out at the sunshine I'm pretty sure I want to spend time lying outside on the lounger. It's done me good all week. Louise told me I looked well. Looked better. And I feel it. But that's for later.

Instead of lounging, I drive along to Knighton and wander around the little town. It's so different to all I've known. So distant from the experiences I've had. I like it.

Could I settle somewhere new? I've no idea. Change, whenever it's happened to me, has been nothing more than a series of impositions, or actions based on my assessment of what is normal. This growing desire I'm feeling, to drop everything and do or be something different, is nothing to do with the more pleasing surroundings of a place miles from home, or the river flowing slowly past where I sit.

It's Louise. It shouldn't be. But it is.

In nine days, we've gone from a chance encounter in a supermarket to something less fateful. Last night was fun. There is something between us. Which is a confusing way of describing it. Mainly, I think it's what others call *chemistry*. But there is something else. Things we can't say. I know what I wasn't able to say; that I couldn't admit to the things that are crushing me, grinding me, closing me down.

But what she isn't telling me is really fucking obvious.

It doesn't matter that she's married. What matters is why she can't say it.

We need to talk. I'm quite surprised she answers.

'Morning, Joe. This is a lovely surprise. What's up?'

'Hey. I had fun last night. The music, your company, those messages. I liked it. All of it.'

'Good. I did too. It was needed.'

She's already praised me for not holding back. That time we talked about her parents. So, I don't.

'You're married, aren't you?'

'Hold on. Give me a moment.'

I hear her moving. Footsteps. Doors opening and closing. The sudden sound of a television or radio. Footsteps on gravel.

'You still there?'

'I am.'

'Okay, yes, I am married. Except, really, I'm not.'

'But married enough to have barriers. There is another word. What is it? Boundaries?'

'Yes, both. Boundaries with barriers. And vice versa.'

'I'd like to know what that really means, Louise.'

'It means there are complexities.'

'Are they too complex?'

'That maybe depends on you.'

'It depends on both of us. Right now, I'm sat on a bench by a river, miles from home. I feel like maybe I could change my life, move somewhere new, close the door on whatever my life has been. I've had an amazing few days getting to know you. But I can't tell what it is that I've got to know.'

Her footsteps have stopped. 'Everything you know about me is completely real. Completely true. I'm telling no lies.'

'I've no doubt at all about that.'

She exhales loudly. 'It sounds like you're creating some sort of goodbye.'

'No. Really what I want is to say *hello*, but to a different Louise. The real one...'

'I am completely real, Joe. No different because of my situation.'

'... where I can understand why there are whole days without messages or calls. And understand all the middle of the night voicemails, which really don't make any sense. The Louise who has pulled me into something exciting, yet who has things I need to know, because they affect me and how I feel and whatever I might do next.'

'I'm sorry.'

'Louise, stop apologising. Please. What has happened between us means something. And will mean other things, things we want to experience. I'd like to feel we have a future.'

'It still sounds like you are planning to say goodbye.'

'It's you that keeps using the word *goodbye.* But I'm definitely not saying it. I just want you to know that regardless of the fun and laughter, regardless of the sudden and special way we've become close, I don't believe we can keep on being *that*. The last week and a bit. Lovely. Fun. You've made me feel happy. You're like no one I've ever met. But I have this horrible sense that there is a built-in ending.'

'You make me happy too. What did you mean, you can't tell what you've got to know?'

'I meant that I'm ready to jump in. But scared there's just a crash landing. In my head, we have something incredible here.'

'We do.'

'I just need to know that I can stay. I want to stay.'

'Joe. Slow down. Please. I've told you that I will explain. I maybe should have done it last night, but it wasn't really the time and place. What are you doing next weekend?'

'Seeing you, I hope.'

'You couldn't have given a better answer.'

<>

After she leaves me on the bench, I scroll back through the messages from last night. Hot. A blaze. Whatever we'd seen and felt during the hours together earlier in the evening, it had switched on all that desire at a distance. It wasn't completely new to me, but I'd never felt anything like what was caused by the messages we exchanged. Then the final thrill: two breathless voice loops; loving what we'd just done; wishing sweet dreams; hoping there will be more.

And now we're back to the silence she has to impose. But now I understand it, because Louise has told me why, in a series of messages. Friday is the day her husband works from home so it's the day that will always mean silence. Not forever, she said. She feels relief that she told me, she said.

<>

It feels like there's nothing for me to do. The sun has done a good job. The aches and pains are gone. While I make some tea, late in the afternoon, a thought crosses my mind that I should just go home tonight. The thought turns into a plan. Leave at seven, back to the house by eleven, latest, but probably sooner. Then I get a whole day to sort stuff. Get some miles in on the bike. Get ready for work on Monday.

That's what I do.

<>

When I wake up on Saturday morning, she's sent messages.

A photo of a hotel booking for the following weekend. Some places to do stuff nearby with the words,

Bring walking shoes.

A song by Oleta Adams.

Part 3
Porcelain

3.1

My return to work was neither good nor bad. There were new things, old things, and mainly happy reactions to me being back. Neal asked for a chat and apologised that he'd been so critical. I told him to forget it. Josie was over the moon that a client I'd been wooing before my holiday had decided to sign while I was away. I told her it's what I do. She said I'm her *enfant terrible* and no one should forget it.

In the end it was like I hadn't been away. I marched through the week, long days, and meetings. It seemed the right thing to do.

Louise and I were in touch. Daily messages. Occasional calls. Long silences.

<>

My journey was slow, especially around Manchester. When I called to explain this, Louise answered and told me it didn't matter. Just get here safe, she said.

And there she is, sitting by a window, reading a book. A glass of cola, or something that colour, is on the table near her left hand. When she sees me, her smile is contagious. She stands. We kiss and hug. It doesn't feel like it's only the third time we've met and the second time we've touched.

She hands me the room key and I head up there to drop my bag. I find an amazing small space with a big bed. The lights are discreet, and the room smells of something I don't know. It's like spices in a cake.

Louise's bag is on the bed. A pair of trainers lie several feet apart, one upside down. A leather jacket is draped over the small sofa. I open my bag for some things and get into the shower.

<>

I ask her about the book she's reading. It's called "Machines Like Me" and the way Louise describes it I almost want to read it with her. An alternative history. A love triangle involving a robot.

She says I can have her copy.

We talk about drinks and food. She thinks the meals here in the hotel are probably delicious but seem smart and highbrow, so she wants to go into town. Get something less posh, without the constant jazzy lift music.

She drives.

<>

Ashbourne is busy and it takes ages to park then find a place to eat. But we're walking hand in hand and that feels good. When we try a pub, just off the high street, they find us a table. It's a good place to settle for the evening as it's mainly families and couples. One or two blokes can't stop staring at Louise but soon have to get back to the wife and kids.

Everyone is eating. It's not a drinker's pub. There's a background of talking and noise. This is a good place for us. When I ask Louise about her week at work, she shakes her head and smiles. It doesn't matter. It's gone.

'Lots to talk about, Joe, and work isn't on the list. I've been wondering how to tell you all this. I even had a panic at one point that I wouldn't be able to say any of it.'

'Is this the right place?'

'Yes. It is. Not sure I could have done it back at the hotel. It's coldly quiet there. Here is good, and I need to do this. It's part of why we're here. It shapes things.'

Interruptions happen. Would you guys like to order? We would and we do. Louise gets a burger and I have a pie. Chips with everything. Then they want to know if we want more drinks. Then they come back and ask if it's okay that the pie I wanted might take a little longer so does Louise want her meal brought anyway, or wait until mine is ready to serve? Wait please. They're sorry. But it's all okay.

Louise starts by saying she doesn't know where to start. But then she just rolls into it, her pale green eyes holding mine during each word and sentence. There aren't many smiles.

She hates using the word *my* alongside any of the words, *marriage* or *home* or *husband*. So, I need to know that he's called Nick, but she will refer to him as Prick.

They met when she was out with friends, celebrating her 25th birthday. Eyes across a room. Chat up, smooth, co-ordinated. The usual. Reciprocal. Days of phone calls and flirting. Lunches. Wine and cocktails. Eventually a night together after drinks and a candlelit dinner.

After a few months getting closer, they lived together part time. He had a place just outside Birmingham. She was in central Worcester. Anyone in the know was happy and encouraging about the affair. Her parents liked him. She liked his father. There was a lot going on.

Prick was a marketing manager. It didn't matter who for, but he was doing pretty well. Louise worked for a retailer in Human Resources. She calls it *Human Remains*. None of that mattered either. Their careers were in good places, evolving places. Money. Cars. Success. Promotion. Nights out. Weekends away. Holidays in the sun. Then, without a second thought, that house they saw one day was too good to ignore and they became joined by new responsibilities. The mortgage. The furniture. The decorations. The garden. Space for two ever-changing cars on the drive, side by side. The switch from nights out to nights in with like-minded couples around a massive, shiny dining table drinking wine from glasses with long, frail stems.

Then the final bond. A decision to get married. Mutual. Everyone joined in with the notion. Five years together had been good. They were in love. They agreed that needed to be made formal. People said they were perfect. A big day in a small church and an elaborate hotel.

They both became directors. Leaders. It was all written in the stars. An honourable estate.

Marriage and success changed nothing. They still had each other, and they liked what they had, but they still kept upgrading it. The kitchen. The bathrooms. The sofas. Televisions got bigger. Holidays got further and further away.

Maybe empathy got smaller.

Friends they'd made before they met seemed to have drifted away now.

Her company changed things. Louise got squeezed out and took the package they offered. Despite the shitshow in global markets, the austerity for others, it was a good time to go it alone. Corporate life had ended up being something she disliked but it left her with all that was needed to set up her own business.

Prick was away a lot, but they kept moving forwards.

After seven years, nothing was wrong, but something wasn't working. Her days were often long, and his trips involved whole weeks away. Three loving calls each day became one, then one every three days. Whatever they needed as partners, lovers or friends was being condensed into tiny, unplanned opportunities. Everything was a reaction.

Louise, even with hindsight, couldn't recall the first thing they stopped being. Lovers, probably.

But then he was good when her dad died. It gave them a renewed bond. Prick rekindled the stability she needed, cancelled his trips away and worked at home or local office as she grieved and cared for her mam.

When she told him she was back on solid ground, he quickly resumed his routines. Perhaps too quickly.

Neither was unfaithful. Louise believed it. But they lost touch in the day-to-day things. Meals didn't get shared. While he was away, Louise slept in the spare room. Nights together lacked any kind of real meaning. Sex was processed, packaged, perfunctory. Then unwanted.

Their tenth anniversary was celebrated with a weekend in Rome. It was a mutual decision, arranged with a degree of optimism that there could be another renewal.

Something went badly wrong while they were there. Prick was distracted by work, dipped into his phone too much. When she started to dive into the reasons, he was evasive and dismissive. This wasn't work, she decided. There was someone else. When he didn't deny it, Louise travelled back alone. They hadn't been together since.

Not together in any way, except that they still lived in that house. Two angry lodgers with unbreakable tenancy agreements. At first, it was a place maintained for the sake of appearances and schedules. He said the affair was over. She assumed it was a lie, but it wasn't. Instead, he was just fucking whoever he could get his hands on. Still smart, connected, linked in; Prick was off the leash.

Their social life as a couple was over. Wherever he landed for work, he had whatever social scene was needed. Louise turned to the solitary nights she grew to love, watching music and fighting off the charmless men who treated the way she chose to dress as a signal for harassment.

She stayed faithful to herself.

There was no agreement about anything but, in the fleeting conversations they had as they passed each other between meals or on the driveway, they couldn't find any way to face what they knew was inevitable. Decisions about money, possessions, legacies. Going solo meant double the costs. Starting from zero was too hard to face. Wants were more important than needs. They stayed in a tried and tested safety net. It wasn't possible to take the steps needed to face a divorce. To be victorious and defeated, all at once.

Louise made the fifth bedroom her office and spent most of her time in there, silent, and dutiful, even when Prick was away. Pre-dawn starts, long hours with no real difference between day and night. When her mam took her own life Louise was plunged into profound isolation and loneliness. The only connection she had to anyone, and anything was lost and that closed, solitary existence began to chip away at her confidence and assertiveness. A daily re-set gave her enough, just about enough, to fulfil her working life and deliver something in that world.

Prick didn't lift a finger to help. He came to the funeral, but not to the wake.

During the times when lockdowns were imposed, they endured being in the same space. When the rules were relaxed and removed, Prick went back to his travels. He stayed away most days then began his routine of being home at the end of every week. Louise soon realised it was to check up on her and her nights out. He sneered at the way she dressed, called her a slut, accused her of seeing other men or one other man. Or anyone. The accusations formed into abuse. You're just an adulterous bitch. Aren't you? There was this constant challenge. Who is he? Where does he live? Do you love him? She just said *no one, nowhere, no*. She wasn't interested in men, unless they were singing and playing and drumming.

'And, as I was distractedly waiting for my basket of shopping to be scanned, I realise the filthy twat behind me is close enough to threaten paternity and has his hand up my dress. Then a handsome stranger stepped in.'

It's the first time she's smiled for ages. During her monologue, Louise's expression had lost any kindness or happiness. Her face had become frozen. Now, she moves her hand towards me. It's almost a formal gesture, like a signal to shake hands. But I see the tiny movement in her fingers, and I enclose her hand in mine.

'Still want to be here?'

Without hesitation, I say more than ever.

It feels like she expects me to ask lots of questions, but I don't feel the need to check or query what she's told me. Louise spoke with such certainty and calm about all these events. An unbroken speech, the story of a broken, failed marriage, was made in a way that left nothing in doubt apart from whatever the ending might be.

Plates get cleared away. Drinks get refreshed. We get called *guys* maybe six times.

'I've never had to tell anyone this. Never really wanted to. Feels like I've released a great cloud of pointless, inert gas.' She laughs. 'I don't mean I've farted.'

'That's good to know.' But I do a cartoon sniff.

'I just meant that I was holding back the truth from myself. Letting it bubble away inside. Telling you was like telling myself. Revealing something I couldn't process.'

It makes me think she has more to say but I can't phrase the way to ask her what it is. Watching her take a sip of cola I see elegant, gentle, deliberate motions. She takes what appears to be enough then, like an afterthought, she gives her lips a tiny lick. Her eyes don't leave mine during these moments.

She hasn't finished.

'This was a good decision. This pub. It's the perfect setting. The ambient noise helped me open up. And...' She looks around. 'I actually quite like it here. I haven't been in a pub or restaurant or anything for ages, not without a band helping me forget things. I hardly eat anything. Just enough, but some days nothing. That food was perfectly wrong and right, bad and good. I could get used to it. In fact, for the first time in a long time I feel like I could happily drink too much.'

Her situation has no end in sight. There are uncivil speaking terms between them. His accusations about her infidelity have taken a recent turn for the worse. An overheard conversation, when he'd had a few, in which he was telling someone he is currently celibate, building up a case that his fidelity couldn't be questioned if it came to a fight. It would make him the innocent party.

That whole sorry mess has left Louise questioning whether she ever really loved him, ever really cared, was ever really happy. Staying together in a house seemed to have no logic, aside from the financial and logistical.

'It's not like we've got kids, the ultimate reason to stick together in a broken marriage.'

'Is it?'

'Some people say it is.'

'Did you never want kids?'

'Never. We were having fun, falling in love, being a couple. We had spontaneity. Trips away, often on a whim, a last-minute *fuck yes, let's do it*. Once we had a place to live together, there was all that acquisition. Furniture. Decorations. *Objets*. Designer dreams. Makeover after makeover. That felt like our destiny. Our reason to co-exist. We saw other couples who talked about *life before the kids* as if it had made their own relationship a sideshow: like they regretted and resented their kids; like they longed for those good old days. Their situations sounded terrible. I don't think there was ever a moment when I felt it was necessary to give up something that felt like freedom.'

'So, no maternal instinct?'

'None whatsoever. We were well-paid and we were crafting all the things we felt were needed to show the world exactly how much we earned and how our respective power games were won. It was never discussed, and it was never a problem. I had no desire to have a child. Nor did Prick, or at least not with me. We had our freedom. A baby would restrict us. A child would prevent us growing old with the comforts we'd accrued. A teen would cause little earthquakes of disquiet.'

'That makes perfect sense.'

'Really?'

'Yes. That whole thing about family and children and togetherness seems like a kind of oppression to me. Like you're not normal if you remain single, or a couple without kids. It's like some people see it as a crime.'

Louise has hold of both my hands now. 'Thank you.' Her expression changes, slightly. 'You look like you have more questions.'

'I do.'

Our hands slip away, and she sits back. It's like she resents me.

'What happened to your friends?'

'They've all gone, and I will never know how perfectly everything turns out for them. That whole social scene was as brittle and unrewarding as the marriage. Once it was clear there was no longer an '*us*', a lot of people stopped calling. I guess some of them know what is going on and disapprove. I've remained acquainted with no more than half a dozen, but what all of this has done is to make me closed and discreet.'

'Don't you ever feel you need some sort of support group?'

'In my mind, telling anyone what has happened, and is still happening, would suggest that I care. That there's a problem I want to solve by seeking guidance. Sharing it with someone would be the start of a process to create reconciliation.'

'But they don't care either, do they? Otherwise, someone would be by your side; constantly dropping by; discussing things.'

'Correct. In the final analysis, none of those people were friends.'

'And parents? Did they offer nothing?'

'Prick's parents are divorced and, for more than ten years, he has been estranged from his mother. His father lives half the year in Spain and the rest of the time in Kent. They never spent any time imparting wisdom about how to make a marriage tick because, quite clearly, they didn't know.

Mam and Dad wanted me to be happy and would check-in on me, and on us as a couple, to make sure all was well. And, when they looked in on the happy house, they saw nothing that needed fixing. Because, back then, nothing did. Fuck.'

That one word comes out as if Louise is suddenly broken.

'Dad never saw the end. Mam was too unwell to notice. It's a huge relief to me that I never had to tell them about this mess, this whole sorry shitshow. I couldn't have done it.'

'What do you think they'd have done?'

Her eyes shift away to look over my shoulder, as if she's in a trance. When she resumes eye contact, I see great sadness.

'That's a terribly difficult question, Joe.'

'Then don't answer it.'

'I have to try, because it's also a very good question.' Louise still seems lost somewhere. 'The biggest lie in all of this remains the one to my mam and dad.'

'But you said they didn't know things were going wrong.'

'They didn't. But that's not what I mean. The thing in my head is that if they'd known about Prick and me having problems, they probably wouldn't have done a thing. They'd have just acquiesced in the drama by carrying on regardless. Because that's what they'd always done. Something had made them remote, so they never saw the things I told you earlier. That I wasn't happy, wasn't in love, didn't truly care.'

'And you wouldn't have told them.'

'I couldn't have. And that's just awful, Joe.'

'Not in my eyes.'

'Oh God, please don't be nice to me. And stop smiling.'

'It's the best and only thing I can do.'

'How much have you had to drink?'

'Two pints. Three if you count the one at the hotel. Why?'

'Because I am about to lose it completely and I'm not sure I'll be able to drive.'

3.2

It's a grey day when I wake up. Louise is in the shower, but the bed's still warm where she'd slept.

We rested well, despite the sense we might not. All we discussed last night, and all we felt once we were alone in this room, was pretty sad. It upset Louise. Yet she's singing away.

I lie, listening to the cascading water and her words about friends in need, who tease. Compressed thoughts and stormy weather. Confessed. Never severed.

I forget to ask her what song it was.

The hotel breakfast is good and, after eating too much of it, Louise tells me she wants to go walking. No plan. Just desire. When I get my phone out to look for a route, she tells me not to. Let's just set off from here, she says. There'll be footpaths, some with signs, and plenty of things to see. We're in the countryside.

She asks, 'Have you brought shorts?'

'Why?'

'No reason.' But her smile and eyes say otherwise.

'Well, as it happens, I have.'

'I'd love you to wear them.'

So, I do.

We walk and talk and the things we say reflect on our environment. Louise points at things. I take photos. Not long after we leave the hotel and its village, we're in the woods. It's silent and calm. Every so often we stop to kiss. Her nails still dig, and gouge and her eyes still go dark green. I know why that is now.

There's no sense of distance or time. Sometimes we walk quickly, others we're slow. It doesn't matter at all. This is time we need. Out in the open.

Last night, away from the pub and under the covers, there were closing words about all Louise told me. Did it matter to me? Yes. Was it important? Yes. How did it make me feel? No different.

She told me to be crystal clear that nothing could or would change quickly.

I said it didn't matter.

Within a mile of the hotel, and with no kind of community, village, or town in sight, we're talking about all the places we've lived.

All I know or knew about Blackpool. She says I don't seem to like it, and maybe that's true. It's never given me anything. It just exists as the place where I learned to hustle. I didn't care if I stayed or left, but I took the first chance to leave. I didn't go far but it was *away*. That was the future, then.

Louise lived near the coast, east of Newcastle, then a spa town near Worcester. University at Manchester. Back to the spa then on again to Worcester where her parents settled. Short term lets around the south of Birmingham, close to work and play. Back to Worcester for the first place in her own right, sometimes shared with Prick. Finally, that grand house, in a small village, with links to wherever they needed to be.

I ask where she would live if she had a completely free hand. She's dismissive at first; says she has no idea; tells me it's a cliché. I say it's not. I want to know. Louise goes quiet then tells me about the one place where she felt like she belonged: a holiday destination where the family went a lot, almost every year. When I ask where, she says it doesn't matter because it's history. She will never go again.

Louise asks me the same question and I can't answer. Until my road trip I'd never considered what places can be. The travelling made me unsettled, that I was trapped by my thirty something years living in that tiny corner of the country. I saw new places with nothing new. Maybe there was a shared set of rules or behaviour. Shops. Houses. Bars. Parks. Road systems. Tower blocks. Zones, demarcated. People doing the same old stuff, pretending to be different but really all sharing a single illusion: that where they are and what they have is unique. Until it's seen through a stranger's eyes.

Louise tells me I'm being deep.

Maybe that's what I am.

At a pretty village, so we stop and stare. A square with a monument, a shop, small houses with neat gardens and a church. We get sweet snacks and sit on a bench to eat. I eat slower than Louise, so she lies with her head on my lap. At one point she reaches up and wipes something from the side of my mouth. When she starts to laugh, I ask what's wrong. She tells me she's never looked up someone's nose while they're eating. She says it's the polar opposite of sexy yet still vaguely arousing. Her laughter makes her fall off the bench.

We walk back slowly, with no urgent need for words but very little silence. The little hotel is a welcome sight. A shower each, then the kind of passion we seem to have fallen into, like it was always there. Sleep, then another shower but this time together. Under the jets of water, the mass of her crazy hair turns into something shiny and slippery, like it's part of a waterfall.

<>

The dining room is busy. The place was a pub once and they upgraded it to something grander, but it's still just a pub. With endless fucking jazz. We probably could have guessed that, unlike the town centre pub last night, the atmosphere here is a bit too quiet. We order food and some wine, and everything we get is good. The missing piece is any kind of conversation. Louise says there is still so much to talk about, but it can't be here. Instead, we do what everyone else does. Rave about the food. Drink wine like it's a ritual. Smile to the gallery. Lower our voices to say the things we really mean.

Back in our room, we lie on the bed doing small talk. For ages we're side by side on our backs, holding hands, things popping into a conversation. It feels good.

Louise is curious, so we turn on our sides. Eye to eye.

She asks about the things I couldn't say to her at the pub in Worcester. The agreement that we owed each other time to tell. In my case, about that one thing I can't speak about.

Me.

I still can't organise how to say it, but Louise has a gently persuasive way of saying *please try.* She reminds me of that list of attributes, her contradiction to my low self-esteem. Her eyes are more demanding when she repeats, *please try*.

My throat tightens. Louise puts a hand on my forearm and watches while I say it all. That roll call of things I didn't want to tell her, or anyone. The all-consuming sense that how and what I feel can only ever be seen as weakness. The nights with my chest pounding like its shock. The need for people to connect, combined with constant running away from any kind of social interaction. The episodes of complete shutdown of everything except sobbing. The inability to see good in me. My failing system. Failing, but not broken, because every once in a while, I function without faults.

'What do those faults look like, Joe?'

'Silence. Dismissal. Pretence. Routine.'

'A routine? Are you sure?'

'Yes. One in which I carry on being Joe the ace employee. Delivering.'

'Is there any other routine?'

'Yes. One in which I avoid people.'

'Then who or what is the recipient of the silence, dismissal, and pretence? Who are you avoiding?'

I'm tearfully mute.

'All you've told me suggests you don't really avoid people. You've dug yourself into a hole so deep that you're invisible. Or you think you are.'

I nod.

'Keep looking at me, Joe. Please.'

I nod, and watch her through a blurred, rippling film.

Louise asks if I've considered speaking to my doctor about this because it's possibly quite serious.

I shake my head.

'When you get home, call your surgery, and ask to speak to a doctor. Tell them it's to discuss your mental health. You'll be seen quite quickly.'

I frown, and now she nods. 'Don't worry. Just take that step, okay?'

Now I can speak. 'I'm not sure I can say any of it without breaking down.'

'And that's part of what they need to see and hear.'

We agree that this will happen. Her smile backs up the kindness in her eyes. She is so very kind.

'I'm lucky. Aren't I, Joe?'

'How come?'

'With all the people in the world that you're avoiding, you decide to climb out of your hole and rescue me from danger. Perhaps that was a release for both of us. Why on earth would you choose me?'

I look at her. All of her. Then only at her eyes. It's because I love her. Should I say? It's ridiculous, isn't it?

'Perhaps I was asking a rhetorical question, Joe. I'd like to know the answer but, maybe, it's just a very happy accident.'

I shake my head.

'Stop thinking. Let's sleep. This has been difficult for you, stepping out of your matter-of-fact way of speaking and thinking. When we wake up, and at any time, you can tell me the things about what's on and in your mind. Make sure you do.'

3.3

We drive our cars to Ashbourne and spend most of Sunday there. Arm in arm, or hand in hand, we stroll around, and Louise calls it *mooching*. It's a good word, and this is a good place to do it.

We talk absent-mindedly about the day, the weather, the pretty buildings, the town's attractions. We grab food from a stall in the market square and Louise calls it a picnic, so we find a place to share the snacks and drinks. In this setting, she wants to know about Natasha.

What went wrong?

I tell her how it was real and loving but maybe never serious, or how could it end like it did? With no loose ends, no discussion, no attempt to find a way to stay together. Maybe I wasn't capable of changing, but she didn't give me the chance. It went from everything being okay to the end, with no attempt to make things work. The combination of my inability to create time and my drive to succeed was decisive.

Louise doesn't stop.

Any regrets?

I blame myself for it all, which still grabs me by the throat sometimes. We'd loved each other but I wasn't far enough inside Nat's head to see what was in there about us, about me and about whatever she really needed from me. I regretted that I didn't try.

She leads me on through more questions. It doesn't feel wrong to tell Louise these things. That I haven't seen Nat for ages, and we never tried to be mates. There was something really difficult about how she was at the end, how she made it crystal clear she didn't want me in her life and needed a really, really clean cut. I must have wanted that too. I didn't try to stop her. There'd been good things between Nat and me. The right mix of friendship and love. The physical. The laughter. Problems solved together; ideas turned into actions. A bond, and companionship. And, in the end, none of it mattered because, despite Nat wanting my hard work to be a driver for success and to create benefits for us as a couple, my career and commitment ended up as the breaking point.

Louise says I did nothing wrong and says we should change the subject. I tell her she just did. She says it's my turn to ask a question and I say I want to know about the favourite place she mentioned. Why is it such a happy memory?

'It was the place we went as a family, more or less every year after we moved to the midlands, so from around my 8th birthday. Have you heard of Ilfracombe?'

I say I haven't.

'Then you probably haven't heard of Woolacombe, either. But that's where we went. A couple of hours down the M5, turn right and another hour on pretty roads to the coast.'

'Why did you stop going?'

I've already learned the ways in which Louise shows sadness. 'Can we discuss that another time please? It's not something I can tell you here.'

I shrug and smile, and she rewards me with a hug and whispered thanks.

While Louise tidies away our rubbish, I look at Devon on Maps and recognise a few names and see a cathedral I could have considered. But it's fucking miles away. The last but one bit of England.

Late in the afternoon, neither of us wants to go but we have to face that difficult truth. In the days and weeks ahead, we will continue to write and talk of the things we need from each other. There will be another weekend like this. It might be soon. It might be weeks away. To seal this fate, we have a long, needy embrace and it doesn't feel like goodbye.

Once mobile, almost every moment of our journey is taken up with a phone call. We review the things we said and learned, and how it felt to be together. She thanks me for being attentive and never once glued to my phone, engaged somewhere else. We do funny stuff, sombre stuff, reassuring stuff and describe, in great detail, the ways our bodies and emotions were turned on. We liked how intense our intimacy had been.

Louise gets back first. She tells me she's going straight to bed and soon, my car is filled with moans and gasps then a long final shout.

'Joe. Fuck.'

<>

When I wake up on Monday morning, I find a chatty, loving message from Louise about the time we spent together. She's attached a photo of me, busy taking my own photo. The final overnight message is her voice telling me all the things she loves about what she can see in the photo. My concentration. My relaxed frame. The way my legs look in shorts.

I edit one of the photos I took in Ashbourne, and send it over with the message,

> *As usual, here's the one photo I want you to see, and the reasons why I think you'll love it. In fact, there's just one reason. It's the place where we maybe realised, we are in love*.

She sends a big red heart.

<>

Later that morning, she calls but I'm in a meeting. I reply with a message that we can't talk. She calls back and leaves a voicemail. 'That's a really beautiful thing to say. I think maybe you're right. Might not get much more time to chat or message today, Joe. Lots on.'

At the very end of that short message, I sense a shake in her voice.

3.4

On Tuesday morning, Louise leaves a voice clip. It's very short. It's very sad.

'Joe. I think we're making a mistake. I'm sorry. Please don't hate me.'

I leave work early to rush home. Need to be somewhere safe for difficult conversations and need Louise to answer her phone. So far, she hasn't.

This can't happen. I can't accept that she means it. Whatever she means.

Time after time I get her voicemail. I leave the same message. 'You mustn't do this, Louise. We have to talk. We're not making a mistake. Yes, it is strange to have what we have so quickly. None of that is a problem. Please call me. I don't and will never hate you. Pick up. Louise. Please pick up.'

She doesn't answer in any way. She hasn't been online for hours.

Call after call.

Finally, I speak a different message. 'A middle of the night voicemail won't do it, Louise. So please don't bank on that being your get out from this.'

Within a matter of minutes, I wish I could retract it. It sounded spiteful and hurtful. That's what it was but that wasn't the idea. Whatever was in my mind wasn't well projected.

It's late in the evening when a message pops up. The tone tells me it's Louise. I don't want to look. A little shot of anger grips me. It's a message, not a call.

> *Joe, please stop the voicemails. That last one... I realise and understand that you're upset, but the spite in your voice was too much. I had no intention of calling in the middle of the night.*

I'm sorry. I didn't mean to be like that.

I know. But I can't talk if that's how you will be, whether you mean it or not.

OK.

Nothing happens. Then the phone pings another WhatsApp arrival.

Let's talk then.

Almost instantly, she calls. My voice is shaky. Hers is hesitant, resistant, and upset. Over the next several minutes, Louise stumbles her way through her reasons.

All the good things don't matter. There's a single issue. She calls it *the over-arching problem*.

It's our age difference.

That's *the over-arching problem*.

Just 24 hours back in her hopeless, helpless routine, alone in an empty house, had caused this. Made her see this. Prick wasn't there and Louise began to wallow in things that resulted in her change of heart.

She repeats. *The over-arching problem* is our age difference.

She's 47, I'm 35. That's 12 years.

We both know it's 12 years.

Several times, in the pub, in the hotel and walking in the town on Sunday, Louise realised that I was being hit on. Looks from women as we passed. Comments between women as we passed them. Stares from car windows. Even the waiters and receptionists.

The only place we were free from it was in the middle of distant fields. Otherwise, it was endemic. That's the word she uses. *Endemic*. I don't know what it means.

I say I don't care about people hitting on me, staring, comments, looks. None of it. Why would I when I'm with someone so beautiful?

'Can't you see what it means?' she asks. 'I'll be fifty before you're forty. The feelings I have about you being drawn away to younger fitter models will get worse and worse and worse. People will think I'm your mother.' Her voice is desperate. I try again. I tell her she's beautiful.

Louise says she thinks she's just a fat, ugly old woman. There are long pauses between those words. I lose it, voice raised. I tell her this is ridiculous. She's not my mother. I don't need a mother. She's neither fat, ugly nor old. I can't believe she even thinks it.

This horrible, sorry exchange goes on and on, around and around. She won't change. I can't change her. She throws in another dismissive remark about herself. That she'll be an old crone, a witch, a hag while I'm still gorgeous and lithe and desirable. Louise says she isn't even desirable now so can't possibly be, won't ever be, in future.

'And what if you decide you want children, Joe. You asked so many questions about that. What if that's something you need? It's an impossible thought.'

I say nothing is further from my mind. It's never been in my mind, and never will be. It's just not a thing. But she's adamant about it. Determined that one day, if we stay together, I will want us to have a child, and will hate her for not wanting one.

Nothing in all of the discussions, in all of the talking and chatting and messages has ever indicated she could be this self-destructive.

I wish I'd known.

I end up lost for words. Then, she says it all again. Don't hate me. If we stop now, you'll be better off. Soon. You deserve much better than me.

Strange. It's me that says goodbye.

3.5

A week goes by in unbearable silence. Then another. Except there is noise elsewhere.

I can do my job without thinking, on autopilot. Nothing is derailed and I've discarded the brief notion that I should quit. It would solve nothing, mean nothing. Not even to me. I'm being supported there. They know I'm their cash cow, a bit of a handful and more complex than they'd like. Something has changed since Neal instructed and/or suggested my holiday. I'm essential. A necessity. And he's on the back foot.

But the times at the house hurt like hell, whether I'm stuck in the living room or bedroom or lying in the bath. It's the same when I'm out cycling, which I do every evening. I struggle to cope with Louise's terrible words about herself. All the support and love she has poured over me, her long list of the wonderful things she sees in defiance of my own self-hatred, made me see a woman completely at one with herself. I thought all that kindness, all those positive views, the comforting smiles, were formed because she was able to value herself. Not quite that she loved herself or was brimming with confidence and self-belief. She simply had a reserve of strength and projected it at me.

It was a disguise. It was Louise deflecting her own troubles by being strong for me. I think. But I don't know. How could I know? Perhaps it all just means we don't know each other. It wasn't a mistake. But was it all too soon? More haste, less speed.

I end up hitting the drink. Nothing to make me a liability to others. But a risk to myself, alone in the house. Beers, at home or in the alehouse, every Friday, Saturday and Sunday night, followed by whisky or rum or both into the early hours. No stop buttons. Eventually, there's no discernible start button either.

Just a rolling programme. More and more of a state. Less and less of an asset. Endless mornings where I wake up on the sofa, often with no idea where I am. Binge eating whatever is in the fridge to feed the notion that it suppresses the effects of alcohol.

Consumption that I tell myself is manageable, due to stop any time now.

Except the rolling doesn't stop. Cans and bottles pile up in the recycling bin. Housework is left for others. The garden becomes a former playground. One in three meals is a takeaway, and I throw away more fresh food than I eat.

Over these weeks, I slowly slip into a mode where I drink at least a couple of cans of beer every evening, almost always silly-strength brews. They replace the bike rides. My fabulous machine sits unloved in the garage. I'm at loggerheads with fresh air.

It ends up that I don't get drunk. That initial buzz becomes the only sign of anything happening. The one when I down a beer in two gulps and the fuzzy interference with normality kicks in. I can walk in a straight line, talk if anyone calls, climb the stairs to the bathroom, undress myself when I finally get to bed, research things on the internet, reject cold callers who knock on the door, write down my plans for the coming week at work, do online shopping and shake my head, tutting, at the news headlines.

Maybe, once in a while, I take delivery of something I don't need and can't remember ordering.

Having no real friends means I don't ever need to tell anyone this is happening. No cheery wave across the clouds to like-minded boozers on social media. It's just me and a one-way trip to Cirrhosis-by-the-Sea.

One Monday, someone at work says I smell of drink and I don't hesitate to look sheepish, then lie about someone's birthday ending up as a late one. After that, Sundays involve afternoon drinking, but it stops sharp at 5pm.

I believe that doubling my weekday visits to the gym will minimise the effects of this stupidity. It's a futile gesture. One morning, two lads laugh at the absolute state of my useless efforts. It makes me work hard. I'll show them. But the exercise is harming me almost as much as the drinking.

Each session sees me slip from the hissing zip of a ring-pull then glide, like a bowling ball, along a well-varnished path. I just drink and drink and drink and, you know what? It works. It makes me forget *the over-arching problem*.

Right up until I remember it.

One evening, absolutely off my face, I compose a message to Louise. The descent into stupor means I don't finish the words and never hit send. When I see what I'd written, planned to send, words I thought were hopeful and calm, I tumble into a trough. It's a deep one, but before I hit the bottom, I have the sense to delete the message.

As I delete the words, I see Louise is online.

I have to say something.

The truth.

Hey. I'm missing you x.

She goes offline and doesn't return. Maybe she's off in some other place, some other app, sharing messages, songs, and laughter.

I lie down in the bottom of the trough and hope someone fills it in.

The sound of an arriving message drips down onto me in the pit. It's a tone called Pulse. I chose it because Louise made me glad that I had one.

Hey honey. How are you feeling?

I have no idea what to say, so all I do is send that screaming face.

That good, eh?

Like I said, I'm missing you.

A big red heart drops into the trough. I blow it back, with another alongside.

The fact that those brief moments of messaging ended without resolution leaves me feeling I should forget it all. That's what she wants. For me to fade away from her, with nothing left to cling to or remember. So, I don't feel pain, or loss. One of those brief affairs that was easily erased, even though I'd felt something indelible. Her voice is in my head telling me it was fun, but what was it really? A chance meeting. Some scanning of each other's real intentions over a week or two. Two nights tasting each other. Like a holiday fling, she'd say it was. One of those wild, crazy, gorgeous times when people are least expecting it and know it can't move forwards, even if they do share numbers and promise to visit later in the summer. That's what it was, Joe. That's all it was.

No.

It wasn't.

Carolyn tells me to get off my arse and go to Worcester. I piss her off by saying I've no idea where to start and have no idea where to go and look for Louise. We have a relatively shouty few moments in which Carolyn tells me to stop being a cunt. She says that if I'm not taking *no* for an answer then I have to go and have the conversation face to face. Fuck messaging, Carolyn says. Fuck voicemails and dictated fucking crap on WhatsApp. Fuck waiting for the phone to ring. Above all, fuck sitting around not making phone calls. Fuck being inert, Joe. Go. Go to Worcester on the one night you know she'll be in the city.

Then she calms down and asks me how she can help.

In the end we narrow it down to two options. The pub where *Latin Tags* will be playing. Or the pub where

Louise and I had our first sort of date, all those weeks ago, and which is holding an open mic night. The *Latin Tags* gig is sold out, and Carolyn says it has been for nearly a fortnight. It's like a coin toss. Which will Louise have chosen? Heads? Tails? The open mic tickets are available online, so I buy one and make a load of plans to find Louise, meet her and tell her we should be together. If she's not there, I'll just have to go and stand outside the pub where the other lot are playing and hope she doesn't leave by the fire exit. Or with somebody else. Where have I heard those words? *Looking through you, looking through your phone*.

This useless lack of real certainty flows over into my travel and accommodation plans. In a dreadful mess, reality crushing in, I realise I need at least one day off and potentially a second. Neal says maybe. Josie says no. Too much going on.

I end up sulking.

Then something clicks. My thoughts regain clarity. The apartment is available all week. It's in a place called Pershore, and I can work there during the day to avoid time off work. It's about fifteen minutes to Worcester by train. Predictably, the last train back is stupid early. I'll just have to get a taxi. Or walk. There'll be a way.

Josie is okay with my new plan. Neal does as he's told.

I throw any old stuff in a bag, forgetting I need things like work tools, toothpaste, and underpants. When I leave the house, I've packed more responsibly and am ready for business as well as pleasure. Or maybe it won't be pleasure. It will just be disarray. Final. Once and for all.

3.6

The advert wasn't truthful and, when I arrive, the host greets me with the news the place has no broadband and no Wi-Fi hub. When I say what the actual fuck, he laughs and says yeah, I know. Better get something sorted.

We end up like mates. He's totally wired, and I reckon he's done a lot of drugs. When I ask him what he's on, he confirms it's coke, then laughs and says that's why he's a super host. And fair play to him, he spends most of the time between 3pm and 5pm on a Sunday sorting out a connection that works on my kit.

It's very strange indeed to be working from home in an inadequate setting. After three days in this place, directing people and things from 200 miles away, I feel like I could be in any strange, mystical place and still working. Rotterdam, or anywhere. Liverpool, or home. I'm tuned in and it feels suddenly like I'm in control because I'm not in the office, not on the train to St Annes or driving along the M55. Not stressing about how much of a cock Neal might be under his smooth façade. Not thinking I don't talk to people enough and they all hate me. I'm working. It works, and it's really, really easy on my own. I even stay sober.

The train to Worcester gets in at just after seven but some bloke who's befriended me tells me to go to the next station because it's nearer the city. When I walk down to street level, I realise the bloke was right, and I soon find the pub.

Louise isn't here, and I can't drink any more sparkling Italian water. I look at the venue where *Latin Tags* are playing. It's a short walk but I can't work out if it's worth the effort, and can't see any way I'll get in. So, it will have to be standing outside hoping she walks out and doesn't scream.

Then it occurs to me. I have means. I can hustle.

Back at the door, I ask the security lads if Louise has been tonight.

They are okay with me. Not seen her for a bit, actually. We've missed her.

Me too.

They look at me like I'm all right. We exchange names and fist bumps. Then the solution comes to me. Ten minutes later I get to the other pub because I know Louise is there. A bit of chat did its job. The security lads didn't want to do it at first, then Devon said he would make a quick call. Had his back to me so I couldn't hear or see.

Yes, Joe. Louise is at the *Latin Tags* gig.

There's a queue but no one's getting in. Ticket only. These lot must be hoping for an ejection or an early leaver. Maybe fifteen of them?

So, I blag it. Up to the evening's second lot of security with a bright, breezy Blackpool *hello*. Just been speaking to Devon along at the Grapes. Said he'd called ahead about mixed up ticketing.

The two lads exchange glances. I'm a chancer.

No, go on, call him, call Devon, he'll tell you.

He makes the call. The lad looks at me all the time he's talking. Then he smiles, and it might be a bad smile. But he nods at his mate who opens the door and, with a wink at my new mates, I'm in.

It's busy as fuck. The support band is on, and I think they sound shocking. It's a long narrow room, almost like a cellar, but at street level.

I can't see Louise.

The bar is heaving, three deep in places. I want a beer, but don't want to stand with that lot. Someone passing mentions a lounge bar and I follow them and soon have a pint. I still don't know where Louise is. The guy behind the bar says the support band has another 30-45 minutes at least, so I realise Louise will be somewhere down the front, probably with twats wanting to molest her. Or actually molesting her.

I have a pretty serious palpitation when I see her. There are people around her, and it looks like they're all together. Two blokes, four women. She's with one of them, isn't she? This is who she's on WA with when I see her online but not messaging me.

I make my way to where they are and stand directly behind Louise but not really close. Not yet.

They aren't her friends. They aren't together. I know it now. While one of them goes to get drinks, the other five move away. Louise takes no notice and keeps moving her ass to the rubbish band. I watch, remembering how her beautiful body looked when we walked and talked, and when we held each other. In bed. Or in other places. She's half dancing, half swaying. Her legs are impossibly long.

'Don't look round.'

3.7

I put my hand on her hip and squeeze. Louise keeps moving and swaying.

'I came to find you. I came back.'

She nods, as if it's part of the dance. I move my hand round to her tummy, and we melt. The band is absolutely destroying a song I know. We sway together, regardless. I press her tummy harder. She pushes backwards. We keep a kind of dance in motion. I move my face up close and nuzzle away her hair so I can say something into her ear.

'I've wanted to hold you, to feel you and to dance with you all this time. You feel amazing. Like fluid.' I sense her head and neck tensing. 'We should not be apart, Louise. We should be like this.'

She nods again then Louise turns her face slightly, so I turn mine too. She whispers in my ear. 'I missed you. Like I couldn't believe. Keep up close to me.'

She takes my hand and moves it to the hem of her skirt. Another turn of her head. More whispers.

'But Joe, why did you come back, honey?'

I disconnect my hand from hers and run my fingers up her thigh.

'You know why.'

'Tell me.'

'I'm in love with you.'

Another nod. Another turn of her head to say, 'Joe, stop. I need to kiss you.'

It's a kiss like you'd do before a tidal wave hits your shoreline. Deep, frantic, and final. The last chance.

We move to a place with more light and stand looking at each other, an uncertain feeling growing in my stomach. The green eyes say *don't worry*.

Don't worry, Joe.

When *Latin Tags* come on, we go back to the way we'd been before. Louise in front, me holding her and moving in time, saying the things I've missed saying. Occasionally, she moves her arm, so her hand is behind my head, pulling it closer to her neck. I kiss her there. Occasionally, she pulls my hand down and guides it between her legs, so our hands work in time with the music.

<>

We leave just after eleven. I've no idea how I'll get back to Pershore, but it won't be for a while. Louise and I agree we have things to sort out. She knows a place that does late food. It's close.

Over a plate of steamed dumplings, with bowls of sauces, she tells me I'm crazy. She says she really is a fat, ugly old woman and, if we go on, I will hate her for it. She says that's why we can't be together. I pick up one of the dumplings and move it up to her mouth. She takes a bite with the same pristine care she uses to sip drinks. I tell her that watching her biting the food has turned me on more than our dance moves.

She laughs.

Louise laughs, and it sounds beautiful. But then she shakes her head with a kind of despair.

I ask, 'What have you been up to?'

'Feed me more food, you monster. Maybe I'll tell you stuff with more of these inside me.' I move another thing so she can nibble it. In between tiny chewing movements she says, 'What about you, honey? I hate that I hurt you. And you look fat. Why aren't you taking care of yourself?'

I didn't want to, but I tell her about the drinking and misery, the sobbing and troughs that feel like graves. Louise puts her head in her hands and wrestles with her hair until it's twisted and taut.

'I didn't want that to happen, Joe. I can't stand that I did that.'

I shake my head. I want her to stop assuming blame. I tell her my own indecision was part of the problem. My own internal misery.

'But I brought it all out of you, Joe.'

'And you can help me bury it, once and for all.'

She nods. Then inhales and exhales with great force. 'But should I help you, Joe? I'm so troubled by the things that I told you. There are real reasons why this can't work. I do believe you will leave me, someday, somehow, for someone your own age.'

'When did you ever tell me how old you are?'

Louise frowns. 'What do you mean?'

'Answer the question. Please. Humour me.'

She shakes her head, almost in resignation. My question has pissed her off. She still wants closure. I'm not letting go. I keep my foot stuck in the door.

'I've never told you my age. In all of our conversations, we've never discussed our ages.'

'How do you know I'm 35?'

'You told me.'

'So, we did discuss it.'

'No. You just slipped it in, by accident I think.'

'Right. Then what do you think I'm thinking about your age?'

She watches me dip another gyoza into some sauce and seems to resent that I eat it myself. 'I don't know. We haven't discussed our ages.'

'Why do you think that is?'

They bring another plate of food and accompaniments. Louise asks for some water.

'Yes, all right. I get what you're saying. We didn't discuss it. So, it isn't a problem. Except it is.'

'It really isn't, Louise.'

Our eye contact is unbreakable. She says, 'We'll just have to disagree.'

'There's no disagreement. There are just your fears.'

'Yes. I'm afraid.'

She purses her lips, so I push another morsel of food that way and change tack.

'You didn't tell me what you've been up to.'

'There isn't much. Nothing has changed. I've worked a little harder to compensate for being mad at myself. This is more or less the first thing I've eaten in weeks that isn't either fruit or cheese. And I've hardly had much of either.'

We keep talking about the things we've done; alone; separated by a rash decision. It's all tinged with regret. Louise keeps saying she didn't want me to be hurt. I tell her she has to change her mind.

A final plate of food arrives. The place is busy but has a contented atmosphere. We can talk quietly without anyone knowing it's a conversation about uncertainty and the need for something to be fixed.

Louise asks where I'm staying, and I tell her about the apartment. She says taxis will be stupid money, so she'll drive me there. She won't stay. I tell her I wasn't expecting it.

I can't tell if this was a reconciliation. We've hinted at renewal. I'm not inside her head. I've no idea what she's thinking. My great plan hasn't worked.

<>

Once clear of the city, Louise speeds up and seems to be taking risks overtaking. She says she has to get back soon. I tell her I understand but don't want us to die together.

She says that maybe she does.

That causes many moments of silence.

Louise breaks it, words spoken into the windscreen. She wants to know how we can make something work, small steps, ideas about how things can be. She wants to try but can't hold back all the thoughts she has that nothing between us can be permanent. Not just because of her situation, or *the over-arching problem*, or the 200 miles we live apart. She says she'll probably always let me talk her out of those because I'm persuasive. It's because she's a mess and will keep sliding into the kind of doubt and trouble that caused her to end things. It's because she can't open up the way she wants to without being destroyed by how it makes her feel.

I tell her she opened up about something incredibly complicated during our weekend together.

She says perhaps that was why she changed her mind so soon after we parted. Because, really, she didn't want to tell me. When I say she can't leave me every time we have a difficult or unspoken conversation, she laughs so loud she nearly loses control of the car. Once recovered, Louise says she really did miss me and there is lost time to make up. A few moments later, she pulls into a quiet lane and, very soon after, her impossibly long legs are wrapped tight around me.

3.8

Two days later, I pack my car early and drive back to Lancashire. She messages me constantly, but Louise can't call, and I can't read.

We're back to being that.

But being back to that feels good. This new flow of photos, fun, music, and affection is a foundation, and we keep building. Our discussions cover many subjects. Feelings. Beliefs. Doubts. They aren't arguments. They have no agenda. They aren't always detailed or well thought out. But we come back to them, often, checking and testing.

Is all this too soon, too fast, too improbable? We are often troubled by those questions. If we compare our experience – that sudden acceleration from random encounter to two nights in a hotel – with previous relationships, it seems mad. Is that what it is? Off-the-rails mad?

So, we talk about love.

It was months before Louise felt she might be in love with Prick. She was busily moving up through the gears of her career and gladly accepted each hint about her feelings for him as they dripped into her head. His appearance in her life meant something, but no neon sign flashed, *you're in love with this man.*

I fell into the relationship with Natasha because she was so pushy. The spilt coffee was an accident, but the unsolicited messages were direct. I think I distrusted her motives until she found ways to make me feel special. I was in love when she told me she loved me.

We share these thoughts, Louise, and I, over several conversations and messages. One evening, Louise gets me on FaceTime and, after we've smiled through some catch up, I ask if we've decided our story is either all too soon or is exactly what it needs to be. Were the ways in which we'd once fallen in love with the people we thought would be the great loves of our lives, any kind or template? Was there a set of rules governing the timing and certainty?

Louise laughs at me and asks where I've learned to be so florid in my observations. I say it's because she uses words like florid, and I'm trying to keep up. She wonders if it's the end of me being so straightforward and literal when I tell her things. I say I doubt it.

She says the only thing that really matters about whatever she may have felt for Prick is that it evaporated the day he revealed he was fucking someone else. That was the end; yet their complex, and inexplicable decision to continue living in the same house meant there is no closure. It may have taken Louise some time to realise that she loved him. But living together in their open jail left her in no doubt that she never had.

There is definitely no rule. Louise is certain of it, and it means she doesn't see the suddenness of our attraction as wrong, or inappropriate. She says all this with great conviction. It gives me courage to say more: that I can see the value of questioning what has happened between us. It was sudden, prompted by something inexplicable. Anyone looking in on us would perhaps scratch their heads and say, *what?*

Yet, once upon a time, we'd both done the same thing, hadn't we? Our experiences with Nat and Prick followed a well-travelled path. An initial chance encounter: proceed until the germ of a notion forms into the words, I love you. Then stay on that path, entwined. It was only at the end that our experiences differed. Closure. Louise had none. But I had nothing else. Nat made out she wanted to throw me a lifeline. Twice, that happened. The rescue ring she chucked at me was made of stone, had no rope attached and was not designed to save me, or us.

Whatever was right or default about our previous relationships, the speed with which they developed was an irrelevance. Louise and I reached a smiling agreement that there is nothing to fear from the timing of what has happened.

We share notes about success.

Louise has no idea how she achieved anything, or even if success was ever a reality. More often than not, it is a status bestowed by others.

My working life went from selling seaside curiosities to what I have now. I had to create a foundation. I could read the signs, follow the lines. My eyes, ears and nose were quick to pick up what needed to be done.

Louise sailed through her teens and degree with no idea about anything. A lucky break resulted in the discovery of a simple truth: she understood how to process rules. That's all *Human Remains* is, she says. Create rules; abide by the spirit and letter; understand people; read people if you have to, but really, that's padding. The simplicity of thought, and the application of it, helped her climb quickly.

I really don't know how I did it. I can't explain what makes me tick. I just have these in-built skills that people see and soon know they will also succeed if they just let me fly.

Neither of us wanted working life to be about being noticed or rewarded. Louise despairs at the cult of corporate celebrity and the ways it harms us. I despise that the craving for status makes people claw themselves up, or drag others down, lacerating everything.

She asks what I feel is successful between us. Not the sex and passion and laughter and loving. What else? I don't know what to say. It's an intimidating question. I mutter something about it being our ability to close off everything outside of our world. What we have is closed. It's just us. It means we stay obsessed. She laughs at that word, *obsessed*; says it seems such a difficult one to use as a description of what might be making us a couple, because it suggests something troublesome.

Later, she calls me because she's checked *obsessed* in a thesaurus and, in the end, decided it is perfect. We *are* obsessed. Pre-occupied. Possessive. Consumed. Engrossed. Gripped. Maybe those things will keep us going? Maybe they mean we can be friends.

And we talk about friendship.

About how neither of us seem to have friends the way other people do.

Louise never once made friends with men. Not with boys, or teens and definitely not with lovers. Successive changes of home and school, then time at university, meant the friends she made were transitory. Work provided alliances, acquaintances, and alternatives. Then marriage created a veneer; a social life in which each unit was as likely to compete as to collaborate. Inside all that, the one person that should have been her friend turned out to be just another prick.

When I ask if her parents had been her friends, Louise shakes her head minutely.

I had Alice Acton and Carolyn Harrison, and she knows all about them. For years, those were the only people left from the life I had before I was twenty. Now there's just Carolyn. The others, my mates, the lads, all that, wasn't like having friends. That was tribal and scripted. More likely to end with an argument than any kind of sympathy.

My relationships with Alice and Carolyn intrigue Louise. She isn't resentful, doesn't object to their place in my history, but can't understand what kept those relationships alive for so long and with such distances involved, especially while I was in a loving relationship and partnership with Natasha.

It seems neither of us became friends with our partner. It seems both of us sleep-walked through all those years, believing love and affection were the same as friendship. There wasn't a single moment in either relationship when we were the best version of ourselves, and neither were Prick and Nat.

It ends with us both saying, simultaneously, *you're a bit fucked up, aren't you?*

That causes chaos; several moments of the laughter people do that won't stop and seems to be regenerated every time one of you starts to speak.

Then Louise makes me quiet. She tells me Alice and Carolyn were my family. Two women who provided the certainty I never had. From parents that went missing. From a sister too consumed by the need to be a parent.

And we talk about family.

About Gareth. Her older brother. I'm shaken that Louise never mentioned him till now. Made out she was the only child. She tells me it's because he died and, sometimes, she just doesn't know how to talk about him. He was part of the family that moved from one end of the country to the other; that spent happy weeks rambling on the clifftops and beaches in Devon; that became a well-knit unit. Gareth was the apple of her mam's eye and the rock of her dad's existence. He was Louise's hero, but all her love and thoughts of him are locked inside memories from the painfully few years they knew each other. The years that ended when she was twelve.

He took a blow to the head playing rugby, and it left him dazed but conscious. They let him play on. Gareth wanted to; insisted; a team player. Sitting in the car that day, Louise watched him stroll out of school, chatting to a couple of friends and one of the girls they all fancied. He smiled when he saw Louise in the car, the bold handsome smile of a 17-year-old Adonis. Blond. Rugged. Wicked. His smile slowly faded and Gareth's walk towards the car became a stumble, then a stagger, then collapse. He never recovered consciousness. Vital signs dwindled and the rock and the apple were gone. The hero was fragile, in the end.

A well-knit unit unravelled. Her mam and dad were incapable of any kind of function and for several years drifted along without the love that had once kept them so close and happy. It left Louise to handle Gareth's loss with neither guidance nor help. She couldn't find the ways to support her mam and dad but felt that wasn't her job. She was still just a kid. The endless searching by her mam, through Gareth's photos and his accrued possessions or trophies. Her dad crying, baying like a wounded wolf. All the memorials, support and love from Gareth's friends and school were like liquid dripping through a paper towel. Preachers brought good books, full of hope. Comforting blankets of faith and belief. Convincing. Warming. So now you can cope.

Louise lived through it all, saw through it all, and was left in a clouded world where no mask could make her happy. A world without heroes. Parents who lost any sense of how to be happy and recognise happiness in others.

I watch her say all this and it leaves me dazed. Something makes me hold out my arms towards the tiny lens on my laptop, to pull her through all the wires and microwaves and dissolve in my arms. She makes the same gesture. She tells me there's more but can't find the strength to say it all.

I say she should try.

The unit recovered, one segment gone, to form new ties. But only because Louise made it happen. She ran away. Took off alone and jumped on a train with some saved pounds and a sports bag of things she might wear. From Worcester towards London, where she hoped to get lost and anonymous.

She got off at Reading, her thoughts scrambled by the idea that a 13-year-old could ever survive on the streets of London. The town she walked through was just a mass of things she didn't want to see, and it made her scared; of herself as well as these forbidding streets.

When it got dark, and she knew she had no choice, she asked a police officer what she should do.

Mam drove to collect her; dad sent his love. No scolds or anger.

Tears and disbelief turned to determination. Mam and Dad found the strength of their love for each other, and it transmitted into all the care Louise needed. Three years after his death, Gareth became their hero, rock, and apple once more.

Her telling of Gareth's loss causes something new. For the first time ever, Louise and I jump in our cars and drive to meet. It means hours driving and no time at all together, but the need to spend whatever moments we can get in each other's arms is overwhelming. I leave in a rush, then head back inside to find something - anything - that could be a gift.

The phone call during our journeys keeps us up to date about where we've reached, and then we knew which destination was nearest. She drives past it, turns around at the next junction then meets me on the southbound side. Deep into the night, we sit at a table in a closed café and just talk about all the love we never got to share with our siblings.

Driving home in the early hours, on the phone again, we talk about isolation. Within a few moments of each other, we arrive back at the places where we live alone.

I sit staring at the house and total up the time I have shared living with others. Not the years of childhood or as a teenager. The other ones, where I lived in places that I might call sharing: the flat with Leigh after I left school; the house with Helen and whoever; the fragments of cohabitation with Nat. That was it. In part, all of that time was actually me living alone because the company was in some way manufactured, necessary but temporary. Then there was just me, living in the collection of bricks, tiles, and timber in front of me now.

Louise's experience is similar. Recent years trapped in that house, a volunteer for the imprisonment caused when she and Prick passed sentence on each other. A period spanning ten years in which her domestic life was deemed to be happy, shared with a man in the name of love and togetherness. Building. Evolving. Accumulating. She's grown to see that time as nothing more than another lonely existence, because what she shared with Prick evolved into nothing. She doesn't say *nothing*. She says *fuck all*. Before that, bedsits. Before that, halls of residence. Before that, a parental home where Louise was never alone even when Gareth's death might have made it feel that way.

Our journeys and our call end with a question hanging in the dawn. After so much time living alone in our respective ways, can either of us ever find what it takes to live together?

Part 4

The Frozen Lake of Life

4.1

Louise calls, and says she wants to come and see me. To stay for more than just a night.

'But will it be okay for me to stay?'

'Is Luxembourg small?'

'I've no idea, Joe. Geography.'

'Then let's try *do bears shit in the woods?*'

She says she got the idea first time. We're laughing.

Of course, there is no doubt or question that her trip will take place. It was always going to happen but had to be when Louise was ready. I tell her she will be welcome. I can't wait.

There are strict instructions that there can be no frantic tidying or cleaning. 'Maybe change the sheets. Other than that, your house doesn't need polish for me to be in it. Promise me it will look like it would any other night of the week.'

I promise.

We agree the date and time. A Sunday, Monday, Tuesday, and Wednesday for us to live together and do whatever we need to be a couple. We're already a couple. That's agreed. But this will be another version of us. An update to version 2.1.

She arrives later than hoped, but the timing doesn't matter. She hands me a small parcel and says it's by way of thanks for what I gave her that day at the service station. Book shaped, tied with a cross of coloured string over brown paper. Louise tells me to open it. It's a book about photography. Inside the front cover is a card telling me she's booked five lessons for me at an online course.

I blink with astonishment. My gift was nothing: fancy biscuits in a fancy container that I'd bought for a rainy day. She says it was everything. A gift from me. The first.

Louise wants to see the place I like to go for beer, so we walk into town and drink. There's none of the usual crowd. I know faces but aside from the friendly words shared with James and Katie while they serve us, the talking is just me and Louise.

We agree not to make plans. I've taken the next few days off and all we're going to do is wake up each morning and decide which of our ideas is the thing we want to do that day. Louise doesn't want to see me in my world or create the illusion that my house can be our home. No trips down memory lane are needed, no introspection about my life in this place. The whole point of her journey is for us to get time together that we've earned ever since that night eating *dim sum*.

She says she likes the ale and orders us another pint, but we don't have a third. Our walk, the long way round back to my house, is another chance to talk. It's true that we have earned this.

Back at the house, Louise asks me why I'm living in a town like this. She takes fifteen minutes to describe all the things she feels are oppressive about it and about its effect on me and my mental health. She says I've put down roots that bind me instead of nourishing me. It took me more than ten years, but Louise needed just four hours in this place to appraise all the things that made me decide to leave that Friday night.

It leads to a longer discussion about why I ignored her advice to see my doctor. She isn't angry. She just thinks it's stupid that I've tried to apply self-help to something that's incredibly complicated. Something that needs profound skills and expertise to assess, review and resolve. While I cook some food, Louise continues to challenge me and push me to get help. It doesn't matter that I might be happy with her, and with us. Depression isn't fixed by any of that, she says, and it's wrong of you to think otherwise.

The food we eat, the first ever meal one of us has prepared for us to share, is simple because that's what

I do best. Louise says she was worried about me cooking because I've never talked about food, but also because she still doesn't eat. Tonight, she leaves nothing and says it's because I made it, and it tasted amazing. As she helps me tidy up, she says she could get used to eating food.

But these things haven't distracted her. I haven't cajoled her into a change of heart. She's adamant. I have to see my doctor.

<>

We drive to the Lakes and set off on a walk from the car park at the northern end of Wast Water. I can't stop taking photos, making progress slow as we head up the path that leads to a smaller lake. We keep moving, despite the suggestion that we should take our clothes off and jump in the water. It's a bit public. And the tarn is fucking freezing.

More climbing takes us to the top of the scree. As we look down on the lake, Louise says it's not what she expected. She thought the Lake District was more of a theme park. She can't believe the stretch of water below us is so silent and unspoiled. Sinister. Louise is intrigued by the notion that bodies might be lost in those depths.

I take a photo of Louise, the lake, and mountains in the background. She says it's the only photo ever in which she's wearing walking boots, leggings, fleece, and bobble-hat. I tell her I'm glad it's me that took it, but that's because she's never let me take her photo before. The clothes aren't important. She asks if I'd have preferred the seven-inch heels and micro dress, then admits not even she could climb 1500 feet in that attire. I tell her I would seriously consider paying her to try. We laugh loudly, but her humour evaporates, and her expression quickly becomes hard to understand. When I take a step towards her, she raises a hand, so its palm is facing me. Stop, it says. Then it's not her hands talking.

'One of the things I've grown to love about you is that you've never once looked at me and judged. You might be the only man in the world who doesn't think I wear clothes solely for his benefit. You've never said *maybe that's a bit too much* or *is that appropriate* or *cover yourself up*. And you've never watched me like those leering cunts in bars and cars, and like the police who tell me I was asking for it, and like Cruella the Shopkeeper and especially not like Prick. He used to love it all. All those hints, all that revelation, the guessing games about what might lie beneath. Loved it, right up until exactly the same clothes that once made him cream his boxers signified I'd become a whore. His word.

But it's not for him or them, and never was. It's all for me. For me to stay in the one place I've always felt sane and fulfilled. A product of myself, drawing from all I've ever been, all the fashion and influences I've ever been consumed by. And, in the end, holding on to what matters most. Me. My identity. My confidence and self-assurance, my pride in my femininity but especially in my independence. I don't need any of the things those wankers think I'm looking for. I just don't want to lose the one thing I can still get right.

But you, my lovely Joe; you see me through such different eyes. Don't you?'

I tell her I do. It's because I want to be another thing she gets right.

<>

We've walked miles when we get back to the car. Louise stopped constantly as we marched up the western side of the lake, taking photos of all the colours from the scree reflected on its surface. It seems we are creating the kind of memories that my previous visit never did.

It's a slow drive away and we decide to stay at a hotel because it's late and we're both incredibly horny.

This proves to be a big part of her stay. We fit in other things, *cerebral things* she calls them, but mainly we spend a lot of time naked and wet.

<>

Despite what she said about not wanting to see my world, I drive Louise around the places nearby. Across to the northwestern tip of the coast then down to the promenade, the piers, a tower, and the pleasure islands. Through the genteel and homely stretch to Lytham, where we park and walk along the front. She says it hasn't changed her mind about what this place might be doing to me. It's all varying shades of monochrome. Louise expresses endless concern that I seem to do nothing more than exist. I've no hobbies, except the odd bike ride and session in the gym. Social life is just work life in a different setting. I never seem to treat myself. No music. No books. No television. No cinema.

I fight back, quietly, by saying *kettle / pot*.

So, we spend her last day in Manchester. It's the first place we've been where Louise suggests we take selfies and we take four, two on each of our phones. Every single one of them shows how good we look. Warm, smiling, and alive. Close. Together.

We go to an art gallery, then look at the buildings and bustle. Louise gets sentimental about the time she spent in the city as a student. We buy each other silly gifts from a shop in the Triangle, then more special ones at a small jewellers off Deansgate. In the end we head to a bar in the northern quarter because Louise says she doesn't want to drive home late this evening, as planned. We have cocktails and snacks then catch a late train. Louise says she'll head back really early in the morning.

We don't get much sleep.

After she leaves, I'm incredibly worried about her safety.

Louise doesn't answer when I call so I send a voice clip about how much I'm missing her and hope she's missing me too.

There's a long pause.

'It's two hours since we saw each other, Joe. Of course I'm missing you. Really missing you. And it's about three hours since we had sex. I will miss that for days and days, even though I can still feel us coming, like an explosion in a fuck factory.'

I revert to messages.

Can we talk soon?

Been horrible on the roads honey. It's why I didn't answer.

OK, but how about now?

No. And I need to put the phone down for a while so I can think about us coming all over again.

She calls me shortly after that and talks me through the moments spent in the quietest part of the car park at Stafford Services. I lie on the bed and listen to her words about all she had felt, and I tell her now I feel it too.

It's not even ten o'clock when she gets back. We'd had to stop talking because she said the traffic was terrible and she had to concentrate. Another message tells me she wishes she hadn't returned. Then another says she's annoyed because she left a bag in my spare room.

Not long after, she tells me Prick has arrived home earlier than usual, and we will not get to talk later.

4.2

Another phase starts in which we do the things we've learned to do, separated and together all at once. Louise tells me the days we spent together were just what she needed. It made us both incredibly contented and happy. It will be unbelievably hard coping with the knowledge it might be many days before we see each other again.

I do as she asked and go to see my doctor. As well as describing all the bad things I've felt, I also tell the doctor that I currently feel incredibly happy because of Louise. But doc makes me concentrate on the anxiety and stress and how it affected me over the time since Leigh's death. Once I've said it all over again, I'm left feeling sore and want Louise to be there with me. Doc says she thinks that I should get counselling. Perhaps no need for meds, or time off work, but the good feelings about Louise - doc calls them *a sticking plaster* - can't be used as therapy. She gives me a number to call.

At my next one-to-one with Josie, I mention that I've been referred for counselling. She closes the office door and talks to me for ages. Am I sure I can keep going at the level I'm at? What help can she give me as my boss? She doesn't want her problem child to stop winning things.

I tell her I'm in good shape. I tell her she needs to keep believing in me. I tell her she knows I'm her only winner.

Josie also gives me a number to call.

There's not much real help from doc's referral. It's just people talking in a group, no different from work or being in a bar.

But Josie's therapist is amazing, and we have discussions like I've never known. I say things aloud that I didn't know or couldn't say before. He hauls things out of me, gently encouraging, patient and calm. I'd never let a customer or colleague control a conversation like that. It's always been me controlling the agenda.

Hypnotised, I fall headlong into the counselling.

Things are released from the pit I'd trapped them in. The deep well in which the seen and the known couldn't be found.

Natasha leaving was the event that has been sitting inside me like the punch to my head that made me curl up into isolation. I made it pre-eminent, to the detriment of bigger things. I blamed me, not her, and saw it as the final signal that no one had, or ever would love me. It created the convenient mask I wore to conceal how fucked up I am but never analysed because I didn't recognise that it was the truth. I didn't just wear the mask, I painted it onto myself, head to toe. Except at work. That's the one place I need no mask, because there it's just *leave me to be me, and you'll reap the rewards*.

When Leigh was murdered the mask got peeled back from one edge and sharp, chilly fragments of despair slipped out. I suppressed them, laundered them, made sure my slip was caught by the safest hands I knew. Then I plastered the flaking edges back before anything else could be shed.

It could be that Nat dumping me, then Leigh's death so soon after, crushed me, kicked me, spat on me, pissed on me. Both broke my heart and soul, perhaps in different ways. Except...

I'd been broken forever. Not forever. Just for about 70% of my life. Just since they left. Mum. Dad. They created a world in which nothing existed. No loving married couple. No family unit. No favoured child. No devoted children. No shared meals. No bedside stories. No cheers from the sidelines as I saved the penalty. No pocket money. No trips to see the sights. No guidance.

No moral compass. No faith. No ways to form friendships or partnerships. No warm sense of belonging. No thing. Nothing.

A father that disappeared so completely that not even an illegal check on a government database could find him. A mother whose disappearance was incomplete, so she could taunt her children with the distances we'd grown apart from her. A sister and brother stayed together, our childhood and adolescence swept aside by the necessity, the sheer terror of needing to become adults in order to survive. Love was alien to us. Whatever compartments it might have existed in were locked tight, buried, sunken wrecks. Even if Leigh might have had enough to give me, I had no apparatus of any kind that enabled me to give it back. Except...

Except... what I did was turn all that back in on myself. To see me as the cause and effect. The disease with no cure. Alive, and dead. Present, and absent.

I felt weakened, at first, by the things I didn't know I felt. Then the therapy began to make me stronger, especially once I worked out that I'd been weak for so long. The sessions formed into something I loved in which I realised that there was something good in my heart, soul, and mind. And something good was feeding it.

Then the sticking plaster falls off.

Louise phones me one afternoon while she's walking. It's a lovely, happy conversation.

Then a voice says, *Who are you talking to?*

Louise whispers, 'Fucking hell, no, I've got to go Joe.'

But the call doesn't drop. I hear their argument.

How dare you follow me, you cunt.

I'll do what I like, you slut - who is he? Who is this twat you've got?

I was talking to a customer.

A customer you need to talk to on a walk around the countryside. I don't think so.

Just fuck off and leave me alone.

Your phone records will tell me. I'm going to get them.

Prick keeps saying he knows there's another man. Louise keeps saying it's a customer. It's always a customer.

So, I'm a customer.

I make the call end.

This is how it is.

Our relationship can't be complete because her marriage isn't really over. We can have all the good things, all the love in the world. But in an argument with that man, I am just a customer. She has to lie to him about me. There is no truth in her world. Just layers of indiscretion.

It makes me angry, then upset. I don't know what to do.

After our next phone call, Louise messages me and asks why I sounded so cold.

I tell her I don't think I can deal with being some sort of bolt on to her life. All the things we've built up are too precarious, too lacking in substance. She calls me straight back. She's in tears.

'Where has this come from, Joe.'

'That day, when Prick followed you, I heard your argument with him. You didn't shut the call down.'

She just says *oh*. Then, eventually, 'But why does what you heard make anything wrong between us.'

'I'm just a customer.'

'What? No, Joe. You can't turn the excuse I gave to that cunt of a man into a reason to be angry or upset with me.'

'Well, I have.'

'Do you expect me to tell him about us?'

'I think I do. I didn't before, but when I heard what you told him, how you brushed away the opportunity to tell him the truth, you relegated me to being a customer. I'm not your fucking customer, Louise.'

'Joe, please...' but she can't carry on because massive sobs just erupt into my ears. It's me that fills the gaps between her pain and sorrow.

'It's never going to be any different than this, is it? We can be all the things we love about each other, but all the loving certainty in the world isn't going to have any kind of future because you're never going to leave that house and walk away from that man. Are you?'

'Yes, Joe. Yes, I am.'

'When?'

'I don't know.' She has another episode of being unable to speak. I say nothing. I'm shaking with my own form of incapability.

'I don't know when it can be. But it will happen. I want to be with you, Joe. Our time together at yours proved it. Made me determined.'

I'm shaking my head with frustration. At her. At him. At me.

'I'm completely and utterly crazy about you, Louise.'

'And I am about you.'

'But this is going to turn me into the wrong kind of crazy. In a future that can't exist.'

She ends the call.

4.3

I end up wallowing in the uselessness of it all. I create reasons for arguments with colleagues, get fractious with clients and generally become a difficult person to like. Fuck, maybe I always was.

I know that the company will let me stretch every single limit of what is acceptable, be lenient about my failings, accept that *Joe being difficult* is just the price they pay.

My basic premise is that I, Joe Thompson, will take everything and everyone down with me. Me, a customer in my lover's eyes, will make all my company's customers - real or sought - hate me and my company and, if possible, themselves.

It's a colossal ego trip, and it's really pathetic. But that is what Louise has done. No amount of therapy allows me to see it as something I've done too.

History keeps colliding with the present.

The future is constantly blocked by the present.

The present has no shiny paper, nor a neatly tied bow. The present is the whole fucking problem.

I'm sliding down into the kind of desperation that people in the Daily Mail, or those idiot celebrities with their culture wars would say is *woke*. Woke. Right. Like every problem in the world is because you have a problem and share it.

Somehow, I'm trapped in this sliding, careering mess. It isn't Louise that caused it. It isn't me that caused it. I just can't see anything other than external dramas that make her and me and every fucking idiot in the entire solar system as some sort of barrier to me being happy.

It all ends with a massive row involving Neal and Josie, who joins in on his side. It's the first time I've ever been given this level of bollocking for anything. I ask them to calm down, but they don't. They ask me to get focused on business, not another breakdown. I say I can't.

Josie tells me to get out, then I hear her telling Neal she might need to sack me. I storm straight back in and tell her to go ahead. Sack me. I don't fucking care.

Neal looks like I've had a shit in his desk drawer.

Josie sits down, and smiles. 'At last. A little bit of the real Joseph Thompson. Neal? Why don't you go and make us all a brew?'

She understands that I've got these things breaking me up, breaking me down. She gets that I'm hurt. She realises I need time. What Josie doesn't understand is why, this time, I have lost the will to work. You always worked through things, Joe. Always fought for all this. She makes a grand gesture around the office.

I'm still sulky and she asks me if the counselling has helped. When I say *obviously not*, she tells me to get a fucking grip.

Neal reappears with three mugs on a tray. We sit down and drink. I apologise. Give me something new to do, I say. Something hard, complex, detailed. I'll get you those contracts. They look at each other. Josie hands me a sheet of paper.

Darren and Siobhan tell me to meet them in the Taps later, but when I get back to my house, I message them to say I can't be arsed. They soon arrive and make me go for drinks. They tell me they're worried about what they heard from the Preston office crowd. All the shouting. I say it's a storm in teacup. I've sorted things with Josie. But I'm still angry about everything else. They tell me to switch my phone off. They tell me to concentrate on them. They buy me beer. After a couple of drinks, we decide to stay and eat then, during the meal, they're both raising their eyebrows, shaking their heads, rolling their eyes at everything I say. When they get a word in, the general view seems to be that I'm a clown and I've slapped myself in the face with a foam pie.

It makes me snarky. It's not their place to criticise, I tell them, so back off. But they're good at this. They keep calm. On message. They're great critics. Please don't take this out on us, they say. You're the problem child that, even when he does wrong, still seems beyond reproach. We're still on your side, they say. You've always been on ours. So, *you* back off, and calm down.

I'm still angry, seething, and filled with something terrible. I can't explain it to myself, so I don't try to tell them. They're right though. It isn't their fault. They're lovely. I insist on paying for the meal and I kiss them both goodnight when Darren drops me off at my house.

<>

I'm still awake at 2. When I switch my phone on, a message from Louise is waiting.

> *It's been a week. I'm so worried about you. And I'm missing you. Can you at least tell me you're OK?*

I shout *fuck off* at my phone. Then my head crashes back into my pillow and I have no idea what to do next. It doesn't help that I've smashed my phone screen by throwing the handset at the wall.

Two days later I have a new phone and am as close to calm as I can get. Louise needs a reply. I want to do it and be civil. But little pricks of malice are poking me in the eyes and tongue. I sit around all evening drafting something I should send and know every word in every sentence is horrible.

By the middle of the night, I decide to stick to basics.

> *I broke my phone. It's why I didn't reply on Wednesday.*

She's quickly online.

Broke it how?

Your message made me throw it at my bedroom wall. I knew it was a week without words. I knew you'd be worried. But I'm still so mad. More mad than I was before. Am I mad?

She's typing for ages.

This sounds awful. Can you be calm and patient if we talk?

I shake my head and snort. I know I can't lose how crazy I am about Louise. It is tearing me in two. I want to talk because her voice drives me wild. I want to talk so I can make her feel what I feel. But I don't want to talk if all it does is soothe her worries, create calm, and stop me being mad.

I'm not sure that I can. I'm so tired of all that you've made me feel.

We have to talk. Can I call you?

Yes. Why not? It's 3 in the morning. That's when you communicate best.

She goes offline. I stare like a maniac at my phone screen and think about smashing this one too. Then I stop. Then I breathe in and reflect. I send,

I'm sorry.

I don't think you are. With all that we know about each other and all that you have learned about me, I can't believe you can be

that horrible. I never thought I'd see this from you. To see you so destructive.

I reflect some more.

Let's talk.

It isn't a happy call. Indecisive, but not terminal. Louise really did just want to know I'm all right. She didn't like the spits of spite in my messages. She can handle that I'm angry but doesn't understand the malice. I spend most of the call snorting and pumped up. She asks me why I've gone from where we were to this.

I say it's like when she decided we couldn't be together because of *the over-arching problem*.

Her voice goes incredibly cold. 'I can't believe you're like this, Joe. Call me when you've recovered some of the beautiful you, I thought I knew. That was a decent person. You're a fucking idiot right now.'

The line goes dead.

For the first time since I boarded this rollercoaster I feel like a worm. It is all about me, about my reaction. I know that. It doesn't matter that I've made things shit for Louise.

It's the middle of the night and I go downstairs and pour myself a scotch. Then I don't stop.

It means I can't travel to work the next day and I call Josie to tell her I've lost the plot completely. I expect her to sack me. It's gross misconduct. I've fucked up. I can't work because I'm drunk at seven in the morning. Josie goes quiet. Then she tells me to drink as much water as I can and go back to bed. Throw a sickie. See me when you're sober.

Instead of obeying her, I pour another tumbler of scotch. But I do take that to bed.

Darren calls. I don't answer. He messages me.

What's happened now?

I hate this. Hate what I've done. I gulp half the whiskey down, then cough so most of it sprays out over me and my bedding. This is not how I should be.

Within half an hour I have an empty bottle of scotch on my chest and a full glass in my hand. That's what I've done in the few hours since Louise called me to make peace. I have drunk a whole bottle of spirits, bar the glassful in my hand. So, I drink it too. Now I've done the bottle. Whiskey galore. But this isn't a party or celebration. I'm a useless mess and nothing I can see or think, or feel is ever going to be of use to anyone. Sleep, or some sort of coma, seems the best policy.

When I come to, it's like I'm living in a distillery. Louise has left a message.

> *I don't like that I swore, but I don't like the Joe that made me swear. Please tell me soon that you're not angry. That you're coping.*

The next message was fifteen minutes later.

> *I don't know why I'm asking. I know you aren't coping. So maybe just tell me you're functioning somehow. That you're able to consider the possibility that one day, soon, we might talk without all this hurt.*

I read that message time and again, closing the app in between each view. Then I read everything, all the messages over the last few hours. It looks like it was: cold; distant; unhappy. What's missing is the things we said when I called to shut all this down. When I was just a customer. *Want. Crazy. Be with you. Future. Exist.* Were those words real? Do bears shit in Luxembourg?

My anger runs away to join the spilt whiskey all over my sheets and duvet. The booze is in my consciousness and crawling over my skin.

I don't like the Joe that made Louise swear either.

I write,

I'll call you when I've learned how to behave.

Then I send a big red heart.

<>

I go back to work the next day, accept no sympathy, and get stuck straight into these new clients. We can win big. I can make that win happen. I can do all that whether I'm in love or not. I've proved that for twenty years.

Wheels start to turn. Creaking. Abrasive. But turning.

Louise has clearly had enough, and I don't blame her for backing off. But the one thing I have to do is answer the simple question she started with. Am I ok?

After two days in the grip of the effort needed to woo and make love to potential clients, I tell Louise I'm doing all right. And I ask her to tell me what she's up to. Her reply is two words.

I'm broken.

When I get time that weekend, I send Carolyn a message saying I've broken someone. She calls me straight back.

'You've broken Louise? Or broken yourself?'

'Well, if you put it like that, I've broken two people.'

'Tell me.'

I work through the story. From the time spent together at mine, and on to the word *customer* and how it made me feel and how it ended things. That I am effectively in therapy that had started to fix things. That there is supposed to be a happy place that will fix everything. I don't tell her the term *sticking plaster*.

Carolyn wants to know more about the counselling and why I didn't tell her.

After I finish describing all that, and all that I've gained from the sessions, she is softer.

'Can I come and stay?'

'Your man won't like or want that.'

'I don't give a fuck about that. He and I, we, are capable of sentience. Bertie won't mind that I ride off on a rescue mission.'

She arrives during the middle of Sunday. She has a small bag of clothes and two bottles of posh squash. The first thing we are going to do, she says, is get sober. I make up the bed in the spare room while she makes a roast dinner. Carolyn is amazing in the kitchen. We sit at my round table, and she talks me through the reasons why I'm barking up the wrong tree. And she tells me it's definitely not because I'm barking mad.

When she stops all that, I haven't listened. She gets an unbroken, unpunctuated speech about my paranoid vision that Louise is messing with me. None of it has ever meant a thing. I'm just a convenient number on her list of options, a manufactured set of next steps, ways out of her dilemma.

'Of course, she isn't messing with you. That's plain stupid.'

'It's how I feel.'

'And it's plain stupid. You're better than this, my old friend.'

I really want a drink. Carolyn says go ahead, but she'll get in her car and never come back.

She's always been so strict.

We have a tit-for-tat exchange of *fuck offs*. But I know she's right. The drinking is serious. She asks if she should take it all away when she goes home. I tell her to leave it. I can do my own tough love.

She doubts it.

Carolyn works through the things I've learned since I saw my doctor and therapist. When I finish the list of things that made me feel better, she nods her head. She asks when my next session will be. I tell her none are planned.

'Then plan one. Plan several. You just told me it's made you feel better. What prompted you to seek help?'

'Someone suggested it.'

'Who suggested it?'

I nod. I say yes, all right. She says nothing.

We go and sit in the living room and keep sipping on lemon and ginger cordial until Carolyn accepts that I've told her all the things I feel about Louise.

She has one closing question. 'What the fuck do you expect the love of your life to actually do, Joe?'

Those three immovable things are still there between us. Truth. Talking. Presence. All this time, all the things we have known and seen. Now Carolyn is throwing all three back at me as a reminder. She tells me to look at her while I'm talking. The carpet isn't interested. She repeats her question. And I don't know how to answer it.

She knows me well enough not to be aggressive. It's enough that she shakes her head with the kind of tetchy frustration she's shown me all these years. But Carolyn demands an answer. I can't escape from the words *love of your life*. So, I tell the truth. What I want the *love of my life* to do is let me tell her I've messed up and hate that I got it so wrong.

This is greeted by eye rolls. Carolyn comes and sits with me and kisses me on the forehead. She says it might not be easy, but the *love of your life*, which incidentally is a reciprocal role, probably just wants a call. One without bitterness and spite.

She plays some music on her phone, and we lie, like we might have done as teens, listening to whatever it is. Simple songs. Easy to understand. Not a message. But a nudge, nonetheless.

Carolyn stays two nights. I go to work both days, and when I get home each day, she's got a plan for the evening. On Monday we go for a walk, across the fields and round in a loop back into town. Then more posh squash and food. More queries about next steps. On Tuesday, we do a shorter walk, holding hands and watching the crazy over-tuned cars blasting up and down the quiet roads. She's baked potatoes and we eat them with tuna and cheese. She asks if I can answer the question yet because all I've given her is bullshit.

I say I want *the love of my life* back. Carolyn raises her eyebrows and smiles a wicked smile.

'Then why the fuck are being such a dickhead?' Before I can answer, she fills in the blanks. 'Yeah, all right. It's because it's you.' She looks at her phone. 'Bertie needs me. He is aroused by my absence. Come here.'

We hug. We have our faces cheek-to-cheek and she whispers that she's glad she came. I whisper that she's welcome any time. Then she pulls away. 'I've known you so long, Joe. We are something special, even when you're being a prick or when I'm in trouble for making wrong choices. Believe me. That woman is amazing. You need her back. She doesn't need your silly judgements and incorrect conclusions.'

She drives off and, as she often has, calls me and we talk while she drives.

4.4

Always a perfect guest, she has stripped off the bedding and dumped it near the washing machine. I head to the spare room to check Carolyn didn't leave anything.

Instead, I find Louise's forgotten bag, there under the dressing table. It weighs hardly anything. As I carry it downstairs, something falls out of the end pocket. It's a scroll of paper the size of a tube of Pringles, tied with a ribbon. I undo the bow, but it barely unrolls at all. There's something inside. Material. Dark pink. I pull out the pair of knickers. When I unroll the scroll and press it flat on the workbench, I see words. From one tiny exchange at the hotel in Ashbourne, I know it's Louise's almost impossibly neat, well-crafted handwriting. One side of the paper has what looks like a poem. On the other, a sentence that was hidden in the curl of the paper. *I left these here, so something of mine is with you. Next time I'm here, we can do many good things with them, you, and me. I love that there will be a next time. xxx*

The poem is called 'You Came Back'.

It isn't long.

You Came Back
Don't look round
You said
The words fed
My feelings.
They were all for you.

You were hidden.
A touch
Too much.
Are you stealing
My heart?

I stand in the small space between the units in my utility room. Louise's underwear clutched in one hand. Her words in the other. There's the fragrance she always seems to use. On the paper? Perhaps in the ink? I press the knickers up to my face. It's there too. Subtly. All of this is a privilege. The words and the scent. I read the poem again, then say it aloud, trying to see how it works when spoken. I'm no poet. I'm no narrator. But Louise wrote this for me, so I do my very best.

It makes me need to speak to Louise. To hear her read these words. Then doubt takes over and I can't frame what I want to say to her. Why was it left as a secret in the spare room? Why? Am I still just a customer? A recipient of favours?

Now I'm talking aloud.

'You're a fool. How can you be this thick? It wasn't intended to be a secret, hidden away. Louise forgot the bag, in the rush of her departure that morning. The bag was there because she did her make up in the spare room. *The love of your life* has made up her mind. *The over-arching problem* is forgotten.'

This epiphany, I think that's what they call it, is a recollection of knowledge. I'm in love with Louise. It's such a deeply powerful love that it scares me. What scares me more is the fact that she feels the same. Quite possibly she feels it more powerfully than me. This gift, a poem and lacy perfumed finery, is a sobering reminder. What have I given in exchange? A childish kick of all the toys in my pram. *The love of my life* poured something beautiful into our relationship. It might not be art, or literary: how would I know that? But those 30 words, including the title, are a monument to the love between Louise and me. A great towering statue. Words on paper, in pale blue ink, not a screen of text.

And all I've given her is biscuits.

I feel destroyed by all the things I lack. There is no knowledge in me. No culture. That night in Worcester, the romance I tried to show was just a mask. When I went to grab her, regain her, engage her, it was all a gesture. A badly composed song, with no substance. Louise turned around and, in the moments between that touch, that kiss and all those swaying dance moves, her head and heart composed a poem.

Biscuits.

Poem.

There is no comparison.

Confectionary.

Art.

I've been a complete and utter twat. Whatever I do next won't change that. It won't bring Louise back. Yet that's all my heart desires.

There is no further discussion or message or word from the love of my life. From my Louise.

But work is okay.

The next few counselling sessions I have are okay.

I start to see that the house where I live can be okay. It isn't where I want to spend the rest of my days, but it's a place where I sit with some sense of purpose, at last.

The reduced level of drinking's okay.

Most of what I eat is okay.

My car's okay.

My clothes are okay.

The things in my back garden are okay.

Against this backdrop of things being okay, I have one huge hole that doesn't get filled. The love of my life is literally and metaphorically miles away. Detached. Unconnected. We haven't spoken for days or messaged any signal of hope. I've caused that and it isn't right. I need to fix it.

It's not okay.

I roll up the tube of paper and tie it with the same-coloured ribbon Louise used, then scrunch up the knickers and push them inside the scroll. I've rolled it so the writing about *next time* is visible. I take a photo, then enhance and crop it to emphasise the writing. It isn't long before I unroll it again and take more photos. Two or three of the poem, different angles, sometimes not the whole thing. Then one with the poem slightly hidden by the dark pink lace. Finally, a close up, just of the poem's title.

I mess around with these images until there are four that I really like then use another app, so they are placed in a quadrant.

No. That isn't the right way to send them.

I send four messages to Louise, each with a different photo. The first is the scroll with an accompanying message.

> *I didn't find this until today. In fact, it wasn't me that found it. It was CH. I feel terrible that you left this surprise, and I didn't know. J x*

Next, the poem in full.

> *This is simply the most powerful thing anyone has given me. I love it, Louise, and I love you x.*

Next, the words of the poem with the hint of lace.

> *We really will do good things.*

I add a horny emoji, then after reflection delete it before sending.

Next, the title of the poem.

> *I did, and I will again.*

I add two big red hearts.

These positive feelings, hands across the divide, bring calm. When I see the little blue ticks on the four messages, I feel relief that almost crushes me. When she doesn't reply for ages, I stay calm. I am calm. Not that long ago, the fact that she'd seen the messages and not replied would have made me wild.

Eventually she replies to each one in turn.

> *I've never sent anyone a poem before. Nor a letter. Can't even remember the last time I sent a greeting card. So, you're special. Obviously, I've sent my underwear to everyone on Tinder, but that's a different matter.*

She's added countless laugh out loud emojis. Then she adds,

> *I've never used Tinder. I wish I hadn't said that now.*

In reply to the photo of the whole poem, she simply replies using its own words.

> *The words fed / My feelings / They were all for you.*

She sends a big red heart in response to the photo with the knickers and poem.

And, finally, her response to my picture of the title and its message is,

> *We have to talk about this.*

It's several moments before I reply that I want to talk and hope it can be soon. Louise says it can't be today.

Then she is silent for days.

I keep reading her poem and start scribbling things I might send her. I am inspired to do something I've never done. Like she did.

I should call it *I Came Back,* but I've never written a poem, or anything. Never sent a card telling mum and dad something, or Leigh. Or Nat. There was the occasional attempt to reply to Alice with letters or post cards. Maybe that was the same. Or was it just greetings? Keeping in touch?

I Came Back

It looks strange to write something on paper. Louise's handwriting flows through her words making it neat and attractive. Some letters have little frills. Whatever she used to write those 30 words was broad. It's not a biro.

I Came Back

What do I want to say? That I need to make her forget the 12 years between our ages, because they don't exist and don't matter. That I want to see her and hear her say we are making a mistake so I can prove we aren't. That I have to hold her and start again.

I don't know how to do line breaks, or when. I think it's supposed to rhyme, but that seems difficult. So, I just type it in one long stream.

I Came Back. And I did it to make you see that you and me, have to be together. I came back to rub out the years you fear. To see you hold you kiss you and fold you in my arms. I came back to bring us back to life. That's what I did.

I can't send it to her because Louise won't tell me where she lives. I know the name of the village; she told me that. But no street name. That's completely correct. It's just in case. I get that. But I wish I could write this on paper, fold it in two so an envelope could be sealed around it and sent by post.

It will have to be a photo. Or a video.

Both.

It takes ages practising so I can write it without mistakes and crossings out. Then I need to work out where the lines should begin and end, plus where I put full stops and commas. I've no idea how to set up my camera so it will film me as a write it, like a performance. In the end I have it looking down over my left shoulder with the paper and my hands in view. Four attempts aren't right because my left hand keeps blocking the view. The fifth is much better but I make a mistake in the title. It picks up that I say *wanker* and it reduces me to a laughing wreck.

Then I do a perfect take.

I Came Back.

And I did it to make you see.
that you, and me, have to be,
together.
I came back,
to rub out the years you fear.
To see you, hold you,
kiss you and fold you in my arms.
I came back to bring us back to life.
That's what I did.

My writing isn't bad. It doesn't have Louise's curls and sweeps, but it's tidy. I take a photo.

The video goes first, edited so there's no preamble and the bit with my hand hitting stop is gone. I just send it without any message.

Then I take time editing the photo, so it has some filtering and looks quite dramatic. Noir. Vignette. I send it with the message,

Your feelings fed my words.

It's the middle of the night when Louise calls. I'm awake and I answer, but it doesn't seem to surprise her. She tells me the poem is lovely and so is the effort I made to video it. Then we agree we're both magnificent poets and end up reading our efforts aloud. Then Louise reads mine and I read hers. Then we read them in silly voices and laugh like we'll hurt ourselves. When the laughter stops, we tell each other we are lost and lonely. Louise is hurting. She says there is some truth in what I said about her leaving her life, but she will do the things needed to remove all the complications and walk away. I say we just need to be together now.

4.5

There is no rapid resumption of normal service. Louise and I don't or can't do *normal*. There's this edge to our discussions and messages. We don't hide from it. We discuss it, openly, with no emotion or anxiety. It's not the only thing we say or write. There are good things, hot things, happy things. But something lurks. An icy barrier that comes down to block the fear that one of us will find another thing that ends it all.

Eventually we resume the trips to meet, because halfway is just an hour away. They are late in the evening, but now they're not spontaneous. It isn't even halfway, really. More often than not one of us gets further than the other. It doesn't matter. We meet in these convenient places and get things said and done.

The cool feelings warm. We convert the worry about what might break us into ways to stop it happening. If X is a problem, then Y is the solution. The edge is blunted. Something less anxious is back in play, with more things that feel like friendship. We miss each other, day in, day out. Whenever we meet, our parting seems unbearable. So does our desire.

We knew we loved each other all along. We said it, we felt it, we showed it. Louise tells me she has never felt such powerful attraction to a man. Ever. She says the days we spent together had left her weakened by her feelings. That time made every penny drop. I tell Louise it was the same for me. I knew we were unstoppable in our passion, but I was bowled over by her amazing mind, wicked wit, huge compassion, and uncluttered intellect. And how beautiful she is. Louise tells me she's proud that I've taken steps to review and mend my mental health. She's worried about the drinking and the ways I seem incapable of stopping it being a crutch. I tell Louise I want and need to be better, for her, and for me. But I know we have a long way to go, and I might always lapse. She knows it too. I tell her we work together because we're equally broken. It makes her frown, then nod. We agree that just touching our fingertips together sends jolts of electricity through us.

All this in motorway service stations, at a series of tables with sticky tops or crumbs, wet or dry circles.

To fix the unbearable need for each other, and to create time together that doesn't involve hours of driving and inadequate settings, we make a date. The place I find calls itself *a hotel like no other* and it's more money than makes sense. But I book a room called a *boathouse* and we meet there one Friday afternoon for four days and three nights.

It's a new direction. In the boathouse, we learn that we can sit and talk, watch TV, be together doing completely unconnected things. Louise reads, Joe edits photos. We learn we can argue without sulking, resentment, or a winner. We learn we are friends that care deeply for each other, regardless of the physical or intimate. We love and desire, but no strip of romance connects us, no hearts, and flowers, except for those big red hearts in our messages. We discuss what caused us to split: the age difference; the existence of a marriage certificate.

We feel different when we leave each other that Monday morning. It's because we know that there are places booked, dates for each of the coming weeks, in which I will spend time near or in Worcester. It might be a single night. It might be a long weekend. It might be a whole week. None of it would be built around Louise's ability to sidestep Prick and any agenda he might have. We agreed I will be there, and she will join me for as much as is realistically possible. Unless it is impossible, each stay will cover a Thursday. Music night.

That's what we do. For months. We become a couple that merges its distant bases into whatever single place helps us to meet and find time together that would otherwise not exist. There is less about how things can't work. We see how just an hour together having tea and cake is more valuable than hours of messaging from opposite ends of three motorways. The things we might face at work become things we face together, learning how our minds work to be good at our jobs. We let the disagreements happen and there are no secrets or lies. The sex is sometimes love-making, sometimes wild filth, and sometimes just doesn't work out. But it is always desired, so each version matters.

We don't do toxic positive thinking, never say *everything will work out all right*. There is empathy with, and acceptance of negative emotions. There are things we have to do, both of us, to make sure we can be permanently together. We work through those as a couple and with the realisation that it is going to be hard. We need a tough reality to be in place about things like money. We run into the place that maybe everyone arrives at, in which we realise all we have and love about each other is peppered with imperfections. Little things that make us do double takes, or screw up our noses, and even snap at for being stupid. But like the arguments, those days in the boathouse, we see how to live with the conflict, let it happen and find the place where it needs to be without causing fracture.

It is perfect. I don't even notice that I am sometimes tired for days on end after I return to my house, or that I am putting miles and miles on my car's engine at God knows what cost in fuel, or that I am placing myself at risk while travelling. Louise tells me often that she's never felt like she does when we first see each other at these rendezvous. It is more than happiness. These moments, in rented places that are sometimes terrible and uncomfortable, are transforming us.

<>

Louise tells me that Prick's father has been taken ill, causing concern and potential disruption. It means Prick is working at their house more frequently. We work through how that might affect us and agree it might stop us meeting. It only affects one weekend, and we agree I will cancel the booking for that accommodation because Louise has agreed to go with Prick to see his dad. They travel separately and Louise comes home the same day. The old man was dying but not dead.

Then he does die.

It goes like this.

I am in the apartment where I'd previously stayed, in Pershore, working remotely, being a star and enjoying an occasional encounter with the super host. Louise is coming for dinner and staying over. It's just a few days after her birthday and we are full of anticipation for the celebration. We agree, like always, there is nothing romantic to be done. Just a glass of wine, some food, and a night in each other's arms. I've bought her a coat. One she'd pointed out to me in the street one day. Another woman's coat. So, I tracked one down and bought it.

Where are you?

There is no sign of her by seven. She hasn't been online since two.

'Hi honey. Is everything OK? Getting worried.'

These days, she doesn't ignore her phone without a good reason. My voicemail gets no response.

I am left there, with uncooked bits and pieces and over-chilled champagne. I jump in my car and drive over to the village where she lives, as if I might find a clue about what has happened. There isn't one.

'Joe, I can't believe this, and I am terrified you won't either.'

Her voicemail is scattered with long pauses that sound like each of her sentences are written on a separate page.

'Nick's dad has died.

He is inconsolable and was unable to drive.

I had to bring him here, to Tonbridge.

Here's the worst bit.

This morning, I told him I had consulted a solicitor about divorce.

He was mad as fuck.

As *fuck*.

I thought he might hit me.

He went off on one about money and how he would screw me to the floor.

Would make me fight for every single penny.

Find out about who I am seeing and get that man's income taken into account.

That's your income, Joe.

He was in the kind of rage I didn't know was in him.

Red-faced.

Screaming.

It's going to be so messy, Joe.

This had been going on for ages when the phone rang, and they told him his dad was dead.

He hasn't stopped crying since.

And, on the way here, he begged me not to leave him.

Told me he loves me.

Cried even harder.

I can't fucking believe this, Joe.

There is possibly no good time we will get to talk.

Will you stay at Pershore?

Why didn't you pick up?

I love you so much.'

She'd called him Nick.

Part 5

On Imaginary Shelves

5.1

It's the close of another week without Louise and nothing has changed. Everything she has ever meant to me is encased in a powerfully protected, impenetrable location. It's neither heaven nor hell, purgatory nor limbo. Not a cell, nor a sanctuary. It isn't real and has no post code. I can't go there unless I'm asleep. Even then, I'm not welcome in its vaulted darkness.

We both knew that her wish to support her ex-husband's needs and feelings about a dead father meant something fatal for us too. When we finally spoke, it wasn't an argument or a shouting match, no emotions on fire, no fingers pointed down the streets of blame. Instead, there was a cold assessment that Louise got it right in that voice message. What she needed to do was going to be very messy indeed. And take months. And keeping me out of the equation was hard but had to be done. In doing the right thing, setting off on the route to a divorce and all the nasty shit it would dredge up, Louise had effectively created a built-in end to our relationship, as well as that one.

It hurt us both that she hadn't questioned the need to help Prick and, within her own heart, found a morsel of goodness to do so. It hurt me more that she used his real name in her message that day. It felt like she bore affection for him. Or at least responsibility. Louise had the same realisation. Her actions had been instinctive, a knee jerk. In fact, they had no meaning and didn't signify ownership or accountability. But they still seemed, to both of us, like a signal that there was a lingering, immutable link. In a moment of honesty, because we always had that, I told Louise I understood what might have caused her to be bound up in that moment. I related it to the way Natasha had come to see me when Leigh was killed. We all have something within us that makes us keep feeling emotions about someone we might once have loved. There can be caring, at least, for the devastation of loss that a former lover or friend or partner might suffer. *Can* be. But it isn't universal.

There was no question of Louise folding her arms and refusing to help. Or walking away, with a final remark that her solicitor was on the case, then coming to me as planned as if nothing had happened. I got that. Louise didn't think twice about it because it was nothing more than an act of compassion. Of human decency.

Yet we both felt the shock waves it meant for our own love and growing partnership.

The discussions about it didn't start with arguments or shouting, but they ended with the broken emotions that we couldn't see this ever working. Tears. Disbelief. Heartbreak. Tempered by the knowledge that neither of us had done wrong or was somehow guilty. We just both knew there was no way the things we'd started could ever be finished. Neither of us said it was over. Instead, we just agreed it had no future because we kept seeing things that were too uncomfortable to be endured.

Even weeks and weeks after all that had happened and been concluded, this still kills me. And, this day, the short drive home along the motorway and on through the quiet streets has me filled with foreboding about that place, that impenetrable place, and whether I will ever be capable of cracking the code: that combination of numbers that will release me from all the love and wisdom and sex and intelligence and beauty and humility and tears and loss. And, once released, either embrace them; revel in them; belong to them; smile at their memory. Or write them on a tag, tie it to a balloon filled with helium, and let it go before trying to shoot it down as it floats and disappears over the horizon.

Whatever.

<>

A late finish at work means I've no inclination to make a healthy meal, or any meal. I rarely do these days. I dump my laptop bag and jacket on the dining table, then spread too much peanut butter on a thick slice of toast and bite into it while I head upstairs. One over-big, poorly chewed mouthful of the cloying sticky snack gets stuck in my gullet and, suddenly, I can barely breathe out. The panic and pain this causes mean I am insensate, for many moments. Once recovered, undressed, and showered I get into jeans and a tee, pumps, and a scent.

Considering I had a near-death experience in the last twenty minutes, I'm feeling unreasonably perky. The walk into town is really a march and I order two pints, necking one in three gulps and half the other in one before ordering a third. It's got to be like this.

If I'm here, waiting to see if Gordon or Liz and Gary have forgiven me, or for strangers and dangers unforeseen, it means I'm not at home clicking through the wheels on that damned lock. Here, with my beer, the memory of those dances at a distance is more easily forgotten. The times when Louise sent me songs that I thought were flirting but were something more powerful. We danced to them and fired hearts and kisses across the clouds. Still wished we were together in one place, while all along we both knew we could never co-exist in either of those places.

And if I'm here there's no risk of a surprise phone call, just to say *hi* and *I love you*.

And if I'm here there can't be any memories of those magnetic, enveloping calls when she stopped on her way home from the music venue and sat in her car making herself come while I listened through my headphones and gasped my own pleasure through hers. When those things happened, back at the start of it all, I felt so alive, so needed, so desirable. I felt such total love and attraction and belonging. When we spoke in the moments after those phone calls, breathless at first then giggling and relieved, there was the endless sense of us being perfect for each other. Funny, witty, wise, and open. Together.

None of that was important in the end. We still did it, but it was replaced by the real thing, and then more important bricks helped the wall to be built, slowly and with solid foundations. The huge steps up we were able to take, after the two breakdowns that fell on our relationship, showed there was more to it all than the unstoppable need for sex on the phone. We had much more to be part of; things to learn, a whole world together to create and live in.

Yet, in some of the darkest moments after Louise and I parted forever, the memory of those phone calls was all I had.

Because now, the beer and shabby chic of the craft alehouse are where my jollies are found. Away from the desire and need. In a mundane, real world. The polar opposite of that make-believe intimacy. I'm back to the bar where all of this started.

It's gone.

Louise is gone.

Like everyone.

They all go away in the end. Into the past tense. That is what this is all about. I'm destined to be alone. Maybe it's freedom? Can freedom ever be a prison? That's where I am. Impounded by wire, searchlight beams criss-crossing the air in case I escape into someone's arms.

Beams lighting up and capturing a father and mother stumbling in different directions across the fields before leaving them to escape without challenge.

Friends and acquaintances, sometimes still in the spotlights, arms held up in surrender. They still got away.

Carolyn, constantly roaming in and out of sight, dodging the beams and bullets. Waving to me or beckoning for help. She had keys, dangling from a huge ring on her belt. They were needed to unlock things, and sometimes did, and once the door was opened, she carried away the mistakes and poor choices to bury them at a distance. But, even with all those keys, not even Carolyn could secure the release I might need.

Lovers, floating like faeries around the perimeter, twinkling and sparkling, then bursting into stardust. Except Alice and Natasha. The guards shot and killed them as they tried, time and again, to charge through the gates to help me escape. They hanged those limp bodies on the wires, a reminder of what it means to try to get close to me.

Louise didn't need to break down the fences or shoot out the lights to get inside. She had been inside from the start. That is how the cards are dealt. The right one, the only one, the true one, is there all along. That was Louise. Through every step and word and thought and action. Watching and listening and needing. Shaking her head at the mistakes, smiling on the successes. Floating along in our space, invisible or ephemeral, but there. Ready and waiting to be found so that, when I met her, I knew. Even when things looked and felt wrong, I still knew. I'd found the perfect match. Simpatico and bold, a guide and muse. A powerful foundation for all that we shared. It kept the walls strong even when the craziness of our separations locked all the doors, leaving our love on detention, in two windowless rooms.

I told her everything and she absorbed it all. Made me coherent, sometimes articulate. Cured all the aches and pains, the grazes, and wounds. Deflected the negative and made it positive. Dug me out of all the places where my failing mental health had led me. Pulled me slowly up from the trenches I'd collapsed into. Pointed me at a better me.

She took time to know me. In the end, Louise knew me more deeply than she knew herself and, with all that knowledge, showed me something I'd never known.

That I could love and be loved. The sadness and crushing reality of our ending didn't change that.

<>

It's a slow evening, and I'm more or less on my own by nine. I'd brought a notebook and, over the course of five pints and two hours, jotted down my summary of the working week just past, and the things I will do on Monday. Two short lists but I take my time, so the contents are correct with no crossings out. I'll type it in an email to the team on Sunday.

As James brings my sixth pint, I'm definitely not drunk but no one would say I'm sober. It's still like that. Not getting drunk. At the point when others need to stop, I reach the point where I'm safe from the harm in my head and heart. So, I keep drinking.

A babble of laughter and a cheer filter through from the small area behind the bar. I didn't know anyone was in there, and James tells me it's a leaving do. Then he's distracted by the main door opening and, when I look at the bar, I see Katie looks a bit concerned. James walks off to serve other tables.

5.2

'Don't look round.'

Something touches my neck. A tiny scratch, something sharp, drawn slowly from my earlobe down the line of my jugular and under the neck of my shirt.

'Just move along the seat so I can sit with you.'

The air all around us is filled with fragrance. Her leg touches mine causing a zap of sensuality to burst up through my core. Her hand, with elaborately coloured nails - those talons - rests on mine. 'You can look now.'

Louise looks terrible.

'What's happened?'

She shakes her head. 'Why didn't you answer my messages?'

I look at my jacket, thrown on the bench opposite. I purse my lips. 'My phone's not here. Haven't looked at it since I left the office. Not even sure where I left it.'

'Unhelpful.'

'I was ignoring everyone, the whole world. Not you.'

James sidles up and asks Louise if she wants a drink. She asks for a diet cola with lemon then, when he raises an eyebrow at me, she tells him I've had enough.

'When you ignore everyone, that includes me. I thought you told me I was singled out by a special tone on your phone, so you knew it was me calling or messaging.'

I tell her I changed it, made her just another person with the default ringtone.

'I'll tell you how it all went. Spoken shorthand.'

Her eyes are filled with what might be pain, but she tells me it's exhaustion and emotion. A little fear. I want a sup of lager but feel damned by the comment she made about how much I've drunk.

Louise tells me her messages.

She'd asked if I was home, and could she stay?

Her journey was necessary, critical, because he'd threatened her, lashed out verbally and almost struck her. Thrown something, that bounced off her hip. The final divorce papers did it. The settlement agreed between the parties. His and her solicitors had shaken on the contents and there was no more to pick over. He'd come back to the house and, despite the legally binding details, his rage re-emerged thanks to the defeat he felt from one minor financial finesse in which a few quid were switched from his stash into Louise's war chest.

In her voicemail to me, that I no longer needed to hear, she said she might not be safe if she stayed, and was about to leave, regardless of my answers to her messages. Louise needed me to call, not text.

It was miles and miles of slow Friday night traffic before she stopped to check. The motorway services were the first place she could look, only to find no answers, then send more, increasingly doubtful, frightened questions and voicemails.

She'd pleaded that I mustn't blank her. She was nearly free and the first, deepest thing she felt was how lost she was without me beside her to celebrate that news. Yet I wasn't there, hadn't been for months and wasn't replying to her messages and calls.

All the way up the M6, my lack of responses left her with a desperate dilemma. Nowhere to go, back there. No certain destination in my life.

I didn't want to ask why she kept going, but she told me anyway.

'I couldn't turn round. The worst that could happen was that you would slam the door in my face after pointing back down the road in the direction I'd travelled. And that was preferable to being somewhere and not knowing. I'd be okay in a hotel or something if that's how things turned out.'

'Why didn't you call?'

'But I did. And now I know that you couldn't answer. Who completely ignores their phone, Joe?'

While she squeezes the juice from the lemon into her drink then takes a sip, demure as ever, I register that she's dressed in different things. Jeans, trainers, a top with buttons done up to her throat. Her hair is still that mass of mess. Eyes still lined with care, pink pout still a cross between a challenge, a dare, and a sign of the lost child inside.

I tell her she's welcome to stay and will be safe there for as long as she needs it.

Now, her eyes register something new. The pain or exhaustion or whatever it really was is replaced by relief. She puts her arm around my shoulder, pulls me towards her and we kiss. Then she puts her head on my shoulder, runs her hand over my pecs and falls asleep.

<>

It's late, and we walk in silence back to my house. We ignore the shortcuts and the house with all the smackheads. Past the vapers, the whitewashed windows, the long-gone banks. We are blasted by the shattering noise from the endless stream of speeding cars, and we ignore the leering, slavering passengers. We laugh, briefly, at the kids playfully stepping on and off the pedestrian crossing. The young men, pestering the young women make no discernible sound.

We smell the weed, and the hooded, baying pedestrians ignore us. We all walk the same path.

The empty fast-food places, and all the litter they pile high, come, and go. The two takeaways, Indian and Chinese, cause the same brief cloud of tempting aromatics but we won't be eating food.

We pass the pub's bouncers and flopping customers. We're bathed in the red, amber and green of the traffic lights. Past the last loom, the drooping union flag, the funeral parlour and the care home. Then we cross the road diagonally and swerve around the dog shit.

We look at the house, the mess of overgrown things, the litter, windows and doors. Her car, two wheels on the pavement.

We ignore the police car, its blaze of neon and wailing siren.

Louise and I hold hands. This ugly, decaying place is beautiful now.

It's time to get inside.

5.3

Over the weeks and months following her decision to be with me, and my acceptance of that decision, we become contented, grounded and beautiful.

Louise redirects her business to find new clients in a new region. I make steps forward in my career when Neal leaves the company.

We sell one of the cars and Louise buys a bike.

We merge into social relationships, especially if live music can be shared.

I stop drinking, Louise starts eating.

A decree nisi flies by.

After many months cohabiting and wrapping ourselves in these experiences, new but without frills or bows, we spend a warm summer's afternoon in the closed privacy of our garden. I tell Louise I want to go and live somewhere else.

'Where do you have in mind, honey?'

'Somewhere that isn't here. Not because of ghosts or memories. Just because it's never felt like home. But not just this house. Let's escape from this whole town and region.'

'Fuck yes. I'll go anywhere with you. My Joe. And I love that word, *escape*.'

For weeks, the sun shines brightly and warms the air late into the evening. We spend those evenings developing plans and plotting tasks. Things to unravel, jobs and possessions. Things to tie down, pre-nup and wills. Things to be done, with great smiles, for our future.

We agree there is no need for too many possessions. The house sells more quickly than expected. We begin the search for where we will live and, when that place is found, do the work needed for our lives to thrive there. The house we will rent is available early the following year, so we spend time traveling and dreaming. It doesn't matter that there is this hiatus. Nothing is ever a problem anymore. We are patient and certain and focused. We know nothing can get in our way.

That Christmas is the first we spend as a couple. We wake up in the tiny rented flat, go out on our bikes and, when we return, make a fuss of ourselves with gifts and a meal. As dusk starts to fall, we wander over to Lytham Green and watch the sun setting.

<>

It's a cold, sunny morning when we depart. Louise asks me how I feel about leaving the place where I've always lived. In all of the time we'd been working towards this day, in all of the ideas and rejected options and laughing, dreaming aspirations, I'd never once wondered about that question.

Louise is driving and, instead of heading east on the M55, she turns left. We drive along Yeadon Way, all the while with the Tower on the horizon. Then into the southern end of Blackpool. Past the back of the pleasure beach, past the south station, Bloomfield Road, and Jimmy Armfield's statue. Out onto the Prom, for a last glimpse at Blackpool Tower, central pier, and the front of the pleasure beach. Trams rattling past. Fun, already, on the faces all around. Under Starr Gate, one last time. Out past the dying, dead airport and, finally, to the M55.

I can't answer Louise's question. I don't need to.

5.4

It takes ages. We'd known it would and, anyway, we have time, and swap over the driving duties every couple of hours.

At every junction, and with every sign, we note all the places with cathedrals I no longer need to visit.

The M6 becomes the M5, and we pass Worcester. Louise doesn't want to see it, but I say we should call in. She is adamant we must not and, instead, turns in at the next services. In the car park we have one last dance in Worcestershire.

The Sound never felt so perfect.

We sail past Bristol, and on into Somerset. Then, just after 3pm, we leave the M5 and head north-west. Louise smiles and giggles. I watch the scenery, rolling hills, endless green fields, an undulating, winding road and keep shaking my head at it all. It's like nothing I've ever seen.

Louise is talking constantly; her memories of this same journey; of Gareth; and of her mam and dad; place names; favourite beaches and walks. Eventually, the first tantalising glimpses of the sea appear to our right. Those patches of blue make her quiet.

A narrow lane, with passing places full of muddy water, takes us on the last couple of miles. Through a tiny hamlet then, finally, we arrive. We pass a sign saying *LEE, Please Drive Slowly.* Louise says, 'Yeah: for fuck's sake, Lee'. I laugh so much I nearly hit an oncoming bus.

The lane drops steeply and water from the fields races alongside us. The church and adjacent schoolhouse look solid and charming. A memorial hall is clearly loved for all its memories. All three buildings are beautifully maintained. Pretty houses, one thatched with ochre paint on its rendering, seem to be omnipresent. The lane rises again, before a final slope down that turns sharply onto a bridge.

The tide is in at Lee Bay and, ahead of us, slightly up the hill from the sea front, is the white stonework of an old, battered-looking house where Louise and I will live till the end of our days, because we have found the road home.

ACKNOWLEDGEMENTS

Sarah Muldowney read the manuscript in May/June 2023 and presented me with written feedback that resulted in amended and new writing. Her enthusiasm and love came at a good time for me. As a talented, darkly splendid writer herself, it meant a great deal to me that Sarah invested so much time in her reading.

Likewise, **Diane Jones** read the manuscript much earlier in 2023 and we spoke at length about things she felt needed attention. Much of what she told me resulted in change for the better.

Jenny Warren reviewed the opening few thousand words and found things that needed to be fixed. So, I did.

Anna Burtt, and the team at **Jericho Writers** took a look at the opening 500 words of the draft, resulting in a *Highly Commended* prize as part of the York Festival of Writing 2022. Alongside the quality of the other writing and writers in that competition, that was a truly special award for my work.

Provoco Publishing continue to provide enthusiasm for what I've written and am planning to write. The Road Home is our second collaboration and exciting times are ahead.

Liz Hughes met me while I was roaming the sea front at Hunstanton. Aside from helping me explore and discover stuff in that lovely town, she made me laugh like I might not stop. She is a fine friend.

Nia Bragg provided some amazing insight that helped me lose concerns I had about some of the story.

I visited the five cathedrals mentioned here in a different order than Joe. Ripon was first, then Chester, Lincoln, Worcester and finally Coventry. In each case, someone kind took time to say hello and chat with me about the building. At no point did anyone look troubled about a scruffy bloke roaming around taking dozens of photos while muttering to himself about what someone called Joe might think about the building. I also had the splendid company of **Gary Potter** (at Ripon) and **Andrea Homer** (at Worcester) which made those visits doubly enjoyable.

And last (but in fact first - always) my lovely muse **Dawn**, whose guidance is never far away and always spot on.

To all of them, my love, and thanks.

MORE FROM NIGEL STEWART

Justinian's Daughters

Introit

The bishop looked at the men around him. This Chapter of clerics, priests, and canons, who despised him and all he stood for. He knew of their treachery, that report declaiming him as a heretic. It had enraged him. But now, his smile filled with the strength of a King's mandate.

'It is 1538. These things you venerate - pilgrimage; relics; saints - are superstition with no place in today's world.'

It was true, they hated this weathercock reformer. Gwilym spoke for them all. 'Your Grace, I beg to differ. None of this is superstition. David is the saint of Wales. Kings and conquerors have travelled here to pray with him. His relics are sacred, as are those of his friend, Justinian.'

The bishop's smile grew wider. 'Ah, yes. Justinian. Tell me, Canon, what this other great Saint means to you all and to this place, this land.'

'Justinian came to Wales in the sixth century, your Grace. A Breton who sought sanctuary. When Dewi-Sant visited his hermitage on Ramsey Island, he quickly grew to admire Justinian's ascetism and the way he prayed while standing in the sea, no matter how cold. They became friends and Dewi asked Justinian to be his confessor, then made him Abbot here on the mainland. He was a powerful, faithful force for Christian good, your Grace.'

The bishop bristled at the use of Welsh. From the chatter of weak-willed peasants on his travels, he knew some of this nonsense and did not care for it. This emigré, Justinian, had soon grown weary of the monks in his charge and rejected David's patronage. Back on the island, with loyal monks supporting him, he founded a stricter, more holy, more spiritual community.

Then reality became lost in mythology. Unable to abide the monastery's codes, the brothers and their servants rose. They attacked and beheaded Justinian, only for his body to pick up the severed head and walk across the sea. Such errant, witless bilge. Yet these fools, this Chapter, sustained it as if it were fact.

Gwilym was still talking. 'Justinian's chapel and shrine were built near the coast, your Grace, but his bones were eventually brought here to the cathedral, where they remain in peace.'

'Until now.' The bishop had heard enough. 'It is time for me to suppress this cult. Your Welsh Saint, and this Saint of Dubious Legends. No one needs these relics.'

Bishop William Barlow plundered jewels from St David's shrine and confiscated the relics of St David and St Justinian.

No one has ever found them.

Elementary

They flew in from the sea. Over the island, then up and over the cliffs, resonating and echoing in the coves and caves beneath them, caressing the stones of St Justinian's ruined chapel.

They filled the air over that tiny city, rattling the cathedral's stained-glass windows, then sped onwards to the drawing on the ground. Those three lines. That imperfectly drawn letter A.

They accelerated down the longest line, from west to east, clouds of dusty earth and pollen billowing up as they passed. Then over the quarry, down the river valley, back to the sea.

They dashed through the harbour, skimming the water, and the boats rocked at their moorings. Then back to the letter A and a different line. Barely off the ground, close enough to touch it and feel what was buried. Away over the fields to the sea.

In from the sea again, they flew between those bright, white obelisks atop the cliffs at the entrance to another harbour. They swept down to the letter A, tracking the final line. On to the clifftops and bays with their sandy, rocky beaches and mysterious caverns.

The rippling white-capped waves flowed to the shore, remorseless, regardless, relentless.

They soared over another saint's relics, along the shoreline, around the island then started all over again, repeating the paths they'd flown.

Now, a vaporous sea fret followed them, smothering the land in dampness. It seemed that hypnotic, lilting voices were borne on the rolling, boiling mists. 'The last two are coming. We are ready to complete this work. Come, beautiful child; come soon. We are waiting to help you.'

The land on and around the letter A became dark and

opaque, lit sporadically by jagged streams of light.

Erin heard the news and its report of a mysterious fog enveloping parts of Pembrokeshire. There was disbelief in the reporter's voice when he said that zero visibility had caused roads near St Davids to be closed.

She headed west out of London; she knew that the apparently inexplicable fog would dissipate as quickly as it had arrived. She would be there soon. It was time to finish their work. Time to blow out the last three lights.

Act One

March 2023. Saturday

'You twats. Why aren't you in the car?'

Ben's walking boots took the fifth. He almost always forgot them, nearly left without them, had to go back to fetch them. He accepted, though, that it wasn't their place to remind him. He gave the left boot a small kick, so it fell on its side, then grabbed a bag and packed his recalcitrant footwear away into the car. Loading complete.

He waved at Mrs. Brice, looking out at him from number 18 across the street. Her smile in return seemed sincere, but she let the net curtain drop so that her face became blurred.

Back indoors, Ben squeezed the last flavour from a teabag and spooned sugar into the mug. Stirring gently, causing tiny tings of metal on porcelain, he took another look at the newspaper and the page where his face smiled from the bottom left corner. One date on his autumn tour already bore a *Sold-Out* overlay.

A cheeky one-liner would be needed that night.

Something with intrinsic local knowledge which, right now, he didn't have. It would probably just be *'Thank you, Reading. You're the best.'*

The tea was just right, and he had a taste for more. Instead, he washed and dried his mug then put it next to others in a cupboard. Ben completed a final roam around the house, checking stuff, switching things off, pulling out plugs, muttering an accompaniment as he went. 'Cabin crew, doors ready for departure.'

Fifteen minutes later, he'd left Clitheroe and was pointing his car down the A59, wondering if it really would take nearly six hours to get there.

Erin stared down at the water. Just a couple of hundred metres downstream, this river formed the border between two countries, but that was nothing to Erin. Borders, barriers, lines in the sand. She belonged on neither side.

The journey from London had been what it always was. Slow, then fast, then a frustrating grind, stuttering along the final miles. Perhaps the scenery was notable? Worth a look? But she never stopped. It was a flashing blur.

Erin looked at the map. Her destination was just over a hundred miles away to the west. She expanded the view. As a child, she'd always believed the peninsula looked like the profile of a creature. The small lake near Rhosson, its eye. St Brides Bay, its mouth. St Davids Head, its ears. Ramsey Island, its prey, or perhaps its plaything. Inland, coloured lines linked the places from her history: a legacy of connections.

In the middle of it all, the airfield sat there, stamped like a faded postmark on an envelope. A letter from a loved one with well-thumbed pages. Hidden away, like treasure in a box under the bed.

Erin had work to do, and she began an assessment of

what was needed. The slow steady flow of the river Wye helped her concentration.

One of them had travelled to a halfway house, a place he knew from childhood and adolescence. Erin would be there too, in less than an hour, to check on Jacob George Wallis. He was predictable, practical, and liked his plans and to-do lists. His booking at the house had been backed up with dozens of questions about spurious details. She'd let him play his little games, bullying and entitlement made respectable by calling them a negotiation. He would be first, and easily dealt with. Something routine to close that chapter.

The other one was still in Lancashire, going through the motions. He was cautious and easily distracted, often by the lyrical or pastoral. He had choices about the best route to Pembrokeshire and might take any of them. There would be a waiting game. It would be the same when he got to the property. Erin expected that Budd would be difficult to corral into a routine. She would need time and patience. He was the last, and she had more than enough time to enjoy whatever would be done with him.

Erin returned to the Old Black Lion, collected her car, and drove away.

He'd meant to stop sooner, but Ben pressed on because he liked the look of the word *Oswestry*. So many ways to say it. Which could it be? He guessed the key would be about emphasis, or stress. He liked emphasis more than stress. His mind settled on Os**wes**try. It had to be that. He loved it.

'Yeah, I'd like a grande latte; extra shot.'

'Anything else?'

'A muffin. The raspberry cheesecake one.'

The young man at the window knew it was him but stayed cool. 'How will you be paying, sir?' In the background, two other baristas had clocked that it really was Benjamin Budd waving a phone at the pay machine.

'Tell me: how do you say Os**wes**try?'

The young man laughed. 'It definitely isn't like that.'

For the next five miles, Ben was grinding his teeth in defeat. Why wasn't it Os**wes**try? Or even Oswes**treeee** would be better than the reality. Then the road signs included instructions and place names in Welsh, and that was a whole new box of delights.

It was a couple of hours before he got to Aberaeron, where the pretty, multi-coloured buildings made him calm. Ben decided this was a good place to stop and stretch his legs. Perhaps grab a bite. He parked near the beach.

It was chilly, but the sun shone, and the waves made a pleasing set of sounds. Ben hadn't been to the seaside for years. It triggered something. He felt close to these smells and sounds, weaving familiar tunes. A gust of especially cold wind, strong enough to blow spray from the wave tops, drove him away from the shore.

The road through the village was noisy, invasive, and made him feel sad that somewhere so pretty was spoiled by the fumes and grinding gears.

But there was still a pleasing bustle, the happiness of people who stopped to talk, listen, and learn. As he scanned the buildings, Ben saw a café with an improbable name and fell in love with the word *cwtch.*

JUSTINIAN'S DAUGHTERS IS AVAILABLE ON AMAZON AND IN GOOD BOOKSHOPS

Printed in Great Britain
by Amazon

31975801R10175